He took his job seriously.

Nick stood at the foot of Laura's bed and watched her sleep for several minutes. He closed his eyes and willed away the need to hold her. She looked so small and vulnerable. And Nick wanted more than anything to protect her, but could he do that? He opened his eyes and stared at the soft blond hair spread across her pillow.

Laura had almost cost him his life once before. But that sure hadn't kept him from hanging around when his assignment was technically over. Giving himself credit, there was more to his being here than simply bone-deep need and desire.

Something wasn't right with this whole picture.

One way or another he would get to the truth. He owed it to himself…and he owed it to Laura. He simply couldn't walk away without looking back. No matter what had happened in the past. He just couldn't do it.

Happy New Year, Harlequin Intrigue Reader!

Harlequin Intrigue's New Year's Resolution is to bring you another twelve months of thrilling romantic suspense. Check out this month's selections.

Debra Webb continues her ongoing COLBY AGENCY series with *The Bodyguard's Baby* (#597). Nick Foster finally finds missing Laura Proctor alive and well—and a mother! Now with her child in the hands of a kidnapper and the baby's paternity still in question, could Nick protect Laura and save the baby that might very well be his?

We're happy to have author Laura Gordon back in the saddle again with *Royal Protector* (#598). When incognito princess Lexie Dale comes to a small Colorado ranch, danger and international intrigue follow her. As sheriff, Lucas Garrett has a duty to protect the princess from all harm for her country. But as a man, he wants Lexie for himself....

Our new ON THE EDGE program explores situations where fear and passion collide. In *Woman Most Wanted* (#599) by Harper Allen, FBI Agent Matt D'Angelo has a hard time believing Jenna Moon's story. But under his twenty-four-hour-a-day protection, Matt can't deny the attraction between them—or the fact that she is truly in danger. But now that he knows the truth, would anyone believe *him*?

In order to find Brooke Snowden's identical twin's attacker, she would have to become her. Living with her false identity gave Brooke new insights into her estranged sister's life—and the man in it. Officer Jack Chessman vowed to protect Brooke while they sought a potential killer. But was Brooke merely playing a role with him, or was she falling in love with him—as he was with her? Don't miss *Alyssa Again* (#600) by Sylvie Kurtz.

Wishing you a prosperous 2001 from all of us at Harlequin Intrigue!

Sincerely,

Denise O'Sullivan
Associate Senior Editor
Harlequin Intrigue

THE BODYGUARD'S BABY

DEBRA WEBB

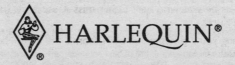

HARLEQUIN®

TORONTO • NEW YORK • LONDON
AMSTERDAM • PARIS • SYDNEY • HAMBURG
STOCKHOLM • ATHENS • TOKYO • MILAN • MADRID
PRAGUE • WARSAW • BUDAPEST • AUCKLAND

ISBN 0-373-22597-0

THE BODYGUARD'S BABY

This edition published by arrangement with Harlequin Books S.A.

® and TM are trademarks of the publisher. Trademarks indicated with
® are registered in the United States Patent and Trademark Office, the
Canadian Trade Marks Office and in other countries.

Visit us at www.eHarlequin.com

Printed in U.S.A.

ABOUT THE AUTHOR

Debra Webb was born in Scottsboro, Alabama, to parents who taught her that anything is possible if you want it badly enough. She began writing at age nine. Eventually, she met and married the man of her dreams, and tried some other occupations, including selling vacuum cleaners, working in a factory, a day care center, a hospital and a department store. When her husband joined the military, they moved to Berlin, Germany, and Debra became a secretary in the commanding general's office. By 1985, they were back in the States, and finally moved to Tennessee, to a small town where everyone knows everyone else. With the support of her husband and two beautiful daughters, Debra took up writing again, looking to mystery and movies for inspiration. In 1998, her dream of writing for Harlequin came true.

Books by Debra Webb

Don't miss any of our special offers. Write to us at the following address for information on our newest releases.

Harlequin Reader Service
U.S.: 3010 Walden Ave., P.O. Box 1325, Buffalo, NY 14269
Canadian: P.O. Box 609, Fort Erie, Ont. L2A 5X3

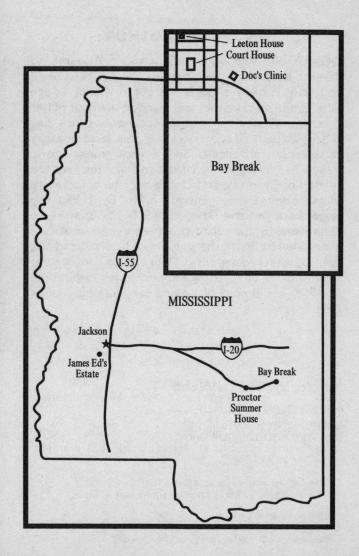

CAST OF CHARACTERS

Laura Proctor—Her child was missing, and she can't prove that he even exists. Can she stay alive long enough to find him?

Nick Foster—He has been burned once—left to die by the woman he trusted. Now she needs his help, but can Nick risk his heart to her again?

Victoria Colby—The head of the Colby Agency. She allows Nick to take Laura's case despite her misgivings.

James Ed Proctor—The governor of Mississippi. Does he love his sister or does he only want her trust fund? He stands to gain the most by Laura's death.

Sandra Proctor—James Ed's wife. She has always been good to Laura, but Sandra has one too many deep, dark secrets.

Ray Ingle—The Natchez homicide detective who has worked with Nick in the past. Can he help Nick and Laura when it really counts?

The Stalker—Laura is worth a great deal to him dead. Who hired him? What has he done with Laura's child?

Ian Michaels—A Colby Agency investigator. No one at the agency is better at digging up the facts than Ian.

This book is dedicated to some of the people I love most—my family. Erica, Melissa, Tanya, Johnny, Chad, Chris and Robby, you mean the world to me. A special thanks to Robby for being the adorable inspiration for Laura's child.

Prologue

Victoria Colby studied Nick Foster's handsome profile for a long moment as he stared out the wall of glass that made up one side of her office. Nick kept his dark hair trimmed at precisely the perfect style and length, fashionably short, to accentuate his classic features. His attire received the same attention to detail. He dressed well and in a manner that drew one's eye to the breadth of his shoulders and the leanness of his waist. He looked more model than investigator.

The man was a perfectionist, personally and professionally. In this line of work those traits could be a definite plus. Victoria had worked hard to make the Colby Agency the best in the business. And carrying on the dream that had driven James, her beloved late husband, was all that mattered to Victoria now.

The Colby Agency was much more than just another private investigations firm; it had a staff second to none. All personnel recruited and employed were on the cutting edge of their field. And Victoria made it a point to see that they stayed at their best, physically and mentally.

Victoria cleared her throat, unnecessarily announcing her presence, and crossed the thick, beige Berber that carpeted her spacious office. Nick was probably aware of her the moment she stepped off the elevator. He missed nothing. "Good afternoon, Nick," she said, smiling pleasantly as she settled into the chair behind her desk.

"Victoria," he returned warily before taking the two steps necessary to reach the overstuffed wing chair in front of her desk. "You wanted to see me?" He grimaced slightly as he lowered his tall frame into the chair, but quickly masked the pain of the old injury and relaxed fully into the supple leather upholstery.

"Yes," she confirmed. Victoria had dreaded this meeting all day, but there was no putting it off any longer. She had noted the deepening lines around his mouth, the darkening circles beneath his eyes. The man was on a full-speed-ahead trip toward crash and burn. Firming her resolve, Victoria began, "Nick, we've worked together for five years, and I know you too well to pretend any longer that nothing is wrong. I've watched the change in you over the past two years. You haven't been the same since—"

"I do my job," he interrupted sharply, his assessing green eyes growing more wary.

"Yes," Victoria agreed. "You're a valuable asset to this agency. You do your job *and more.*" She understood all too well what Nick was attempting to do. She had been there. After losing James she'd buried herself in work, too. "And I'm sure you'll understand that what I'm doing now is *my* job." She paused a beat, allowing Nick to prepare himself for her next words. "As of today, you're on mandatory R-and-R. You will not set foot back in this building, nor will you conduct any business even remotely related to this agency for a period of fourteen days."

Instantly his gaze hardened, as did the usually pleasant lines of his angular face. "That's not necessary, Victoria. I'm ready for—"

"No," she cut him off, her tone final. "I've always

trusted your judgment, Nick.'' She shook her head. "But not this time. I'd hoped that your need to assuage your conscience would fade with time, but it hasn't. You're still struggling with demons you can't possibly hope to conquer by driving yourself into the ground.'' Victoria raised a hand to stay his protests. He snapped his mouth shut, but his tension escalated, manifesting itself in his posture and the grim set of his jaw.

Regret weighed heavily on Victoria's shoulders at having to call her top investigator, her second in charge actually, on the carpet like this. "You can't run forever, Nick. You'll either burn out or get yourself killed trying to prove whatever it is you feel the need to prove. When Sloan left I wasn't sure I would ever be able to work so closely with anyone else, but I was wrong. I don't want to lose you, Nick, but I won't allow you to self-destruct on my time either. Go home, spend some time with your brother, or find yourself a hobby.'' Victoria raised a speculative brow. "Or maybe a woman. Lord knows you could use one...or both.''

Nick's gaze narrowed. "I don't recall seeing a category marked 'personal life' on my performance evaluation.''

Necessity and irritation overrode Victoria's regret. "You see this desk?'' With one manicured nail she tapped the polished oak surface of the desk that had once belonged to her husband. "The buck stops here, mister. When you go home at night you can thank God in heaven for whatever blessings you may have received that day. But here, in this building, I am the highest power. And, despite your long standing at this agency, whatever I say is the final word. You, Mr. Foster, are on vacation. Is that understood?''

He didn't flinch. "Absolutely.''

"Good.''

Nick got to his feet. The only indication that the move

cost him was the muscle that ticced in his jaw and the thin line into which his lips compressed.

"Two weeks, Nick," Victoria reiterated as he strode slowly toward the door, his trademark limp a bit more pronounced than usual. "Get a life, and when you return to work I want to see a new attitude."

He paused at the door and shifted to face her. The other trademark gesture for which Nick Foster was known spread across his handsome face. Victoria imagined that the intensity and appeal of that smile had made many a heart flutter wildly.

"Yes ma'am," he drawled, then walked out the door.

TWO WEEKS.

What the hell was he supposed to do for two weeks? Nick slammed his final report into the outbox on his desk. Victoria just didn't get it. He had a life—*here.* Nick surveyed his upscale, corner office. Work was his life. He didn't care what the shrinks said—Nick Foster didn't need anything else.

Especially not a woman.

Ire twisted inside him when he considered Victoria's words again. Yeah, he always did a hell of a job on his assignments. Especially this last one. Victoria could always count on him. No one else at the agency would have gone so far out on a limb for a client, but unlike the rest, it didn't bother Nick.

He had nothing to lose.

If he had gotten himself killed, who the hell would have missed him?

Nick shrugged off the answer to that question. He stood, gritting his teeth at the pain that radiated through his right knee and up his thigh. Nothing like a needling reminder from the past, he mused, to keep a guy in touch with reality.

Reality had royally screwed him three years ago when he'd gotten this bum knee while protecting a client. Bad knee or no, he still did the best job possible. In fact, in all his years of service to the Colby Agency he had never failed—except once. He brutally squashed the memories that accompanied that line of thinking. That would never happen again. You couldn't lose if you weren't looking for anything to gain.

Nick jerked on his suit coat and grabbed his briefcase. What the hell? He hadn't been camping or fishing in a while. Maybe he would hone his survival skills with a couple of weeks in the wilderness. And maybe he would call Chad and make it a family venture—considering the two of them were all that was left of the Foster clan. Nick's right knee protested painfully when he skirted his desk too quickly.

He muttered a colorful expletive and then forced his attention away from the burning throb. He had ignored a hell of a lot worse.

The ergonomically modulated buzz from the telephone halted his thoughts as well as his indignant exit. Nick stared at the flickering red light with a mixture of annoyance and curiosity. Everyone else at the agency, including Victoria, had no doubt already left for the day. No one ever stayed this late but him. Why should he bother answering the phone? Hadn't Victoria ordered him to take a vacation starting immediately?

Just when he thought he could walk out the door without answering the damned thing, he snatched up the receiver and barked his usual greeting, "Foster."

"Nick, it's Ray Ingle."

Nick froze, his tension rocketed to a new level. "Ray," he echoed, certain that he must have heard wrong. Maybe his mind was playing tricks on him. Maybe he should have listened to the shrinks after all.

"It's been too long, buddy." Ray's chastisement was subtle.

"Yeah, it has," Nick said slowly as he leaned one hip against the edge of his desk, taking the weight off his bum leg. He dropped his briefcase to the floor and raked his fingers through his hair as he waited for Ray to make the next move.

"I haven't called in a while." *Since we gave up on finding her,* he didn't have to add. "You haven't returned any of my calls in so long, I guess I didn't see the point anymore."

"I've been really busy, man," Nick offered by way of explanation, but the truth of the matter was he just hadn't wanted to make time. He and Ray, a Natchez police detective, had worked closely for months on that one case. And to no avail. Guilt congealed in Nick's gut.

"Sure, I know," Ray acknowledged quietly.

Nick straightened. "Look, I was just on my way out the door, is everything okay?" He hated himself for trying to cut the call short, but just hearing Ray's voice evoked more memories than Nick was prepared to deal with right now. He didn't know if he'd ever be able to deal with those memories.

"I saw *her.*"

The hair on the back of Nick's neck stood on end as adrenaline flowed swiftly through his rigid body. "Laura?" he murmured in disbelief, the sound of her name sending an old ache through his soul. If Ray had seen her...she couldn't be dead. Nick had known it all along.

"If it wasn't her, it was her frigging twin."

Nick moistened his suddenly dry lips. "Where?"

"I was following up on a possible homicide witness down in Bay Break and—"

"You're sure it was her?" Nick prodded, suddenly impatient with the need to know.

"I'm pretty sure, Nick. Hell, we turned a good portion of the good old South upside down looking for that girl. And there she was, plain as day." Ray sighed. "I don't know how and I don't know why, but it had to be her. I haven't told anyone else yet. I hate to upset our Governor on the eve of an election." He paused. "And, I figured you'd want to know first. I can give you a few hours head start, but then I'll have to inform him."

Emotion squeezed Nick's chest, he swallowed tightly. "I'm on my way."

Chapter One

She was being followed.

Oh God, *no*.

Panic shot through Laura Proctor, the surge of adrenaline urging her forward. The November wind whipped her hair across her face as she turned toward the town's square and scanned the sidewalk for the closest shop entrance. The last of autumn's leaves ripped from the trees at the wind's insistence, swirling and tumbling across the empty street. Someone bumped Laura's shoulder as they walked by, making her aware that she had suddenly stopped when she should be running.

Running for her life.

Instinctively her feet carried her along with the handful of passing pedestrians. She hadn't taken the time to disguise herself as she should have. The desire to avoid the possibility of being recognized was no longer a priority. The only thing that mattered now was finding a place to hide.

Any place.

She had to get away.

To get back to her baby. She couldn't be caught now.

Not now.

The knot of people crowding into the eastern entrance of the courthouse drew Laura's frenzied attention.

Election day. Thank God.

Laura rushed deep into the chattering throng. Once up the exterior steps, she allowed herself to be carried by the crowd into the huge marbled lobby. Weaving between the exuberant voters, she made her way to the stairwell. Almost stumbling in her haste, Laura flew down the stairs leading to the basement level.

If she could just make it to the west end, up the stairs, and onto the street on the opposite side of the square, she would be home free. She had to make it, she determined as she licked her dry lips. The alternative was unthinkable.

Don't dwell on the negative. *Think, Laura, think!*

Okay, okay, she told herself as she glanced over her shoulder one last time before starting down the dimly lit, deserted corridor. If she cut through the alley next to Patterson's Mercantile, then circled around behind the assortment of shops until she reached Vine Street, she would have a straight shot to the house.

Mrs. Leeton's house.

And her son. God, she had to get to Robby.

Laura skidded to a halt at the foot of the west stairs. "No," she muttered, shaking her head. The door to the stairwell was draped with yellow tape. A handwritten sign read, Closed—Wet Paint. Laura grasped the knob and twisted, denial jetting through her.

She was trapped.

Laura blinked and forced herself to think harder.

Slow, deliberate footsteps echoed in the otherwise complete silence. She swung around toward the sound. He was coming down the stairs. In mere seconds he would cross the landing and descend the final steps leading to the basement...

To her.

Oh God. She had to hide. Now! Laura ran to a door, but it was locked. As was the next, and the next. Why were all the offices locked?

Election day.

Only the office serving as the voting polls remained open today. Fear tightened its mighty grip, shattering all rational thought. Laura bolted for the next possibility. Blessedly, the ladies' room door gave way, pushing inward with her weight. Moving silently past each unoccupied stall, Laura slipped inside the last one and closed the rickety old door behind her. She traced the flimsy lock with icy, trembling fingers only to find it broken. Climbing onto the toilet, she placed one foot on either side of the seat and hunkered into a crouch. Knowing her pursuer to be only seconds behind her, Laura uttered one more silent prayer.

Trembling with the effort to remain perfectly still, she swallowed the metallic taste of fear and concentrated on slowing and quieting her breathing. The heart that had stilled in her chest, now slammed mercilessly against her rib cage. Laura refused to consider how he could have found her. She had been so careful since returning to Bay Break. She fought back a wave of tears as she briefly wondered just how much her brother was willing to pay the men he sent after his only sister.

How could this keep happening?

Why didn't he just leave her alone?

How did they keep finding her?

And, God, what would happen to Robby if she were killed in the next three minutes as she fully expected to be if discovered? Anguish tore at her throat as she thought of her sweet, sweet baby. She wanted to scream…to cry…to run!

Stupid! Stupid! How could she have been so careless?

She should never have left the house without taking precautions to conceal her identity. But Mrs. Leeton had insisted that Doc needed her at the clinic—that it was urgent. After all Doc had done for her son, how could Laura have refused to go? She closed her eyes and banished the tears that would not help the situation.

The slow groan of the bathroom door opening temporarily halted Laura's galloping heart. Everything inside her stilled as her too-short life flashed before her eyes.

She had failed.

Failed herself.

Failed to protect the only man she had ever loved.

And, most important, failed to make the proper arrangements for her son's safety in the event of this very moment.

Now she would die.

What would become of Robby? Who would care for him? Love him, as she loved him?

No one.

The answer twisted inside her like a mass of tangled barbed wire, shredding all hope. She had no one to turn to…no one to count on. A single tear rolled past her lashes and slid slowly down her cheek only to halt in a salty puddle at the corner of her mouth.

Something deep and primal inside Laura snapped.

By God, she wouldn't go down without a fight.

Laura's heart pounded back to warp speed. She swallowed the bitter bile that had risen in her throat as she heard the whoosh of the door closing and the solid thunk of boot heels against the tile floor. Each harsh, seemingly deafening sound brought death one step closer.

The first stall door banged against its enclosure as the hunter shoved the door inward looking for his prey. Then the second door, and the next and the next. Hinges whined and metal whacked against metal as he came ever closer to Laura's hiding place.

To her.

Her heart climbed higher in her throat. Her breath vaporized in her lungs. Tears burned in her eyes. She focused inward to her last image of Robby, all big toothy smiles, toddling across the floor, arms outstretched.

Blood roared in Laura's ears as her killer took the final step then paused before the gray, graffiti-covered metal door that stood between them. Did he know that she was there? Could he smell her fear? Could he hear her heart pounding?

Bracing her hands against the cold metal walls, Laura gritted her teeth and kicked the door outward as hard as she could. The answering grunt told her she had connected with her target—his face hopefully. Laura quickly scrambled to the floor, beneath the enclosure and into the next stall. Hot oaths and the scraping of boot heels echoed around her. Her body shaking, her breath coming in ragged spurts, Laura crawled from one stall to the next to retain cover. She had to get out of here. Had to run!

To get to Robby!

The door of the stall she had just wriggled into suddenly swung open. "Don't move," an angry male voice ordered.

Laura frowned. There was something vaguely familiar about that low, masculine drawl. As if in slow motion, her gaze traveled from the polished black boots, up the long jean-clad legs to the business end of the handgun trained on her. She blinked, feeling strangely disconnected from her body. Then her gaze shifted upward to look into the face of death.

Nick.

It was Nick.

"DON'T MAKE ME SORRY I put my weapon away," Nick growled close to her ear. Awareness punched him square in the gut when he inhaled the gentle fragrance that was Laura's alone. No store-bought perfume could ever match that natural sweetness. He clenched his jaw and simultaneously tightened his grip on her arm as they moved toward his rental car.

Hell, the Beretta had been overkill, he knew. Laura hadn't even been carrying a purse, much less a weapon of any sort. But Nick wasn't taking any chances this time. She hadn't had a weapon the last time either.

His right leg throbbed insistently, but he gritted his teeth and ignored the pulsing burn. He had found Laura, alive and well, and that's all he cared about right now.

Lucky for him Bay Break streets were deserted as far as he could see. He supposed that most of the residents out and about this morning were huddled in and around voting booths inside the courthouse, or sitting around a table in the local diner discussing how the election would turn out. Nick didn't keep up with Mississippi politics, but James Ed Proctor III's sensational reputation was hard to miss in the media. And, from what Nick had heard, whomever the man supported for Congress or the Senate was a sure winner.

The cold wind slapped at Nick's unshaven face. After a late night flight, a long drive, and an even longer surveillance of the little town's streets before Laura made her midmorning appearance, Nick welcomed the unseasonably cold temperature to help keep him alert.

He had fully expected Bay Break to be a good deal warmer than Chicago, but he'd gotten fooled. According to the old-timers hanging around the general store, all the signs warned of an early snow. Nick didn't plan to hang around long enough to see if their predictions panned out. Between twelve hours of mainlining caffeine and the unanticipated cold, Nick felt more alert than one would expect after virtually no sleep in the last thirty hours. But by the time he drove to Jackson and did what he had to do, he would be in desperate need of some serious shut-eye. And, of course, there was that R-and-R Victoria had ordered. Yeah, right, Nick thought sarcastically.

Laura struggled in his grasp, yanking his attention back to the here and now. Nick frowned when he considered the woman he was all but dragging down the sidewalk. There was something different about her, but he couldn't quite put his finger on it. She seemed softer somehow. He scowled at the path his thoughts wanted to take. He knew just how soft and delicate Laura Proctor was in all the places that made a man want a woman—except one. It took a woman with a cold, hard heart to walk away from a man who lay bleeding to death.

"You can't do this," Laura muttered heatedly. She scanned the sidewalks and streets. Looking for someone to call out to for help, Nick surmised.

"Who the hell do you think you are? You're not a cop," she added vehemently. "And I have rights!"

Anger kicked aside his foolish awareness of her as a woman and resurrected more bitter memories. Nick paused, then jerked her closer, his brutal hold eliciting a muffled yelp of pain, or maybe fear, at the moment he didn't really care which. "When somebody put a bullet into my chest and *you* left me to die, you lost your rights as far as I'm concerned."

Seconds ticked by as Laura tried her best to stare him down, her sky blue gaze watery behind thick lashes. She could cry a river of tears and he would still feel no sympathy for her. Nick mercilessly ignored the vulnerability peeking past that drop-dead stare, and turned the intimidation up a couple of notches. Laura's defiant expression wilted.

His point made, Nick escorted her the last few steps to the car. After unlocking the driver's side door, he pulled it open and ushered Laura inside. Her long blond hair trailed over his hand, momentarily distracting him and making his groin tighten. He squeezed his hand into a fist and forced away the unwanted desire. He had come here to take her back, not take up where they had left off. Laura Proctor would never make a fool of him again. And this time, he would be the one walking away.

As he had anticipated, once in the car she bolted for the passenger side. With a smug smile, Nick slid behind the wheel and started the engine, almost drowning out her surprised gasp when she couldn't open the door.

"You bastard," she snarled, her eyes unnaturally dark with anger. Her breasts rose and fell with her every frustrated breath. "This is kidnapping!"

Nick's smile widened into a grin of pure satisfaction. "Consider it a citizen's arrest," he offered. Before he could back out of the parking slot Laura flew at him, a clawing, kicking tangle of arms and legs.

Nick shoved the gearshift back into park. After several seconds of heated battle he subdued her, but not without a slash across his throat from her nails. He shook her, none too gently. "Look," he ground out. "I'm trying *not* to hurt you."

"Sure," she hissed. "You don't want to hurt me, you just want to get me killed."

For one fleeting instant Nick allowed himself to feel her fear. There had supposedly been a couple of attempts on her life two years ago. Could she still be in danger? Even now, after all she had put him through, Nick's gut clenched at the thought. Hell, he couldn't say for sure that there had ever been any real danger in the first place. According to the reports he had been privy to, Laura had possessed a wild streak, not to mention an overactive imagination. Her older brother, Mississippi's esteemed Governor, was always getting her out of one scrape or another. Who was to say that the whole thing was anything more than her vivid imagination? And the guy she had been romantically linked to back then was over the edge in Nick's opinion. He doubted her poor taste in associates had changed since.

Nick swallowed hard at the thought of Laura with another man.

Did he care?

No, he told himself. The lie, unspoken, soured in his throat.

''You don't have to worry, Laura. I'm taking you back home, to your brother. I'm—''

''My brother?'' She quickly retreated to the passenger side of the car, as far away from Nick as possible. ''I can't go back home! Don't you understand? It's not safe.''

Nick leveled a ruthless gaze on her panicked one. Her lower lip quivered beneath his visual assault, he suppressed the emotion that instantly clutched at his chest. How could she look so innocent? So truly frightened for her life? And, damn him, how could he still care? ''You don't have an option. In fact, if you'll remember correctly, the last time *you* were supposedly in danger *I'm* the one who almost bought the farm.''

Something in her eyes changed, softened with what looked like regret. But it was too late for that now. Way too late.

Their gazes still locked, Nick shifted to reverse. ''Buckle up, baby, we're out of here,'' he ground out, then glanced over his shoulder before backing into the street.

Laura Proctor was going back to face her brother and

the law. Nick had every intention of uncovering the real story about what happened their last day together at her brother's cabin as well. Protecting Laura and seeing her safely returned to the new Governor after the election two years ago had been Nick's assignment. But things had gone wrong fast, and Laura was hiding at least part of the answers.

Including the part where she recognized the man who almost killed Nick. The one she had obviously disappeared with that same day. Ironic, Nick thought wryly, that he had found her and would be delivering her to her brother right after an election—just two years later than planned.

LAURA HAD TO DO something. Nick, the arrogant bastard, was going to get her killed. She glared at his perfect profile and winced inwardly. God, the man was breathtaking. It hurt to look at him and know what she knew. He had haunted her dreams every night for the past two years. He'd ruined her for anyone else. A dozen snippets of memory flashed before her eyes. The way it felt to be held by Nick. The way he made love to her. Her heart squeezed with remembered pain. He had been fully prepared to give his life to protect hers. Yet she could never trust him with her secret, and she sure couldn't go back to Jackson with him.

The small sense of relief Laura had felt when she had realized the man holding the gun on her was Nick instead of some hired killer died a sure and swift death when he announced why he had tracked her down.

He still wanted to finish the job he had been assigned two years ago, to return her safely to her brother. And that was exactly the reason Laura had not been able to go to Nick for help. He was too honorable a man to ignore his responsibility to James Ed. No way would Nick have done things Laura's way. He took his job way too seriously.

She had always known that Nick could have found her eventually if he had really wanted to—but he hadn't. He had apparently stopped trying. Unlike James Ed's men, whom she gave the slip without much difficulty, Nick wouldn't be so easy. He was too damned good, the best. If anyone could have caught Laura during the past two years, he could have. Why now, she wondered, after all this time? But the answer to that question didn't really matter at the moment. Right now Laura desperately needed to think of something fast. Something that would give her an opportunity to escape. She glared at the space where the unlock button used to be, and then at the useless door handle he had somehow disabled. Nick Foster was just a little too smart for his own good.

And hers.

Well, Laura decided, she hadn't eluded her brother this long without being pretty smart herself. She would find a way. Going back to James Ed was suicide. And she could never allow anyone—especially Nick—to discover her secret. She had to protect Robby at all costs. Even if after getting Robby settled some place safe it meant going back to her brother, Laura would do it to lead any threat away from her child.

She would never let anyone harm her son.

Never.

But how would Doc know what had happened to her? Would Mrs. Leeton be able to take care of Robby if Laura never returned? Unsettled by the thought, Laura snapped from her disturbing contemplation, and realized that they were already headed out of town.

To Jackson.

Desperation crowded her throat.

She needed to go back to Mrs. Leeton's house first.

To her son. She couldn't leave without making some sort of arrangements.

There was no other option at the moment.

"We have to go back," she said quickly.

"Forget it." Nick's focus remained steady on the road. A muscle flexed in his square jaw, the only visible indication of his own tension.

Laura frantically groped for some reasonable explanation he would find acceptable for turning around. Nothing came. A new kind of fear mushroomed inside her. She had to think of something.

Now!

"My baby!" she blurted when the Please Come Again sign loomed closer. "I have to get my baby."

Nick threw a suspicious glance in her direction. "What baby?" he asked, sarcasm dripping from his tone.

"My…I have…a son," she admitted, defeat sucking the heart from her chest. How would she ever protect her baby?

Nick's expression shifted from suspicious to incredulous. "I'm not falling for any of your tricks, Laura."

Trembling with the crazy mixture of emotions flooding her body, Laura swiped at the tears she had only just noticed were slipping down her cheeks. Dammit, why did she have to cry? She was supposed to be tough—had to be tough. "Please take me back, Nick. I have to get my son," she pleaded, any hope of appearing even remotely tough dashed.

Something, some emotion, flitted across his handsome face so fast Laura couldn't quite read it. She fought to ignore what looked entirely too much like hurt that remained. She knew just how much Nick had suffered because of her. He had almost died. She winced inwardly at the memory. But she couldn't permit herself to feel any sympathy for him. He certainly harbored none for her. She had to stay focused on keeping her son safe. Robby was all that really mattered. And she could never allow Nick to suspect the truth about her child.

Laura didn't even want to imagine what Nick would do if he found out he had a son.

A child she had kept from him for almost two years.

NICK PARKED the rented sedan on the street in front of the small white frame house Laura identified as belonging to a Mrs. Leeton. Emotions churned in his gut. What was it to him if Laura Proctor had gotten herself pregnant since he had last seen her? Or, hell, maybe even shortly before he had met her.

Nothing.

Less than nothing, he reiterated for good measure.

She had simply been an assignment back then, and Nick's sole motivation for taking her back to her brother now was to clear up his record. Laura Proctor represented a black mark on his otherwise perfect record, and he was about to wipe it clean. If he had kept his head on straight back then he wouldn't have screwed up the assignment in the first place. And he sure as hell wouldn't have allowed himself to believe the woman almost virginal. What a joke.

On him.

Nick reached for the door handle, but Laura grabbed his arm. He stared for a long moment at the small, pale hand clutching at him before he met her fearful gaze. ''What?'' he growled.

''Please don't do this, Nick,'' she begged. ''Please just walk away. Pretend you never saw me.'' She moistened her full, lush lips and blinked back the tears shining in her eyes. ''Please, just let us go.''

''Save your breath, Laura.'' A muscle jumped in his jaw, keeping time with the pounding in his skull. Don't even think about feeling sorry for her, man, he reminded himself. You let your guard down once and it almost cost you your life. "Nothing you can say will change my mind," he added, the recall of Laura's betrayal making his tone harsh.

Her desperate grip tightened on the sleeve of his jacket. "You don't understand. He'll kill me, and maybe even my son." She squeezed her eyes shut, her breath hitched as it slipped past her pink lips. "Oh, God, what am I going to do?"

Nick tamped down the surge of protectiveness that surfaced where Laura was concerned. His chest tightened with an emotion he refused to label. He focused his attention on the street and dredged up the memory of waking up alone and barely alive in the hospital. "Who will kill you, Laura? The guy you watched put a bullet in me before you ran away?" He turned back to her then, the look of pain in her eyes giving him perverse pleasure. "Just how far were you willing to go to cause your brother trouble? Was it all just some kind of game to you?"

Her eyes closed again, fresh tears trickled down those soft cheeks. She was good. She looked the picture of innocence and sweetness. He almost laughed at that. Obviously the hotshot she had been involved with two years ago, or someone since had left her with an unexpected gift. Maybe it had been the guy who had put the bullet in Nick. Laura Proctor would have a hell of a time promoting that innocent act with an illegitimate baby on her hip. Well, that wasn't his problem, even if the thought did make some prehistoric territorial male gene rage inside him.

"Are we going in, or do we head straight for Jackson?" he demanded impatiently, drumming his fingers on the steering wheel for effect.

Laura brushed her cheek with the back of her hand. "I

want to get my son first,'' she murmured, defeat sagging her slim shoulders.

''Well, let's do it then,'' he shot back, trying his level best not to think about Laura having sex with another man, much less having the man's child. Damn, he shouldn't care.

But, somehow, he still did.

Nick called himself every kind of fool as he emerged from the car, years of training overriding his distraction as he surveyed their surroundings. Vine was a short, dead-end street dotted with half a dozen small frame houses. A dog barked at one of the houses on the far end of the quiet street. Two driveways had vehicles parked in them, indicating someone could be home. Either Mrs. Leeton didn't own a car or she wasn't home, he noted after another scan of the house before them. Nick reached beneath his jacket and adjusted the weapon at the small of his back. There was no way of knowing what to expect next out of Laura or the people with whom she associated.

Laura scrambled out of the car and into the vee created by his body and the open car door. It took Nick a full five seconds to check his body's reaction at her nearness. Laura's gaze collided with his, the startled expression in her eyes giving away her own physical reaction. Nick breathed a crude, four-letter word. Laura shrank from him as if he had slapped her. He didn't want to feel any of this, he only wanted to do what had to be done. But his male equipment obviously had other ideas.

''I know you'll never believe me, but it didn't happen the way you think,'' Laura said softly, defeatedly. She looked so vulnerable in that worn denim jacket that was at least two sizes too big, the overlong sleeves rolled up so that her small hands just barely peeked out. But the faded denim encasing her tiny waist and slender hips was breathstealingly snug, as was the dirt-streaked T-shirt that snuggled against her breasts.

Nick swallowed hard and lifted his gaze to the face he had never wanted to see again, yet prayed with all his heart he would find just around the next corner. For months after her disappearance his heart rate had accelerated at the sight of any woman on the street with hair the color of spun gold and whose walk or build reminded him of Laura. Each time, hoping he had found her, his disappointment had proven devastating. And now she stood right before him, alive and every bit as beautiful as the day he had first laid eyes on her. Could he have found her long ago had he truly wanted to? Or was believing the possibility that she was dead or, at the very least, lost to him forever simply easier?

Victoria had ordered him to stop looking for Laura. Her own brother had believed her dead. But Nick had never fully believed it. Yet he had stopped looking all the same. If she was alive and she didn't want to contact him, he wasn't going after her. Then Ray had called and the need for revenge had blotted out all else.

A wisp of hair fluttered against her soft, creamy cheek and Nick resisted the urge to touch her there. To wrap those golden strands around his fingers and then allow his thumb to slide over her full, lush lips.

"Please don't make me go back, Nick," she said, shattering the trance he had slipped into.

Briefly he wondered if she still felt it too, then chastised himself for even allowing the thought to materialize. Laura Proctor had no warm, fuzzy feelings for him. Actions speak louder than words, Nick reminded the part of him that stupidly clung to hope, and her actions had been crystal clear two years ago. She had left him to die.

"If you want to pick up your kid, I would suggest that you do it before I lose patience," he snapped, using his anger to fight the other crazy, mixed-up emotions roiling inside him.

"Yes," she murmured. "I want to pick up my son." She looked away, then reached up to sweep the tendrils of hair from her face.

The ugly slash on the inside of her wrist caught Nick's eye. He captured that hand in his and forced her to allow him to inspect it. He clenched his jaw at the memory that she had allegedly tried to commit suicide only a few weeks before they had met. But the woman he had known for such a short time in that quiet cabin by the river would never have done anything like that. She had been too full of life and anticipation of what came next. She wouldn't have walked away leaving him to die, either—but Laura had.

And that was the bottom line: she couldn't be trusted.

His hold on her hand bordering brutal, Nick led Laura up the walk and across the porch of the silent house. The whole damned street looked and felt deserted. He glanced down at the woman at his side. If this turned out to be a ploy of some sort, she would definitely regret it. He nodded at her questioning look, and she rapped against the door.

Laura held her breath as she waited for Mrs. Leeton, a retired nurse, to answer the door. The woman was old and riddled with arthritis, so Laura waited as patiently as she could for the key to turn in the lock. Until three years ago, Mrs. Leeton had worked with Doc for what seemed like forever. When Laura showed up a week ago needing Doc's help, he had asked Mrs. Leeton to take Laura and Robby in. The elderly woman had readily agreed. Laura hadn't really liked the idea of leaving Robby alone with Mrs. Leeton this morning, but what else could she do? Mrs. Leeton had insisted that Doc needed Laura right away.

When the door's lock finally turned, anxiety tightened

Laura's chest and that breath she had been holding seeped out of its own accord. Would Nick recognize his own child? Would he demand that she turn his son over to him? Nick wasn't the same man she had known two years ago. He was harder now, *colder.*

Would he take Robby to get back at her? Or would he simply take him out of fear for his son's well-being? Just another reason she could never have turned to Nick for help no matter how bad things got. James Ed had convinced Nick and everyone else that she was mentally unstable. Nick would never in a million years have allowed a woman considered mentally unstable to raise his son. He would have taken Robby, Laura knew it with all her heart.

Oh, God, was she doing the wrong thing by even coming back here? Why didn't she just let Nick take her back to Jackson without mentioning Robby? Doc would have taken care of her baby until Laura could figure out a way to escape...*if* she figured out a way.

The door creaked open a bit and old Mrs. Leeton peered through the narrow gap. Laura frowned at the look of distrust and caution in the woman's eyes. Did she not recognize Laura? That was impossible. Laura and Robby had been living here for a week. The idea was ludicrous. Hysteria was obviously affecting Laura's judgment.

"Mrs. Leeton, I've had a change in plans. I have to leave right away," Laura told her as calmly as she could. "Please let Doc know for me. I just—" she glanced at the brooding man at her side "—need to get Robby and we'll be on our way."

"Who are you and what do you want?"

Alarm rushed through Laura's veins at the unexpected question. "Mrs. Leeton, it's me, Laura. I've come back to get Robby. Please let me in." Nick shifted beside her, but

Laura didn't take her eyes off the old woman. Something was wrong. Very wrong.

"I don't know who you are or what you want, but if you don't leave I'm going to call the police," Mrs. Leeton said crossly.

Outright panic slammed into Laura then. "I need to get my son." Ignoring her protests, Laura pushed past the woman and into her living room. Nick apparently followed. Laura was vaguely aware of his soothing tone as he tried to placate the shrieking old woman.

"Robby!" Laura rushed from room to room, her heart pounding harder and harder. Oh God, oh God, oh God. *He's not here.* The cold, hard reality raced through her veins. Laura shook her head as if to deny the words that formed in her head. No, that can't be! She had left him here less than an hour ago. It can't be!

Laura turned around in the middle of the living room, slowly surveying the floor and furniture for any evidence of her son.

Nothing.

Not one single toy or diaper. Not the first item that would indicate that her son had ever even been there.

He was gone.

She could feel the emptiness.

Frantic, Laura pressed her fist to her lips, then looked from Nick, who was staring at her with a peculiar expression, to the old woman who glared at her accusingly. Laura clasped her hands in front of her as she drew in a long, shaky breath. "Mrs. Leeton, please, where is my baby?"

The old woman's gaze narrowed, something distinctly evil flashed in her eyes. "Like I said before, I don't know you, and there is no baby here. There has never been a baby here."

Chapter Two

"There's no need to call the police, Mrs. Leeton," Nick assured the agitated old woman. He shot a pointed look at Laura. "We've obviously made a mistake."

Laura jerked out of his grasp. "I'm not leaving without my son!" She grabbed the old woman's shoulders, forcing Mrs. Leeton to look directly at her. "Mrs. Leeton, why are you doing this? Where's Robby? Who took him?"

"Get out! Get out!" the old woman screeched. "Or I'll call the police!"

"We're leaving right now." Nick carefully, but firmly, pulled Laura away from the protesting old woman. "Now," he repeated when she resisted.

"I can't go without my baby." The haunted look on Laura's face tore at Nick's already scarred heart. "She's lying. She knows where he is!" Laura insisted. Her eyes, huge and round with panic, overflowed with the emotion ripping at her own heart. How could he not believe her?

But he had trusted her once before....

Nick forced his gaze from Laura to the old woman. "I apologize for the confusion, Mrs. Leeton." He tightened his grip on Laura when she fought his hold. "We won't bother you again." This time Nick snaked his left arm around Laura's waist and pulled her against him. His gaze connected with hers and he warned her with his eyes that she had better listen up. "We're leaving—*now,*" he ground out for emphasis. Laura sagged against him, emotion shaking her petite frame.

"If that crazy girl sets foot back on my property I'm calling the police!" Mrs. Leeton shouted behind them.

Nick didn't respond to her threat. He had no intention of returning to the woman's house. If Laura had a son, he wasn't here, that much was clear.

Laura clung helplessly to Nick as he strode back to the rental car, her violent sobs rattling him like nothing else in the past two years had. He automatically tuned out the intensifying pain radiating from his knee upward. He didn't have time for that now. He glanced down at the woman at his side. Whether she had a child and where that child might be was not his concern. He ignored the instant protest that tightened his chest. Taking her back to James Ed was all he came to do, Nick reminded himself. Laura had a brother, an influential brother, who could help her with whatever personal problems—real or imagined—she might have.

Nick opened the car door, intent on ushering Laura inside. Hell, it was too damned cold to stand outside and debate anything. He could calm Laura down once they were in the car. As if suddenly realizing that they were actually leaving, she twisted around to face him.

"I have to find Robby," she said, her voice breaking on a harsh sob. "You have to believe me, Nick. I left him with Mrs. Leeton not more than an hour ago." Another shudder wracked her body.

Nick pulled her close again, his own body automatically seeking to comfort hers. He forced himself to think rationally, ruthlessly suppressing the urge to take her sweet face in his hands and promise her anything. "Show me some proof that you have a son, Laura. Convince me."

For the space of two foolish heartbeats Laura stared into his eyes, the blue of hers growing almost translucent with some emotion Nick couldn't quite identify. Her upturned face too close for comfort.

"He's real," she whispered, her breath feathering across his lips, making him yearn to taste her, to hold her tighter.

"Prove it," he demanded instead. "Show me pictures, a birth certificate, a favorite toy, clothing, any evidence that you have a child."

She shifted, her body brushing against his and sending a jolt of desire through him. "My purse..." Laura frowned, then looked toward Mrs. Leeton's house. "I left my purse and what few clothes we brought with us in there."

Nick followed her gaze and studied the small white frame house for a moment. "We definitely aren't going back," he said flatly, then returned his attention to the woman putting his defenses through an emotional wringer. "I don't want the local police involved."

Instantly, Laura recoiled from him. Anger and bitterness etched themselves across the tender landscape of her face. Her eyes were still red-rimmed from her tears, but sparks of rage flew from their watery blue depths. "Of course not," she spat the words with heated contempt. "We wouldn't want to do anything that would bring the wrong kind of attention to the almighty Governor of Mississippi, now would we?"

"Get in the car, Laura." Irritation stiffened Nick's spine. He had no intention of making the Proctors' domestic difficulties personal this go-around. "Now," he added when she didn't immediately move.

Her eyes still shooting daggers at him, Laura turned to

obey, but suddenly whipped back around. "Doc," she said. "Doc will back me up. He'll tell you about Robby."

Tired of beating a dead horse, Nick blew out a loud, impatient breath. "Who's Doc?"

"My doctor," Laura explained. "Robby was really sick. Doc's the reason I came back here, I knew I could trust him," she added quickly as she slid behind the wheel, then scooted to the passenger side of the car. "Let's go!"

Nick braced his forearm on the roof of the car and leaned down to look her in the eye. He held her gaze for a long moment, some warped inner compulsion urging him to believe her. He straightened, taking a moment to scan the quiet neighborhood, then Mrs. Leeton's house once more. Something about this whole situation just didn't feel right. Maybe there was some truth to Laura's story. Nick had always trusted his instincts. And they had never let him down…except once.

"Hurry, Nick, we're wasting time!"

Still warring with himself, Nick dropped behind the wheel and started the engine. He turned to his passenger and leveled his most intimidating gaze on hers. "If you're yanking me around, Laura, you're going to regret it."

LAURA STARED at the scrawled writing on the crudely crafted sign hanging in the window of Doc's clinic. The breath rushed past her lips, leaving a cloud of white in the cold air as she read the words that obliterated the last of her hope. "Gone out of town, be back as soon as possible." This couldn't be. She shook her head as denial surged through her.

It just could not be.

Her pulse pounded in her ears. Her heart threatened to burst from her chest. Laura squeezed her burning eyes shut.

Robby, where are you? Please, God, she prayed, *don't let them hurt my baby. Please, don't let them hurt my baby.*

"That's rather convenient," Nick remarked dryly from somewhere behind her.

Laura clamped one hand over her mouth to hold back the agonizing scream that burgeoned in her throat. How could she make Nick believe her now? Mrs. Leeton was lying or crazy, or maybe both. Doc had disappeared. Doc's new nurse would be where? Laura wondered. The woman worked part-time with another doctor in some nearby small town. Where? Laura wracked her brain, mentally ticking off the closest ones. She couldn't remember what Doc had told her. His longtime secretary had retired and moved to Florida months ago. He hadn't hired anyone else, preferring to do the paperwork himself now. Who could Laura call? She couldn't think. She closed her eyes again and stifled a sob that threatened to break loose. She had to keep her head on straight. She had to think clearly.

Who could have taken Robby?

Why?

Realization struck like lightning on a sultry summer night, acknowledging pain hot on its heels like answering thunder.

James Ed.

It had to be him, or one of his henchmen. They had found out about Robby and taken him to get to Laura. That would be the one surefire way to bring her home. She had realized that day two years ago at the cabin that her dear brother intended to kill her. She just hadn't known why. But that epiphany had come to her eventually. *The money.* He wanted Laura's trust fund. He was willing to kill her to get it. And now Robby was caught in the middle.

What about Doc? Could he be in on it? Was his sudden disappearance planned? Laura shook her head emphatically. No way. Doc loved her. And she trusted him. He wouldn't do that. Laura read the sign in the window again. But where could he be? He had asked her to come to the clinic. He'd told Mrs. Leeton it was urgent. Had he somehow heard that someone was in town looking for her? Maybe he wanted to warn her. Could he have taken Robby somewhere to safety?

Laura prayed that was the case. But how could she be sure? Could she leave town without knowing that her son was safe? She swallowed tightly.

No. She had to find him.

"I know Doc's here," she said aloud, as if that would make it so. "He has to be."

"Let's go, Laura. I'm tired of playing games with you."

Laura turned around slowly and faced the man who seemed to have set all this in motion. The man she still loved deep in her heart. The man who had given her the child that she could not bear to lose. But she could never tell him the truth.

Never.

Nick's green eyes were accusing, and full of bitterness. Defeat weighed heavily on Laura's shoulders as she met that unsympathetic gaze. Pain riddled her insides. She had lost her son and no one on earth cared or wanted to help her. She was alone, just as she had been alone since the day her parents had died when she was ten years old. Nothing but a burden to her much older brother, Laura had known from day one that he couldn't wait to be rid of her. As soon as she had come home from college, James Ed had tried to push her into marrying the son of one of his business associates, but Laura had refused. Then the attempts on her life had begun.

She supposed that it was poetic justice of sorts. James Ed had considered her a nuisance her entire life, but being the responsible, upstanding man he wanted everyone to believe he was, he had offered Laura an out—marry Rafe Manning. Rafe was young, reasonably handsome, and rich. What more should she want? Why couldn't she be the good, obedient sister James Ed wanted her to be?

If only James Ed had known. Rafe's wild stunts had made Laura's little exploits look like adolescent mishaps. Between the alcohol and the cocaine, Rafe was anything but marriage material. Not to mention the apparently insignificant fact that Laura had no desire to marry Rafe or anyone else at the time. She had been too mixed up herself, too young.

So Laura had thumbed her nose at her big brother's offer, and he had chosen an alternative method of ridding himself of his apparently troublesome sister. Maybe Rafe had been in on it, as well. How much would James Ed have paid him to see that his new bride had a fatal accident? James Ed always preferred the easy way out. Hiring someone to do his dirty work for him was a way of life.

Perversely, Laura wondered if her showing up now would be an inconvenience considering James Ed had no doubt already taken control of her trust fund. Only weeks from her twenty-fifth birthday, Laura would be entitled to the money herself. Then again, that might be the whole point to this little reunion. James Ed would make sure that she didn't show up to claim her trust fund. What would a man, brother or not, do to maintain control of that much money?

Nick stepped closer and Laura jerked back to the here and now. Robby was gone. Doc was gone. What did anything else matter? Panic skittering up her spine once more, she backed away when Nick reached for her. She had to find Robby and Doc. Laura rushed to the door of the house that served as both clinic and home to Doc Holland. She banged on the old oak-and-glass door and called out his name. He had to be here. He simply would not just disappear. She twisted the knob and shook the door. It was locked up tight.

Doc never locked the door to his clinic.

"This isn't right," she muttered. Laura moved to the parlor window. She cupped her hands around her eyes and peered through the ancient, slightly wavy, translucent glass. Everything looked to be in order. But it couldn't be.

"He wouldn't just leave like this," she reminded herself aloud. Bounding off the porch, Laura rushed to the next window at the side of the house. The kitchen appeared neat and tidy, the way Doc always kept it.

But something was wrong. Laura could feel it all the way to her bones. Something very bad had happened to Doc. Her heart thudded painfully. She knew Doc too well. He would never just disappear with Robby without leaving her some sort of word. "They've gotten to him, too," she whispered, the words lost to the biting wind. Forcing herself to act rather than react, Laura ran to the next window, then the next one after that.

That same sense of emptiness she had felt at Mrs. Leeton's echoed inside her.

"No one's here, Laura."

She struggled against the fresh onslaught of tears, then turned on Nick. "He has to be here," she snapped. Her heart couldn't bear the possibility that her child was in the hands of strangers who might want to harm him. Or that something bad had happened to Doc. "Don't you understand? Without him…" Anguish constricted her throat, she couldn't say the rest out loud.

Nick lifted one brow and glared at her unsympathetically. "We're leaving *now*. No more chasing our tails." He snagged her right arm before she could retreat. "Don't make this any more difficult than it already is," he warned.

Difficult? Laura could only stare at him, vaguely aware that he was now leading her back to the car. Did he truly think her situation was merely difficult? Could he not see that someone had cut her heart right out of her chest? Her child was missing! And she had to find him. Somehow...no matter what it cost her.

Another thought suddenly occurred to Laura—Doc's fishing cabin. Maybe he had gone to the cabin to hide Robby. Hope bloomed in Laura's chest. It wasn't totally outside the realm of possibility, she assured herself. She paused before getting into the car and closed her eyes for a moment to allow that hope to warm her. Please, God, she prayed once more, let me find my baby.

Now, all she had to do was convince Nick to take her there. She opened her eyes and her gaze immediately collided with his intense green one. Despite everything, desire sparked inside her. How she wanted to tell Nick the truth—to make him believe in her again. But she couldn't. And when they arrived at the cabin, if her son was not there, Laura would do whatever she had to in order to escape. She would go to James Ed all right. But she would go alone and on her own terms. Somehow Laura would devise a fail-safe plan to get her son back.

Whatever it took, she would do it.

NICK KEPT a firm hold on Laura as they emerged from the car outside Dr. Holland's rustic fishing cabin. The place was in the middle of nowhere, surrounded by woods on three sides and the unpredictable Mississippi River on the fourth. The cabin sat so close to the water's edge, Nick felt sure it flooded regularly. But from the looks of things, there appeared to be no amenities like electricity. It served only as modest shelter for the hard-core fisherman or hunter. So what did a little water hurt now and then? he mused. Most likely nothing.

Now that he had gotten a good look at the place, Nick was surprised there had been a road accessible by car at all. Once again, quiet surrounded them. Only the occasional lapping of the water against a primitive old dock broke the utter silence. The sun had peaked and was now making its trek westward. Nick would give Laura five minutes to look around and then they were heading to Jackson. They had already wasted entirely too much time.

She hadn't spoken other than to give him directions since they left the clinic. Nick glanced at her solemn face now and wondered what was going on in that head of hers. His gut told him he didn't want to know. And his gut was seldom wrong.

At the steps to the dilapidated porch, Laura pulled free of his loosening grip and raced to the door. Nick followed more slowly, allowing her some space to discover what he already knew: there was no one here. Considering nothing about the cabin's environment appeared disturbed in any way, and the lack of tracks, human or otherwise, there hadn't been anyone here in quite a while. Nick swore softly at the pain that knifed through his knee when he took the final step up onto the porch.

Damn his knee injury, and damn this place. He plowed his fingers through his hair and shifted his weight to his left side.

The wind rustled through the treetops, momentarily interrupting the rhythmic sound of the lapping water. Nick scanned the dense woods and then the murky river, a definite sense of unease pricked at him. Maybe it was because the remote location reminded him of the place he and Laura had shared two years ago, or maybe it was just restlessness—the need to get on with this. Whatever the case, Nick's tension escalated to a higher state of alert. If he still smoked, he'd sure as hell light up now. But he'd quit long ago. He had even stopped carrying matches.

"Doc's not here. No one's here."

Nick met Laura's fearful gaze. Drawing in a halting breath, she rubbed at the renewed tears with the back of her hand. She looked so vulnerable, so fragile. He wanted to hold her and assure her that everything would be all right as soon as she was back home. But what if he was wrong? What if someone still intended to harm her?

And what if he were the biggest fool that ever put one foot in front of the other? Don't swallow the bait, Foster. You've seen this song and dance before. "Let's get on the road then," he suggested, self-disgust making his tone more curt than he had intended.

She blinked those long, thick lashes and backed away a step. "I can't go with you, Nick." Laura shook her head slowly from side to side. "I have to find Robby. I...I can't leave without him. If you won't help me, I'll just have to do it alone."

Keeping his gaze leveled on hers, Nick cautiously closed the distance between them. "Don't do anything stupid, Laura," he warned. "If you say you have a kid, I'm sure it's true. And if you do, I can't imagine why anyone would want to take him, can you? What about the boy's father?"

The cornered-animal look that stole across her face gave her away about two seconds before she darted back inside the cabin. She had almost made it across the solitary room and to the back door when Nick caught, then trapped her between his body and a makeshift kitchen cabinet. Anger and pain battled for immediate attention, but at the moment jealousy of a man he had never even met had him by the throat. He leaned in close, pressing her against the rough wood counter, forcing her to acknowledge his superior physical strength.

"Does Rafe know about his son? Or is there some other unlucky fellow still wondering whatever happened to his sweet little Laura?" Nick snarled like the wounded animal he was.

In a self-protective gesture, Laura braced her hands against his chest, unknowingly wreaking havoc with his senses. How could she still affect him this way? Her scent tantalized him, made him want to touch her, taste her, in all the ways he had that one night. Every muscle in his body hardened at the imagined sensation of touching Laura again. When she turned that sweet face up to his, her eyes wide with worry and pleading for his understanding, his resolve cracked....

"He doesn't know about Robby." She licked those full pink lips and a single tear slid slowly down one porcelain cheek. "I'm afraid I won't find him, Nick. Please help me."

...his resolve crumbled. Nick allowed himself to touch her. His fingertips glided over smooth, perfect skin, tracing the path of that lone tear. The sensation of touching Laura like he had dreamed of doing for so very long short-circuited all rational thought.

Slowly, regret nipping at his heels already, Nick lowered his head. He saw her lips tremble just before he took them with his own. Her soft, yielding sigh sent a ripple of sensual pleasure through him. She tasted just like he remembered, sweet and innocent and so very delicate. Like a cherished rose trustingly opening to the sun's warmth, Laura opened for him. And when he thrust his tongue inside her sweet, inviting mouth the past slipped away. Only the moment remained...touching Laura, tasting her and holding her close, then closer still.

Nick threaded his fingers into her long blond hair, reveling in the silky texture as he cradled the back of her head. ''Laura,'' he murmured against her mouth, and she responded, knotting her fists in his shirt and pulling him closer. His body melded with hers, her softness molding to his every hard contour as he deepened the already mind-blowing kiss.

Lust pounded through him with every beat of his heart. Nick traced the outline of Laura's soft body, his palms lingering over the rise of her breasts, then moved lower to cup her bottom and pull her more firmly into him. She slid one tentative hand down his chest, then between their grinding bodies. Laura caressed him intimately. Nick groaned loudly into her mouth as she rubbed his erection again and again through his jeans.

Her tongue dueled with his, taking control of the kiss, just as her body now controlled his. Her firm breasts pressed into his chest, her nipples pebbled peaks beneath the thin cotton of her T-shirt. The urge to make love to Laura—here, now—overwhelmed all else as she propelled him ever closer toward climax with nothing more than her hand, and in spite of the layers of clothing still separating them.

The unexpected blow to the side of his head sent Nick's equilibrium reeling. He staggered back a couple of steps and Laura took off like a shot. He stared at the thick ceramic mug shattered on the primitive wooden floor. He hadn't even noticed it on the counter. Nick shook his head to clear it and took several halting steps in the general direction of the door. When he got his hands on Laura he intended to wring her neck. At the moment he had to focus on reversing the flow of blood from below his belt to above his neck.

She was already at the car when he stumbled across the

porch, his body still reeling from her touch. He rubbed the throbbing place just behind his temple then checked his fingertips for any sign of blood. No blood, just a hell of a lump rising. A half dozen or so four-letter words tumbled from his mouth as he lurched toward the car, his knee throbbing with each unsteady step. Pure, unadulterated rage flashed through him like a wild fire. She would regret this, he promised himself.

Nick knew by Laura's horrified expression that she had just discovered that the keys weren't in the ignition. Did she think he was stupid as well as gullible? In a last-ditch effort to save herself, she locked the doors.

Grinning like the idiot he now recognized himself to be, Nick reached into his pocket and retrieved the keys, then proceeded to dangle them at her. "Going somewhere?" He inserted the key into the door's lock and glared at her. "I don't think so." He jerked the door open and leaned inside.

Laura tried to climb over the seat and into the back but Nick caught her by the waist.

"Let me go!" she screamed, slapping, scratching and kicking with all her might. "I have to find my son!"

Once Nick had restrained her against the passenger-side door, he glowered at Laura for three long beats before he spoke. "You have two choices," he growled. "You can sit here quietly while I drive to Jackson, or I can tie you up and put you in the trunk. It's your call, Laura, what's it going to be?"

Chapter Three

Laura sat absolutely still as Nick parked the car at the rear of James Ed's private estate per security's instructions. She forced away the thoughts and emotions that tugged at her senses. Nick's touch, his kiss, the feel of his arms around her once more. She still wanted him, no matter that her whole world was spinning out of control. Commanding her attention back to the newest level of her nightmare, Laura lifted her gaze to the stately residence before her. The place was every bit as ostentatious as she had expected. Nothing but the best for James Ed, she thought with disgust.

In a few hours every available space out front would be filled with Mercedes, Cadillacs and limousines as the official victory party got under way. According to Nick's telephone conversation with James Ed, of which Laura had only overheard Nick's end, a celebration was planned for the Governor's cohorts who had won big in today's election. Laura was to be taken in through the back. That way there would be no chance that a guest arriving early or some of the hired help might see her. James Ed was still protecting his good name.

But Laura didn't care. A kind of numbness had settled over her at this point. The knowledge that she might never see Robby again, and that she was going to die had drained her of all energy. She felt spent, useless.

She surveyed again the well-lit mansion and considered what appeared to make her brother happy. Money and power. Those were the things that mattered to him. He could keep Laura's trust fund. She didn't care. She only wanted her son back. But James Ed wouldn't care what Laura wanted. He had never cared about her. Otherwise he would have left her alone after she disappeared rather than hunting her down like an animal. She had barely escaped his hired gunmen on two other occasions. And now Laura would answer doubly to James Ed for all the trouble she had caused him.

But he couldn't hurt her anymore, that was a fact. He had already taken away the only thing in this world that mattered to Laura.

Laura looked up to find Nick reaching back inside the car to unbuckle her seat belt. His lips were moving, so she knew he was speaking to her, but his words didn't register. On autopilot, Laura scooted across the seat and pushed out into the cold night air to stand next to Nick. She looked up at him, the light from a nearby lamppost casting his handsome face in shadows and angles. She knew Nick was a good man, but he had been blinded by her brother's charisma just like everyone else. None of this was Nick's fault, not really. He was only doing what he thought was right. His job.

Would Robby look like him when he grew up? she suddenly wondered. Even at fifteen months, he already had those devilish green eyes and that thick black hair.

Yes, Laura decided, her son would grow up to be every bit as handsome as his father. She frowned and her mouth went unbearably dry. The father he would never know…and the mother he wouldn't remember. She blinked—too late. Hot tears leaked past her lashes.

"They're waiting for us inside," Nick said, drawing her back to the present.

Laura swallowed but it didn't help. She brushed the moisture from her cheeks with the back of her hands and took a deep, fortifying breath. She might as well get this over with. No point in dragging it out.

"I'm ready," she managed.

"Good."

Nick smiled then and Laura's heart fluttered beneath her breast. It was the first time today she had seen him smile, and just like she remembered, it was breathtaking. Robby would have a heart-stopping smile like that, too.

"This way, Mr. Foster."

Startled, Laura turned toward the unfamiliar male voice. The order came from a man in a black suit. A member of her brother's security staff, Laura realized upon closer inspection. She noted the wire that extended from his starched white collar to the small earpiece he wore. The lack of inflection in his tone as well as his deadpan gaze confirmed Laura's assumption.

Nick took Laura by the arm and ushered her forward as he followed the security guy. No one spoke as they moved across the verandah and toward the French doors at the back of the house. Laura instinctively absorbed every detail of the house's exterior. Her brother had spared no expense on exterior lighting. Of course that could be a hindrance if she somehow managed to escape. The darkness proved an ally at times. Not that her chance of escaping was likely. Laura eyed the man in black's tall frame with diminishing hope. Still, she needed to pay attention to the details. As long as she was still breathing, there was hope. *Focus, Laura,* she commanded her foggy brain.

A wide balcony spanned the rear of the house, supported by massive, ornate white columns. Three sets of French doors lined the first as well as the second floor. At least there were several avenues of escape, Laura noted, allowing that small measure of hope to seed inside her hollow heart. Maybe, just maybe, she would live long enough to at least attempt a getaway.

They crossed a very deserted, very elegant dining room and entered an enormous kitchen. Gleaming cabinetry and stainless steel monopolized the decorating scheme. The delicious scents of exquisite entrées and baked goods hung in the warm, moist air. Laura remembered then that she hadn't eaten today, but her stomach felt queasy rather than empty. Besides, she had no desire to share her last meal with her brother, or to eat it in his house. She would starve first.

Several pots with lids steamed on the stovetop. Security had apparently temporarily vacated the staff upon hearing of her arrival. As soon as the all clear signal was given the kitchen would quickly refill with the staff required to pull off this late night gala.

James Ed always rode the side of caution. And he never passed up an occasion to celebrate, to show off his many assets.

Laura's stomach knotted with the knowledge that her own brother hated her this much—or maybe it had nothing to do with her. Maybe it was simply the money.

Maybe…

Maybe Robby was here. A new kind of expectation shot through Laura. James Ed could have brought Robby here to use him as leverage to get what he wanted.

Nick firmed his grip on her right arm as if somehow sensing that her emotions had shifted. She had to get away from him. He read her entirely too well. Escape scenarios flashed through her mind as they mounted the service stairs.

Laura's heart pounded harder with each step she took. She felt hot and cold at the same time. She rubbed the clammy palm of her free hand against her hip, then squeezed her eyes shut for just a second against the dizziness that threatened. She could do this. Laura would do whatever it took to find her son and escape. James Ed would not win.

"Governor Proctor asked that you wait in here."

Nick thanked the man, then led Laura into what appeared to be James Ed's private study. Flames crackled in the fireplace, the warmth suffusing with the rich, dark paneling of the room. A wide mahogany desk with accompanying leather-tufted chair occupied one side of the room. Behind the desk, shelves filled with law books lined the wall from floor to ceiling. Leather wing chairs were stationed strategically before the massive desk. An ornate sideboard displayed fine crystal and exquisite decanters of expensive liquors. No one could accuse James Ed of lacking good taste, it was loyalty that escaped him.

Anxiety tightened Laura's chest, making it difficult to breathe. She had to concentrate. If she somehow freed herself from Nick's grasp and found Robby, could she make it off the grounds without being caught? Nick narrowed his gaze at her as if he had again read her thoughts. The man was entirely too perceptive.

"Take it easy, Laura, your brother will take good care of you," he said almost gently.

Laura shook her head, a pitiful outward display of her inner turmoil. "You just don't get it." She moistened her painfully dry lips and manufactured Nick a weak smile, hoping her words would penetrate that thick skull of his. "It would have been simpler if you'd just killed me yourself."

Laura knew she would not soon forget the expression that stole across Nick's features at that moment. The combination of emotions that danced across his face were as clear as writing on the wall. He cared for her, but he was confused. He trusted James Ed, just like everyone else, and he didn't quite trust Laura. Because she had hurt him badly. Left him to die—he thought. But she hadn't. And now he would never know what really happened, and, what was worse, he would never know his son.

"Laura, I'm sure—"

"Laura?"

A bone-deep chill settled over Laura at the sound of James Ed's distinctive voice. Nick turned immediately to greet the Governor. James Ed, tall, still thin and handsome, hadn't changed much, except for the sprinkling of gray at his sandy temples, and that was likely store-bought to give him a more distinguished appearance. Laura couldn't read the strange mixture of emotions on his face as he approached her. Fear sent her stumbling back several steps when he came too close, but his huge desk halted her.

"Laura, sweet Jesus, I didn't think I would ever see you again. I thought…I thought—dear God, you really are *alive*."

Feeling as trapped as a deer in the headlights of oncoming traffic, Laura froze when her brother threw his arms around her and hugged her tight. He murmured over and over how glad he was to see her. Resisting the urge to retch, Laura closed her eyes and prayed for a miracle. At this point, deep in her heart, she knew it would take nothing short of a miracle to escape and find her child.

James Ed's uncharacteristic actions dumbfounded Laura, adding confusion to the anxiety already tearing at her heart. He had never been the touchy-feely type. Then realization hit her. It was a show for Nick's benefit. James Ed wanted Nick to believe that he truly was thankful to have his baby sister home. When her brother drew back, tears clung to his salon-tanned face, further evidence of his feigned sincerity. The man was a master at misrepresentation and deceit. A true politician, heart and soul.

Laura slumped against the desk when he finally released her. She felt boneless with an exhaustion that went too deep. Nick had no way of knowing that he had just delivered her like the sacrificial lamb for slaughter. It was his job, she reminded herself. Nick worked for James Ed. She had known he would do this if he ever found her, just as she had known he would take her son away if he discovered his existence. And suddenly Laura understood what she had wanted to deny all day. It was over, and she had lost.

Robby was lost.

Laura's eyes closed against the pain that accompanied that thought, and the memory of her baby's smile haunted her soul.

"Nick, thank you so much for bringing her back to us. I don't know how to repay you."

Nick accepted the hand James Ed offered. "I was only doing what I was assigned to do two years ago." Nick wondered why it suddenly felt all wrong.

"You're a man of your word." James Ed gave Nick's hand another hearty shake. "I like that. If there's ever anything I can do for you, don't hesitate to ask."

Nick studied the Governor's sincere expression. He considered himself a good judge of character, and Laura's fears just didn't ring true when Nick looked her brother square in the eye. He read no deceit or hatred in the man's gaze. But his gut reaction told him that Laura truly believed in the threat.

"There is one thing," Nick began, hesitant to offend the man, but certain he couldn't leave without clearing the air.

"*Laura!*" Sandra, James Ed's wife, flew across the room and pulled Laura into her arms. "Honey, I am so glad to have you back home. You don't know how your brother and I have prayed that somehow you really were alive and would come back to us.''

Nick couldn't reconcile what Laura had described with the reunion happening right in front of him, and still something didn't feel right about the whole situation. Something elemental that he couldn't quite put his finger on.

''You were saying, Nick,'' James Ed prompted, the relieved smile on his face further evidence that Laura had to be wrong.

Nick studied the Governor for another long moment before he began once more. He knew that what he was about to say would definitely put a damper on this seemingly happy event. A few feet away he could hear Sandra fussing over a near catatonic Laura. What the hell, Nick had always been a straightforward kind of guy. Why stop now?

''Laura is convinced that you're the one behind the threat to her life, two years ago and now,'' Nick stated flatly.

You could have heard the proverbial pin drop for the next ten seconds. The look of profound disbelief on James Ed's face morphed into horror right before Nick's eyes. Nick would have staked his life on the man's innocence right then and there. James Ed couldn't possibly be guilty of what Laura had accused him. Slowly, James Ed turned to face his sister, whose defeated, lifeless expression had not changed.

''Laura, you can't really believe that. My God, I'm your brother.''

''Honey, James Ed has been beside himself since the day you disappeared. How could you think that he had anything to do with trying to harm you?'' Sandra stroked Laura's long, blond hair as a mother would a beloved daughter. But Laura made no response. In spite of everything she had done, Nick ached to give Laura that kind of comfort himself—to see if she would respond to him as she had that one night.

Suddenly, Laura straightened, dodging Sandra's touch and pushing away from the desk that had likely kept her vertical. She took several shaky steps until she was face-to-face with her brother. She stared up at him. Nick tensed, remembering the hefty mug she had used to bash him upside the head. Luckily for James Ed there was nothing in her reach at the moment.

"If you really mean what you say, big brother, then do me one favor," Laura challenged, her voice strangely emotionless, but much stronger than Nick would have believed her capable at the moment.

Nick readied himself to tackle her if she started swinging at James Ed. The lump on the side of his head undeniable proof that Laura could be a wildcat when the urge struck her.

"Laura." She flinched when James Ed took her by the shoulders, but she didn't back off. "I will do anything within my power for you. Anything," he repeated passionately. "Just name it, honey."

"Give me back my son," she demanded, her voice cracking with the emotion she could no longer conceal. Laura's whole body trembled then, her upright position in serious jeopardy.

Nick moved to her side, pulled her from a stunned James Ed's grasp and into his own arms. "Shh, Laura, it's okay," he murmured against her soft hair as he held her tight. Her sobs would be contained no longer, she shook with the force of them.

"Nick, I don't know what she's talking about." James Ed threw up his hands, his exasperation clear.

"What on earth can she mean?" Sandra reiterated as she

hurried to her husband's side. She looked every bit as confused and genuinely concerned as James Ed.

"Please make him tell you, Nick, please," Laura begged, her fists clenched in the lapels of his jacket. "I don't care what he does to me, but don't let him hurt my baby." The look of pure fear and absolute pain on her sweet face wrenched his gut.

Confusion reigned. For the first time in his entire life, Nick didn't know what to do. As much as he knew he shouldn't, he wanted desperately to believe Laura. To take her away from here and keep her safe from any and all harm.

"Tell me, *please*," James Ed urged. "What is this about a child?"

In abbreviated form, Nick recited the events that had taken place in Bay Break, all the while holding Laura close, giving her the only comfort he could. "Laura insists that she has a son," he concluded. "I didn't find any evidence to corroborate her story, but—" he shrugged "—she stands by it."

Laura pounded her fists against his chest, demanding Nick's full attention. "I do have a son! His name is Robby and he's—"

"Laura," James Ed broke in, his tone calm and soothing despite the unnerving story Nick had just related to him.

Laura whirled in Nick's arms, but he held her back when she would have flung herself at James Ed. "You stole my son! Don't try to tell me you didn't!"

"Laura, please!" Sandra scolded gently. "You aren't making sense. What child?"

Laura turned to her. "Sandra, make him tell me!"

Nick tightened his hold on Laura, his protective instincts kicking into high gear. He still felt connected to her; he couldn't pretend that he didn't. "So you don't have her son?" he asked the Governor pointedly.

James Ed closed his eyes and pinched the bridge of his nose. Several long seconds passed before he released a heavy breath, opened his eyes, and then spoke, "It's worse than I thought."

"What's that supposed to mean?" Laura challenged, her voice strained.

James Ed settled a sympathetic gaze on his sister. "Laura, there can't possibly be any baby." He held up his hands to stay her protests, a look of pained defeat revealing itself on his face. "Just hear me out."

Laura sagged against Nick then, the fight going out of her. Nick wasn't sure how much more she would be able to stand before collapsing completely.

"Laura," James Ed began hesitantly. "Until the day before yesterday, when you escaped, you had spent the last eighteen months in a mental institution in New Orleans."

Nick felt Laura's gasp of disbelief. "That's a lie," she cried.

James Ed massaged his right temple as if an ache had begun there. "Apparently when you ran away two years ago, you wound up in New Orleans. You were found in an alley a few months later and hospitalized." He paused to stare at the floor. "The diagnosis was trauma-induced amnesia, and schizophrenia. The doctor says you haven't responded well to the drug therapy, but there's still hope."

Laura shook her head. "That's a lie. I've never been to New Orleans."

"Laura, honey, please listen to your brother," Sandra coaxed.

"You had no ID, no money. They assumed you were homeless and really didn't attempt to find out where you'd come from. And that's where you've been ever since. If you hadn't escaped, we might never have known you were even alive.'' His gaze softened with sadness. ''You were considered a threat to yourself…as well as others.'' A beat of sickening silence passed. ''Detective Ingle spotted you yesterday.'' James Ed looked to Nick then. ''Ray told me you would be bringing Laura home. He received a copy of the New Orleans APB on the Jane Doe escapee just a few hours ago. It didn't take long to put two and two together. We've already contacted the hospital. The treating physician there faxed me a copy of his report.''

Laura turned back to face Nick. ''He's lying, Nick. You have to believe me!''

Nick searched her eyes, trying to look past the panic and fear for the truth. ''Laura, why would he lie?'' All the cards were stacked against her, James Ed had no motivation that Nick could see for wanting to harm her. And Laura had no proof of any of her accusations, or that she had a child.

''Honey, I would never lie to you.'' James Ed moved closer. ''I am so sorry that this has happened. If we had known how sick you were two years ago, maybe we could have prevented this total breakdown—''

''Why are you doing this?'' Laura cried. ''I'm not crazy. I just want my son back!''

''I think it's time to call Dr. Beckman in,'' Sandra suggested quietly.

''Who?'' Laura demanded. Her body shook so badly now that Nick's arms were all that kept her upright. Nick's own concern mounted swiftly.

''Wait,'' James Ed told Sandra, then turned to Laura. He studied her for a time before continuing. ''All right, Laura, tell us where you've been if not in New Orleans.''

''Darling, don't put yourself and Laura through this now,'' Sandra pleaded softly.

James Ed shook his head. ''I want to hear Laura's side.

I won't be guilty of failing to listen again." He gave Sandra a pointed look. "I want to know where *she* believes she has been."

"You know where I've been," Laura snapped. "You've had someone tracking me like an animal."

"Please, Laura, you can't believe that." James Ed reached for her, but she shunned his touch.

"Stay away from me!"

"Surely we can sort all this out in the morning after Laura's had a good night's rest," Sandra offered quickly. "We're all upset. Let's not make things worse by pushing Laura when she's obviously exhausted." Sandra placed a comforting hand on James Ed's arm. "And we do have guests arriving shortly, unless you'd like me to cancel...."

"You're right, of course, dear," James Ed relented with a heavy sigh. "Laura needs to rest. Canceling dinner is probably wise, too. I should have realized that earlier. We've all had a shock."

"I'll get the doctor." Sandra hurried toward the door.

Laura stiffened. "I don't need a doctor."

"Honey, this is for your own good," James Ed assured her. "We've had Dr. Beckman, a close friend, standing by since we found out...what happened. He has spoken with the doctor in New Orleans and understands the specifics of your case. He'll give you something to calm you down, and we can work all this out in the morning."

"No!" Laura struggled in Nick's arms. "Don't do this, James Ed, please!"

Nick didn't like the way this was going. Before he could protest, Sandra rushed back into the room followed by a short, older man carrying a small black case.

"Nick, please don't let them do this to me."

Nick looked from Laura to the doctor who had just taken a hypodermic needle from his bag. Nick's uncertain gaze shifted to the Governor. "I don't know about this, James Ed," Nick said slowly.

"It's okay, Nick, he's only going to give her a sedative," James Ed explained tiredly. "It's for her own good. Considering the state she's in she might hurt herself."

The image of the scars on Laura's wrists flashed through Nick's mind. Maybe James Ed knew what he was doing. She was his sister. If there was no child, then Laura was seriously delusional. But—

"Don't!" Laura shouted when the doctor came closer. "Help me, Nick! You have to help me!"

"Nick, you're going to have to help *us,*" James Ed pressed as he reached for Laura. "You must see that she desperately needs a sedative."

Nick pulled Laura closer, the look he shot James Ed stopped him cold. "This doesn't feel right."

"It's perfectly safe, Mr. Foster," the doctor assured Nick. "She needs rest right now. Her present condition isn't conducive to her own welfare."

Nick felt confused. His head ached from the blow Laura had dealt him. The image of her scarred wrists kept flitting through his mind. He wasn't sure how to proceed. His heart said one thing, but his brain another. He stared down at the trembling woman in his arms. What was the best thing for her? The dark circles beneath her wide blue eyes and the even paler cast to her complexion gave him his answer. She needed to rest. She needed the kind of help Nick couldn't give her. But *this* just didn't feel right.

Sandra reached for Laura this time. "No," Nick said harshly. "I don't think—"

"Your job is over now, Nick," Sandra interrupted calmly, patiently. "You should let us do ours."

"It's for the best, Nick," James Ed said with defeat.

"Mr. Foster, I'll have to ask you to leave now."

Nick's gaze shot over his shoulder toward the man who had just spoken. A suit from James Ed's private security staff stood directly behind Nick. His jaw hardened at the realization that he had been so caught up in Laura's plight that he hadn't heard him approach.

"Get lost," Nick warned.

"Let's not make this anymore unpleasant than necessary, sir," the man in black suggested pointedly.

Nick held his challenging stare for several tense seconds, then reluctantly released Laura. He wouldn't do anything to make bad matters worse…at least not right now.

When Sandra and Dr. Beckman closed in on Laura, the look of betrayal in her eyes ripped the heart right out of Nick's chest. "Please don't let them hurt my baby," she murmured, then winced when the needle penetrated the soft skin of her delicate shoulder.

Nick turned to James Ed, a white-hot rage suddenly detonating inside him. "If you're holding anything back—"

The Governor shook his head in solemn defeat. "Trust me, Nick."

Chapter Four

"She isn't well," Sandra said softly.

"I know."

"What are you going to do?"

"I don't know," James Ed answered hesitantly. His pause before continuing seemed an eternity. "But I have to do something. I can't allow her to continue this way."

"What do you mean?" Caution and the barest hint of uncertainty tinged Sandra's words. "Laura is your sister," she reminded softly. "Now that she's back, there are changes…"

James Ed breathed a heavy sigh. "Do you think I could forget that significant detail?"

"I'm sorry. Of course not."

Laura struggled to maintain her focus on the quiet conversation going on above her. Blackness hovered very near, threatening to drag her back into the abyss of unconsciousness. Her entire body felt leaden, lifeless. She wasn't sure she could move if she tried. She could open her eyes. Laura had managed to lift her heavy lids once or twice before Sandra and James Ed entered the room.

How long had she been here? she wondered. Long enough that the sedative the doctor had administered had begun to wear off. Though still groggy, Laura's mind was slowly clearing. But she couldn't have been here too long. Twenty-four hours, maybe? Though Laura had no way of knowing the precise drug she had been given, she recognized the aftereffects. Whatever it was, it was strong and long lasting. She'd had it before....

Before she had escaped her brother's clutches. Before she fell in love with Nick and had Robby.

A soul-deep ache wrenched through her. Laura moaned in spite of herself. Where was Robby? Was he safe? Oh God, she had to find her baby. But if she opened her eyes now they would know she was listening. Why hadn't Nick helped her? Because he was one of them, Laura reminded herself. He had always been on their side. No one believed her. No one would help her.

"She's waking up," James Ed warned, something that sounded vaguely like fear in his tone. "Where is the medication Dr. Beckman left?"

"You go ahead and get ready for bed," Sandra suggested. "You didn't get much sleep last night with Laura's arrival. I'll see to her, and then I'll join you."

James Ed released a long breath. "All right."

Laura heard the door close as James Ed left the room. Her heart thudded against her ribcage. She had to do something. Maybe Sandra would believe her. She opened her eyes and struggled to focus on her sister-in-law's image. A golden glow from the lamp on the bedside table defined Sandra's dark, slender features. Smiling, she sat down on the edge of the mattress at Laura's side. Laura's lethargic fingers fisted in the cool sheet and dragged it up around her neck, as if the thin linen would somehow protect her. She had to get away from here. Somehow.

"Help me," Laura whispered.

"Oh, now, don't you worry, everything is going to be fine." Sandra smoothed a soothing hand over Laura's hair.

"You shouldn't be frightened. James Ed and I only want the best for you, dear. Don't you see that?"

Her lids drooping with the overwhelming need to surrender, Laura mentally fought the sedative. She would not go back to sleep. She concentrated on staying awake. Don't go to sleep, she told herself. You have to do this for Robby. Robby…oh God, would she ever see her baby again? And Nick? Nick was lost to her, too.

Sandra retrieved something from the night table. Laura's drowsy gaze followed her movements. A prescription bottle. Sandra slipped off the top and tapped two small pills into her palm. Laura frowned, trying to focus…to see more clearly. More medicine! She didn't want more.

"Here." Sandra placed the medication against Laura's lips. "Take these and rest, Laura. We want you to get well as soon as possible. Dr. Beckman said these would help."

Laura pressed her lips together and turned her head. She would not take anything else. She had to wake up. Tears burned her eyes and her body trembled with the effort required to resist.

Sandra shook her head sympathetically. "Honey, if you don't take the medication, James Ed will only make me call Dr. Beckman again. You don't want that, do you?"

A sob constricted Laura's throat. Slowly, her lips trembling with the effort, she opened her mouth. Tears blurred her vision as Sandra pushed the pills past Laura's lips. Laura took a small sip of the water Sandra offered next.

"That's a good girl," Sandra said softly. She fussed with the covers around Laura and then stood. "You rest, honey, I'll be right down the hall."

Laura watched as Sandra closed the door behind her. Laura quickly spat the two pills into her hand. She shuddered at the bitter aftertaste they left in her mouth. Her fingers curled into a fist around the dissolving medication.

She cursed her brother, cursed God for allowing this to happen, then cursed herself for being a fool. Gritting her teeth with the effort, Laura forced her sluggish body to a sitting position. With the back of her hand she wiped at the bitter taste on her tongue. She shuddered again, barely restraining the urge to gag.

Laura took a deep breath and surveyed the dimly lit room. She had to get out of here. But how would she get out? She would most likely be caught the moment she stepped into the hallway. Security was probably lurking out there somewhere. French doors and several windows lined one wall. The balcony, she remembered. The balcony at the back of the house. Maybe she could get out that way. A single door, probably to a bathroom or a closet, Laura surmised, stood partially open on the other side of the room. Still wearing the clothes she had arrived in, Laura pushed to her feet, then staggered across the room to what she hoped was a bathroom. Her legs were rubbery, and her head felt as if it might just roll off her shoulders like a runaway bowling ball.

Cool tile suddenly took the place of the plush carpeting beneath her feet. Laura breathed a sigh of relief that the door did, in fact, lead to a bathroom. She lurched to the vanity and lowered her head to the faucet. Water. She moaned her relief at the feel of the refreshing liquid against her lips, on her tongue, and then as it slid down her parched throat. Laura rinsed the bitter taste from her mouth, then washed the gritty pill residue from her hand. She shivered as her foggy brain reacted to the sound of the running water, making her keenly aware of the need to relieve herself in another way.

After taking care of that necessity, Laura caught sight of her reflection as she paused to wash her hands. The dim glow from the other room offered little illumination, but

Laura could see that her eyes were swollen and red, and her face looked pale and puffy. She splashed cold water onto her face several times to help her wake up, then finger-combed her tousled hair. All she had to do was pull herself together enough to find a way to climb down from the balcony. Laura frowned when the coldness of the tile floor again invaded her senses. She needed her shoes. Where were her shoes?

Laura lurched back into the bedroom. She searched the room, the closet, under the bed, everywhere she knew to look and to no avail. Her shoes were not to be found. Exhausted, Laura plopped onto the edge of the bed. She had to have shoes. It was too damned cold to make a run for it barefoot. She would have to head for some sort of cover— the woods, maybe. How could she run without her shoes?

Think, Laura, she ordered her fuzzy brain. They must have removed her shoes when they took her jacket. She stared down at the stained T-shirt she wore. She had to remember. What room was she in when they took her jacket? The study or in this bedroom? Robby was depending on her. She had to get out of here. But somehow she needed to search the house first. Robby could be here. Her heart bumped into overdrive at the thought of how long it had been since she had seen her son. She let go a halting breath. He had been missing over twenty-four hours now, if her calculations were correct. She scanned the room for a clock, but didn't see one. Laura squeezed her eyes shut then.

Please God, keep my baby safe. I don't care if I die tonight, she beseeched, *just don't let anything happen to my baby.*

Her body weak and trembling, Laura dropped to her hands and knees on the floor. For one long moment she wanted to curl into the fetal position and cry. Laura shook off the urge to close her eyes and allow the drug to drag her back into oblivion. She had to find those damned shoes. Slowly, carefully, she crawled around the large room and searched every square foot again. Still nothing. Too weary now to even crawl back to the bed. Laura leaned her head against the wall and allowed her eyes to close. She was so tired. She could rest for just one minute. She scrubbed a hand over her face…she could not go back to sleep…she had to find her shoes.

To find Robby.

All she needed was one more moment of rest….

The blackness embraced Laura as she surrendered to the inevitable.

LAURA WASN'T SURE how much time had passed when she awoke. Hours probably, her muscles cramped from the position in which she had fallen asleep. It was still night she knew since only the dimmest glow of light filtered through her closed, immensely heavy lids. Groaning, she sat up straighter and stretched her shoulders, first one side, then the other. She frowned, trying to remember what she was supposed to do. Her shoes. That's right. She needed to find her shoes and get out of here. Laura shoved the hair back from her face and licked her dry lips.

"Okay," she mumbled. Shoes, she needed her shoes. She had to get up first. Laura forced her reluctant lids open and blinked to focus in the near darkness. Eerie pink eyes behind a black ski mask met her bleary gaze. Laura opened her mouth to scream, but a gloved hand clamped over her lips.

"So, Sleeping Beauty is awake," a male voice rasped.

Laura drew back from the threat, the wall halted her retreat, his hand pressed down more brutally over her mouth. She shook her head and tried to beg for her life, but her words were stifled by black leather.

"You," he said disgustedly. "Have caused me a great deal of extra trouble." Something sharp pricked her neck. Laura's heart slammed mercilessly against her rib cage. He had a knife. A cry twisted in her throat.

He jerked Laura to her feet. The remaining fog in her brain cleared instantly. This man had come to kill her. She was going to die.

No! her mind screamed. She had to find Robby.

Laura stiffened against him. He was strong, but not very large. If she struggled hard enough—

"Don't move," he growled next to her ear. The tip of the knife pierced the skin at the base of her throat again.

Laura suppressed the violent tremble that threatened to wrack her body. Blood trickled down and over her collarbone. Hysteria threatened her flimsy hold on calm. She had to think! Her frantic gaze latched on to the open French doors. He had probably entered her room from the balcony. If he could come in that way, she could escape by the same route. All she had to do was get away from him...from the knife.

His arm tightened around her as if she had uttered her thoughts aloud. "Time to die, princess," he murmured, then licked her cheek. The foul stench of his breath sent nausea rising into her throat.

Laura swallowed convulsively. She squeezed her eyes shut and focused on a mental picture of her son to escape the reality of what was happening. Her sweet, sweet child. The tip of the knife trailed over one breast.

"Too bad you didn't stay gone." He twisted her face up to his. Those icy eyes flashed with rage.

The air vaporized in Laura's lungs. He was going to kill her and there was no one to help her. No one. Nick didn't believe her. And her own brother had probably hired this man.

"Now you have to die." He eased his hand from her lips only to press his mouth over hers. The feel of wool from his ski mask chafed her cheeks. Laura struggled. The knife blade quickly came up to her throat again.

Laura wilted when he forced his tongue into her mouth. Tears seeped past her tightly closed lids. Her entire body convulsed at the sickening invasion. Rage like she had never experienced before surged through her next. Laura's eyes opened wide and she clamped down hard with her teeth on the bastard's tongue. The sting of the knife blade slid down her chest when he snapped his head back. Laura jerked out of his momentarily slack hold. She flung herself toward the balcony. She had to escape.

"Come back here, you bitch," he growled, his words slightly slurred.

Laura slammed the French doors shut behind her. He pushed hard against them. Laura fought with all her body weight to prevent the doors from opening. Her feet slipped on the slick painted surface of the balcony. One door opened slightly before she could regain her footing. He reached a hand between the doors and grabbed her by the hair. Laura screamed. The sound echoed in the darkness around her. She slammed against the door with every ounce of force she had. The man swore, released her and jerked his arm back inside.

Too weak to stand any longer, Laura dropped to her knees. She held on to the door handles with all her might. The handles shook in her hold. She leaned harder against the doors. Surely someone would come into her room at any moment. James Ed had around-the-clock security, Laura was certain. If they would come, then she would have proof that she had been telling the truth all along.

Seconds clicked by. Someone had to come, didn't they? A sob twisted inside her chest. She was so tired. And no one was coming. No one cared.

Laura screamed when the door shoved hard against her, hard enough to dislodge her weight. She scrambled away from the threat. Panic had obliterated all reason. She had to get away. To find her child.

"Laura!"

Laura stilled. Was that Nick's voice? Hope welled in her chest. He was coming back for her.

"Laura." James Ed crouched next to her. "What happened?"

Laura lifted her gaze to his, disappointment shuddered through her. It wasn't Nick. She must have imagined his voice. "Please help me," she pleaded with her brother.

"Sweet Jesus!" James Ed stared at her chest. "Laura, are you hurt?"

She stared down at herself. Blood. Her T-shirt was red with blood. Her blood. The blackness threatened again. Laura struggled to remain conscious. She was bleeding. The knife. Her gaze flew to her brother's. "He tried to kill me," she murmured.

James Ed shook his head, his face lined with worry. "Who tried to kill you, Laura? There's no one here."

Laura looked past James Ed to the bedroom she had barely escaped with her life. The overhead lights were on now. A man in a black suit stood in the middle of the room. Security. Laura remembered him from when she had first arrived. She frowned. Security had to have seen the intruder. Surely he couldn't have gotten past a professional security team. Could he be hiding somewhere in the house? Why weren't they looking for him?

Sandra was next to her now. "Let's get you back inside and see exactly what you've done to yourself."

"No," Laura denied. "There was a man. He tried to kill me. He had a knife."

"Come on, Laura." James Ed helped Laura to her feet. "Don't make this any worse than it already is."

"I found this, sir."

The man held a large kitchen knife gingerly between his thumb and forefinger. Light glistened from the wide blade. Blood—her blood, Laura realized—stained the otherwise shiny edge.

Sandra scrutinized the knife. "It's from *our* kitchen," she said slowly, her gaze shifting quickly to James Ed.

"Dear God," he breathed.

Despite the lingering effects of the sedative, Laura realized the implications. "No," she protested. "There was someone here. He—"

"That's enough, Laura," James Ed commanded harshly. She glared up at him. "We've had more than enough excitement for one night," he added a bit more calmly. "Now, let's get you back in bed and attend to your injuries."

Shaking her head, Laura jerked from his grasp. "You can't keep me here." Laura backed away from him. "I have to find my son."

James Ed only stared at her, something akin to sympathy glimmered in his blue eyes. For one fleeting instant Laura wondered if she could be wrong about her brother. Probably not.

"Miss Proctor, I have to insist that you cooperate with the Governor."

Laura turned slowly to face the man who had spoken. The security guy from the night before. She didn't know his name. Laura met his cold, dark gaze. He extended his hand, and Laura dragged her gaze down to stare at the offered assistance. She looked back to her brother, then to

Sandra. Laura swallowed the rush of fear that crowded into her throat. How could she fight all of them?

She shifted her gaze back to the man offering his hand. "They're going to kill me, you know," she said wearily. Laura blinked as tears burned her eyes.

"Laura, please don't say things like that," Sandra insisted gently. "Please lie down and let me take care of you. You've hurt yourself."

Laura shook her head. "It doesn't matter." She brushed past the guy in the black suit and walked to the bed. Laura climbed amid the tangled covers and squeezed her eyes shut. "Just go away," she murmured. "Just…go away."

A long moment of silence passed before anyone responded to her request.

"Lock it this time," James Ed ordered, his voice coming from near the door. "And I want someone stationed outside her room. I don't want her hurting herself again."

"Should we call Dr. Beckman?" Sandra suggested quietly.

"I think it's too late for that," James Ed returned just as quietly. "This has gone way beyond Beckman."

"Excuse me, sir," a new male voice interrupted. "There is a gentleman downstairs to see you."

"At this hour?" James Ed demanded. "Who is it?"

Silence.

"I think you had better come and see for yourself, Governor."

NICK STOOD in the middle of Governor Proctor's private study. He was mad as hell. He had no idea what the hell had gone on here tonight, but he had clearly seen Laura on that balcony. Fear and fury in equal measures twisted inside him. If tonight was any indication of James Ed's ability to take care of his sister, it stunk. And Nick had no intention of leaving her welfare to chance.

Maybe Victoria was right, maybe he had lost his perspective. Victoria had wanted to assign Ian Michaels to Laura's case when Nick called and informed her of his plan to hang around. She had stood by her assertion that Nick needed a vacation. But Nick had managed to convince her otherwise—against her better judgment. Nick blew out a disgusted breath. What the hell was wrong with him? He should have flown back to Chicago last night instead of skulking outside James Ed's house watching for trouble. If security had caught him, how would he have explained his uninvited presence? Nick had just about convinced himself to leave after more than twenty-four hours of surveillance, when Laura had flown out onto that balcony screaming bloody murder. Now, Nick didn't care what James Ed thought.

Nick closed his eyes and shook his head. Here he was allowing history to repeat itself—at his expense. Laura Proctor had almost gotten him killed once. And now he was back in her life as though nothing had ever happened between them. Nick swore softly, cursing his own stupidity.

But he just couldn't leave her like this.

"Nick, sorry you had to wait." Governor Proctor breezed in, a suit flanking him. "I thought you had to get back to Chicago? What's going on?"

"I was about to ask you the same question." Nick met him halfway across the room and accepted the hand he extended. "I saw Laura on the balcony." Nick had called out to her, but she hadn't heard him.

James Ed shook his hand firmly, then sighed mightily. Worry marred his face. "I'm not sure I know what happened."

"Where's Laura?" Nick felt a muscle tic in his tense jaw.

James Ed dropped his gaze and slowly shook his head. "She's in her room, heavily sedated." He lifted his gaze back to Nick's and shrugged listlessly. "Tonight's episode was intensely frightening. I was afraid she would—" he swallowed "—fall off the balcony."

Renewed fear slammed into Nick like a sucker punch to the gut. "Is she all right?"

"Physically she'll be okay," he explained. "But she's convinced that someone is trying to kill her."

"And you don't believe that?" Nick noted the lines of fatigue around the Governor's eyes and mouth before he looked away. "You're certain she's all right. I heard her scream and the next thing I knew she was struggling against the French doors as if someone were trying to get to her."

"That was me," James Ed explained. "I'll take you up in a moment and you can see for yourself." He shook his head wearily. "But honestly, Nick, I don't know what I believe." He gestured to the chair in front of his desk. "Please, have a seat. I have to do something. But first I have to think this through." He skirted the desk and settled heavily into the high-back leather chair behind it.

Nick didn't have to look to know that the Governor's bodyguard remained by the door. Slowly, Nick moved to stand behind one of the wing chairs near the desk. He wasn't ready to sit just yet. He watched James Ed's reaction closely as Nick asked his next question. "I don't know what's happening here, James Ed. Your actions indicate to me that you don't believe Laura, yet you believed her two years ago. That's why you hired me in the first place."

"Did I?" He met Nick's analyzing gaze. "Or was I simply desperate for someone else to take responsibility for my out-of-control sister?"

"And the man who shot me?" Nick lifted one brow in skepticism. "Was he another figment of her imagination as well?"

James Ed closed his eyes and let go a weary breath. "I don't know," he said quietly. "I only know that Laura is alive and she needs help." He opened his eyes, the same translucent blue as Laura's, and met Nick's gaze. "The kind of help I can't give her. I'm afraid for her life."

The image of Laura's scarred wrists loomed large in Nick's mind. He tensed. Maybe James Ed had a right to be scared of what Laura might do to herself. Nick couldn't be sure. Too much of what was going on still baffled him. Something had been nagging at him since he left her here last night. And he hadn't been able to leave because of it. Nick couldn't put his finger on it just yet, but something wasn't as it should be. Maybe he just needed to get Laura out of his system. Whatever it was, he had to do this. He needed closure with Laura and both their demons.

"Tomorrow I'm calling a private hospital that Dr. Beckman has recommended to me." James Ed lifted his gaze to Nick. "I don't know what else to do. Every waking moment she rants on about her child, then tonight she claims someone tried to kill her. I'm at a complete loss."

"And what if she's telling the truth," Nick offered.

James Ed searched his desk for a moment, then picked up a piece of paper and handed it to Nick. "There's the report from the hospital in Louisiana. See for yourself."

Nick scanned the report that had been faxed to Beckman. The conclusions it indicated were very incriminating. If half of this turned out to be true, Laura was a very sick lady. He leaned forward and passed the report back to James Ed. "I'm still not convinced."

James Ed stroked his forehead as if a headache had begun there. "What is it that you would suggest then, Nick?

I only want to keep her from hurting herself and to find a way to help her.'' He straightened abruptly and banged his fist against the polished desk. "Damn it! I love my sister. I want her to be well. If these doctors can help her, what choice do I have?''

Silence screamed between them for one long beat. "Give me a chance to see if I can get through to her.'' Nick shrugged. "Let me look into the allegations she has made.''

James Ed's weary expression grew guarded. "I'm listening.''

"Two weeks. I choose the place,'' Nick went on. "And there will be absolutely no interference from you or anyone else.''

James Ed frowned. "What do you mean interference?''

"You won't see Laura until I bring her back to you.''

"What kind of request is that?'' James Ed demanded crossly. "She's my sister!''

"What do you have to lose?'' Nick said flatly. He couldn't get to the bottom of what was going on with Laura unless he had her all to himself. There could be no distractions or interference.

The Governor pushed to his feet, irritation lining his distinguished features. "Fine.'' He glowered at Nick. "I'm only doing this because I'm desperate and I trust you. I hope you know that, Foster. Now, where are you planning to take her?''

"I'd like to take her to your country house near Bay Break. It's quiet and out of the way,'' Nick explained. "And Laura mentioned that her childhood there was happy.''

James Ed blinked, then looked away. "Laura did love it there as a child.'' He closed his eyes for a moment before he continued. "And that would protect Laura from the paparazzi that follows me.''

Nick considered the Governor's last words for a bit. Was his concern for his sister or for his image? Maybe Laura's accusations were making Nick paranoid. One thing was certain, before he left Laura this time, Nick would know exactly what and who was behind Laura's problems—even if it turned out to be Laura herself. That possibility went against Nick's instincts, but time would tell.

"When would you like to begin?" James Ed asked.

Nick couldn't be sure, but he thought he saw something resembling hope in James Ed's gaze. "We'll leave right away," Nick suggested.

"I'll call Rutherford and have him prepare the house." James Ed surveyed his desk as if looking for something he had just remembered. "Sandra will put some things together in a bag for Laura."

"Good." Nick turned to leave.

"Nick."

He shifted to face James Ed once more. "Yes."

"Take good care of her, would you?"

Nick dipped his head in silent acknowledgment.

NICK STOOD at the foot of Laura's bed and watched her sleep for several minutes. He closed his eyes and willed away the need to hold her. She looked so small and vulnerable. And Nick wanted more than anything to protect her. He opened his eyes and stared at the soft blond hair spread across her pillow. He wanted to hold her to him and protect her forever. That's what he really wanted. But could he do that? He had seen the report with his own eyes. He swallowed. Laura could be very ill.

That reality didn't stop him from wanting her. Laura's problems had almost cost him his life once before. Apparently that didn't carry much weight with Nick either, because it sure as hell hadn't kept him from hanging around when his assignment was technically over. Giving himself credit, there was more to his being here than simply bone-deep need and desire.

Something wasn't right with this whole picture. James Ed appeared every bit the loving, concerned brother. By the same token Laura seemed as sane as anyone else Nick knew. He lifted one brow sardonically. That didn't say much for Nick's selected associates.

Nick's thoughts turned somber once more. Laura was convinced that she had a child. He frowned. According to James Ed and the hospital report, that was impossible. Nick massaged his forehead. Well, he had two weeks to decide what the real truth was. And the only way he would ever be able to do that is if he kept his head screwed on straight. He couldn't allow her to get to him again. One way or another he would get to the truth. He owed it to himself...and he owed it to Laura. The image of her stricken face when he had left her haunted his every waking moment. Nick swallowed hard. He simply couldn't walk away without looking back. No matter what had happened in the past. He just couldn't do it.

Nick stepped quietly to the side of the bed. He sat down next to Laura and watched her breathe for a time. She was so beautiful. Nick cursed himself. He wasn't supposed to dwell on that undeniable fact. He lifted his hand to sweep the hair from her face, but hesitated before touching her. He swallowed hard as he allowed his fingertips to graze her soft cheek. That simple touch sent desire hurdling through his veins.

"Laura," he whispered tautly. "Wake up, Laura."

Her lids fluttered open to reveal those big, beautiful blue eyes. It took her a moment to focus on his face. Drugs, he realized grimly. James Ed had said she was heavily sedated.

"Nick?" She frowned, clearly confused.

"It's okay, Laura," he assured her.

She struggled to a sitting position. Nick's gaze riveted to her bloodstained T-shirt. The same T-shirt she had been wearing when he brought her here.

"What the hell happened?" he demanded softly. Before Nick could determine where the blood had come from, Laura flung her arms around him and buried her face in his neck.

"I prayed you'd come back for me," she murmured, her words catching on a tiny sob.

Hesitantly, Nick put his arms around her and pulled her close. "It's okay. I'm here now, and this time I'm not leaving without you." The feel of her fragile, trembling body in his arms made him want to scream at the injustice of it all. How could life be so unfair to her...and to him?

Laura drew back from him, her eyes were glassy, her movements sluggish. "Nick, I just need you to do one thing for me."

"What's that?" he asked, visually searching her upper body for signs of injury. The idea that someone had hurt Laura seared in his brain.

"Please, Nick," she murmured, "find my baby."

Chapter Five

"This child doesn't look neglected to me." Elsa touched the small dark head of the sleeping child. "Where was he found?"

"It's not our job to ask questions."

"I'm only saying that he looks perfectly healthy and well cared for in my opinion," Elsa argued irritably. The child slept like the dead. He rarely cried and ate like a horse. And when he was awake, he played with hardly any fuss. This was no neglected and abandoned child.

"Who's asking for your opinion?"

"I'm entitled to my opinion."

"That you are. You'd do well to remember your place and to keep your opinions to yourself."

"Don't you wonder where he came from?" Elsa wondered how her longtime friend could simply pretend not to notice the obvious inconsistencies.

"No. And if you know what's good for you, you'll put those silly notions out of your head and be about your work. There are some things we're better off not knowing."

Elsa's gaze again wandered to the sleeping child. He really was none of her concern—not in that way anyhow. And asking questions and jumping to conclusions weren't included in her duties.

Perhaps her friend was right.

NICK STARED at a framed photograph of Laura as a child while he waited for his call to be transferred to Ian's office. Perched in the saddle atop a sandy-colored pony, Laura beamed at the camera, her smile wide and bright. Nick decided the moment had been captured when she was about five. All that angel blond hair hung around her slim shoulders like a cape of silk. Her big brother, James Ed, who would have been about twenty-one, sported an Ole Miss letter sweater and gripped the lead line to the pony's bridal. His own smile appeared every bit as bright as his sister's.

A frown furrowed Nick's brow. What happened, he wondered, between then and now to change their lives so drastically? With a heavy sigh, he placed the picture in its original position on the oak mantel. Nick stared at the frozen frame in time for a second or two more. Had James Ed been a doting brother then? Did he really care about Laura the way he claimed to now? Laura certainly didn't think so.

Ian Michaels' accented voice sounded in Nick's ear, drawing his attention back to the cellular telephone and the call he had made. "Hey, Ian, it's Nick. I need you to check on a few things for me." Nick paused for Ian to grab a pen. "Review the file on Laura Proctor again and see if you can dig up anything new." Nick scrubbed a hand over his unshaven face, then frowned at the realization that he hadn't taken time to shave. After getting Laura settled in the Proctor country home, he had stayed up what was left of the night—early morning actually—watching over her.

"I didn't find anything when I ran that background check on her brother a couple of years ago." Another frown creased Nick's forehead. He'd been pretty distraught at the time; maybe he missed something. "I want you to look again. See if I overlooked anything at all. Something just isn't kosher down here. I can feel it,'' Nick added thoughtfully. He listened as Ian mentioned several areas that might turn up something new if he dug deeply enough.

"Sounds good," Nick agreed. "And, listen, check out that hospital in Louisiana that claims to have provided care for Laura for the past eighteen months. I want to know the kind of treatment she received, the medication she took—hell, I want to know what she ate for the last year and a half." Nick smiled at Ian's suggested means of collecting the requested and highly sensitive information. "Just don't get caught," Nick said. "Call me as soon as you have anything."

Nick flipped the mouthpiece closed and deposited the phone into his jacket pocket. He massaged his chin and considered his next move. There really wasn't much he could do until he heard from Ian. He let go a heavy breath. Except for keeping Laura out of trouble and, of course, getting the truth out of her. He should probably check on her now, he realized.

The Proctor country home was a ranch-style house of about three thousand square feet that was more mansion than home. Polished oak floors and rich, dark wainscoting and stark white walls represented the mainstay of the decor. The furnishings were an eclectic blend of antiques and contemporary, complemented by oriental wool rugs. The place was well maintained. The caretaker, Mr. Rutherford, appeared to stay on top of things. Upon James Ed's instructions, Rutherford had dropped by and adjusted the thermostat to a more comfortable setting, even stocked the refrigerator before Nick and Laura arrived. The old man had gone to a lot of trouble in the middle of the night. He also left a note with his telephone number in case they needed anything. Nick wasn't sure the guy could be of any real assistance to him unless the central heating unit died or the water heater went out, but he appreciated the gesture.

From the foyer Nick took the west hall and headed in the direction of Laura's bedroom. There were two bedrooms and two bathrooms at each end of the house. Laura's was the farthest from the main part of the house. Nick's was directly across the hall from hers. Nick opened the door and walked quietly across the plush carpeting to her bedside. She hadn't moved since the last time he checked on her. That bothered him. Laura hadn't shown any true violent tendencies in his opinion. A faint smile tilted his lips. Well, except for the way she crowned him with that coffee mug. Nick touched the still tender place at his temple. But that had been in self-defense, at least from Laura's standpoint. Yet they had kept her drugged as if she were a serious threat.

Nick considered the shallow knife wound on her chest and the tiny prick at the base of her throat. The injuries weren't consistent with anything self-inflicted in his opinion. Anger kindled inside him when he considered that no one had tended the injuries. He had done that himself, and then replaced the bloodstained T-shirt with a clean one Sandra had provided. Oh, Sandra had been apologetic enough. She had tried, she insisted, to take care of the wounds, but Laura had fought her touch. Nick wasn't sure he fully believed the woman, but that really didn't matter now.

Laura was safe for the moment. And one damned way or another he intended to see that she stayed that way. When she was up to it, he would get the answers he wanted. But first he had to unravel the mystery of where Laura had been and what she had been doing for the past two years. His gut told him that the answers he wanted about the man who shot him were somehow tangled in those missing months.

The pills Sandra had given him for Laura right before they left Jackson caught his eye. Nick sat down on the edge of the bed and picked up the prescription bottle to review the label. Take one or two every twelve hours. The pharmacist he had called this morning for information regarding the drug had said that the dosage was the strongest available. He had seemed surprised at the instructions to administer the medication more than once in a twenty-four hour period. Nick sighed and set the bottle back on the night table. The medication was strong enough that Laura hadn't moved a muscle.

Nick watched her breathe for a long while, just as he had done for hours last night. He closed his eyes and resisted the urge to touch her. Touching her would be a serious mistake. He had to stay in control of the situation this time. Nick pushed to his feet. Whenever she roused from the drug-induced slumber, she would likely be hungry. Nick left the room without looking back. A quick inventory of what the kitchen had to offer would keep him occupied for a while. If any supplies were needed he would just call Mr. Rutherford and put in an order.

When Nick reached the spacious kitchen a light knock sounded from the back door. A quick look through a nearby window revealed an older man, in his sixties maybe, waiting on the back stoop. Mr. Rutherford, Nick presumed from the overalls and the work boots.

"Howdie, young fella," the old man announced as soon as Nick opened the door. "I'm Carl Rutherford. Came by to see if you had everything you needed."

"Good morning, Mr. Rutherford. I'm Nick Foster." Nick pushed a smile into place and extended his hand.

"A pleasure to meet you, Mr. Foster." Rutherford clasped Nick's hand and shook it firmly

"Please, call me Nick. And thank you, you've taken care of everything here quite nicely."

Mr. Rutherford beamed with pride. "I've been seeing after this place for nearly thirty years." His expression grew suddenly somber. "How's Miss Laura this morning?"

Nick hesitated only a moment before stepping back. "Come in, Mr. Rutherford. I was about to have another cup of coffee."

"You can call me Carl," he insisted as he stepped inside.

Nick gestured for him to have a seat, then closed and locked the door. "How do you take it, Carl? Black?"

Carl settled himself into a chair at the breakfast table. "No sir, I like a little cream in mine if that's not too much trouble."

Nick shot him an amused look. "No trouble at all. You asked about Laura." Nick withdrew two cups from the cabinet near the sink and placed them on the counter. He had already gone through one pot. "She's sleeping right now." Nick frowned as he poured the dark liquid into the cups. "I'm not sure I can answer your question about her well-being with any real accuracy."

Carl huffed an indignant breath. "Was never a thing wrong with that little girl as long as she lived here."

Nick eyed the old man curiously as he stirred the cream into his coffee. "Tell me about Laura...before," he suggested cautiously. "Maybe that will give me some insight to what's going on now," he added at the older man's suspicious look.

Carl folded his arms over his chest and leaned back in his chair, lifting the two front legs off the floor. "She was a mighty sweet little thing growing up. Everybody loved her. Like an angel she was."

Nick had made that same connection several times himself. There was just something angelic and seemingly vulnerable about Laura's features. "She never got into trouble in school?" Nick placed both cups on the table and sat down across from his talkative visitor.

Carl shook his head adamantly. "No sir." He waved off the obvious conclusions. "Oh, the tale was that she got a little wild right before she went off to college." He made a scoffing sound in his throat. "That's why James Ed rushed her off to that fancy college up north."

"And you don't think that was the case?" Nick watched the older man's swiftly changing expressions.

"Land sakes no!" The chair legs plopped back to the floor. "Wasn't a thing wrong with that little girl except she had a mind of her own. She didn't fall into step like James Ed demanded." He harrumphed. "Why she was just like her daddy, that's all."

"Like her father how?" Nick's interest was piqued now. He sipped his coffee and listened patiently.

"You see, I worked for James Ed's granddaddy, James Senior, when I first moved to this county," Carl explained. "Right before James Ed's daddy, James Junior, went off to college he got a little wild."

Nick eyed him skeptically. "What do you mean wild?"

The old man shrugged. "Oh, you know, running with the wrong crowd. Even got himself involved with a girl from the wrong side of the tracks."

"Rebellious, like Laura?"

Carl nodded. "So the tale goes."

"What happened?"

"Well, James Junior got himself hustled off to one of them Ivy League law schools." The old man frowned in concentration. "Harvard, I believe it was. There was a bit of a stir about it. All the big shots hereabouts have always gone to Ole Miss. James Senior went to Ole Miss."

"But not James Ed's father?"

"Nope." Carl took a hefty swallow of his coffee. "When James Junior got back, he joined his daddy's law practice and married a girl of the right standing, if you know what I mean."

Nick considered his words for a time before he spoke. "What happened to the other girl?"

"Can't rightly say."

"So you think James Ed ushered Laura off to school in Boston in order to keep her out of trouble here."

"Yep." He leveled a pointed look at Nick. "But I think it amounted to nothing more than James Ed being too busy taking care of business and building his political career to deal with a hard-to-handle teenager." Red staining his cheeks as if realizing too late he had said too much, Carl scooted his chair back and got to his feet. "Thank you for the coffee, Nick. I'd better get going. Lots to do, you know." He turned before going out the door and met Nick's gaze one last time. "Give Laura my best, will you?"

Nick assured him that he would do just that. After the old man left Nick paced restlessly. He slid off his jacket and hung it on the back of a chair. For the next half hour he played the conversation over and over in his head, looking for any kind of connection. Each time he came up blank. Not taking any chances, he put in another quick call to Ian and added James Ed's daddy to the list of pasts to be looked into.

Maybe if he looked long and hard enough he would find at least some answers.

LAURA LICKED her dry lips and tried to swallow. Her throat felt like a dusty road. With a great deal of effort she opened her eyes. Focus came slowly. Where was she? Pink walls. Shelves lined with stuffed animals and a collection of dolls brought a smile to her parched lips.

Home.

She was home.

And Nick was here.

The events of the past few days came crashing into her consciousness. Laura wilted with reaction. *Her baby.* Oh, God, where was her baby? Clenching her jaw, she forced the overwhelming grief away. She had to get up. She couldn't find her baby like this.

Her arms trembling, Laura pushed to a sitting position. Her muscles were sore and one leg was asleep. Grimacing at the foul taste in her mouth and the bitter knots in her stomach, Laura stumbled out of bed. She made her way to the bathroom and took care of necessary business, including brushing her teeth. Using her hand, she thirstily drank from the faucet, then splashed some of the cool water on her face. Laura felt like she had been on a three-day drinking binge. She supposed she should be thankful for the dulling effects of the drugs, for if she were to have to face this nightmare with full command of her senses—

Laura couldn't complete the thought. Focus on something else, she ordered herself. Clumsily she fumbled through drawers until she found a hairbrush. Straightening out the mess her hair was in took some time and focused effort. Though still groggy, she felt at least a little human then.

Dressed in nothing but an oversized T-shirt and panties from the bag Sandra had sent along, Laura went in search of Nick. She needed to know if he had made any headway in the search for her son.

Laura's heart squeezed at the thought of her baby. A wave of dizziness washed over her. She sagged against the wall for a few seconds to allow the weakness to pass. *Please, God,* she prayed, *don't let anyone hurt my baby.*

She closed her eyes tightly to hold back the burn of tears. Crying would accomplish nothing.

Robby, where are you? she wanted to scream.

Laura forced her eyes open and pushed away from the wall. She had to be strong. Her son was depending on her. If no one would believe her, she would have to find a way to escape. Somehow she would find Robby herself.

Somehow...somehow.

A touch of warmth welled inside her when she considered that Nick had rescued her. Maybe he believed her just a little. That shred of hope meant more to her than he would ever know.

Laura passed through the foyer and checked both the den and the living room. No Nick. She frowned and for the first time noticed it was dark outside. Had she slept through another day? God, how long had her baby been missing now? She repressed the thought. One thing at a time. She had to find Nick first.

The scent of food suddenly hit her nostrils. Laura staggered with reaction. How long had it been since she had eaten? She shook her head. She had no idea. Following the mouthwatering aroma, Laura found Nick in the kitchen hovering over the stove. She opened her mouth to call his name, but caught herself. She propped against the doorjamb instead and took some time to admire the father of her child.

Nick wore his thick black hair shorter than she remembered, Laura realized for the first time. But it looked good on him, she admitted. Nick was one of those guys who had a perpetual tan, the kind you couldn't buy and you couldn't get on the beach. His skin was flawless. And those lips. Full and sensual, almost feminine. Laura took a long, deep breath to slow the rush of desire flowing through her. From the beginning she had been fiercely attracted to the man.

Laura had only made love with one other man, and that one time had proven more experimental than passionate.

There was just something about Nick. Laura closed her eyes and relived the night they had spent making love. A storm had raged outside, roaring like a wild beast with its thunder. Flash after flash of lightning had lit the room, silhouetting their entwined bodies in shadows on the wall. His kiss, his touch, the feel of his bare skin against hers....

"Laura?"

Laura's lids fluttered open, her attention drifted back from the sweet memory of making love with Nick, of making their baby. Those assessing green eyes, the color of polished jade met hers.

"Feeling better?"

A trembling smile curled her lips. Her heart wanted so to trust this man. Every fiber of her being cried out with need in his presence. "A little," she replied. Laura shoved a handful of hair behind her ear and trudged slowly across the room. Damn, she hated this zombie-status feeling. She leaned against the counter and peered into the steaming pot. Soup. She closed her eyes and inhaled deeply of the heavenly scent.

"Hungry? You slept through lunch."

The sound of his deep voice rasped through her soul. That knowing gaze remained on hers, analyzing. "Yes," she murmured. With Nick wearing jeans and a tight-fitting polo shirt, Laura had an amazing view of all that muscled terrain she remembered with unerring accuracy.

Nick reached for a bowl. "Have a seat," he suggested.

Laura frowned when she noted the gun tucked into his waistband, but the image of those strange pink eyes made her glad Nick was armed.

"Sit down, Laura."

She snapped her gaze to his. Food. Oh yeah. He wanted

her to eat. Though food would never fill the emptiness inside her, she knew she had to eat. But only the feel of her baby in her arms would ever make her whole again.

"Have you learned anything about my son?" she asked abruptly.

Nick shifted his intense gaze to the steaming soup. "I have a man working on it." After thoroughly stirring it, he met her gaze once more. "But to answer your question, no. We don't have any more details other than those you gave me."

Which were sketchy at best, he didn't add. Laura could hear the subtle censoring in his tone. Anxiety twisted in her chest. "I've got to find him, Nick." She sucked in a harsh breath. "Please, don't keep me here like a prisoner when my son is out there somewhere." She shook her head slowly. "I have to find him."

Nick clicked the stove off and turned his full attention to her. "You're not a prisoner, Laura. I didn't wake you this afternoon and give you the scheduled dose of medicine for that very reason. I want your head clear. I want to help you."

Hope bloomed in Laura's chest. "You believe me?" she whispered, weak with relief. Laura blinked back the moisture pooling in her eyes.

He studied her for a long moment before he answered. "Let's just say, I'm willing to go with that theory until I have reason *not* to." He cocked his head speculatively. "Can you live with that?"

Laura gave a jerky nod. "As long as we find my baby I can live with anything."

Warning flashed in those green depths. "If you make a run for it, or give me one second of grief—"

"I won't," Laura put in quickly. "I swear, Nick. I'll do whatever you say."

Tension throbbed in the silence that followed. "All right," he finally said, then gestured to the table. "Have a seat and I'll be your server for the evening." A smile slid across those full lips.

Laura nodded and made herself comfortable at the table. Nick might still have reservations, but at least he planned to give her the benefit of the doubt. That's all she could ask at this point. And he had effectively stalled James Ed's plans to send her away.

Her eyes drinking in his masculine beauty, and comparing each physical trait to that of her small son, Laura watched Nick prepare her dinner and set it before her. Robby looked so much like his father. Laura longed to share that secret with Nick.

But she couldn't.

Not until she proved her case—her sanity. She frowned. She had to find her son, and then prove herself a fit mother to the man who possessed the power to legally take her child from her. Laura's heart ached at the possibility that Nick would likely never forgive her for keeping his son from him. He would probably hate her. She shook off that particular dread. She had enough to worry about right now. Some things would have to wait their turn to add another scar to her heart.

"Water or milk?" he asked.

"Water is fine," she replied with a small smile. "I'm still feeling a little queasy." His answering smile as he sat down across the table from her took her breath away.

Laura squeezed her eyes shut and tried to clear the lingering haze that continued to make coherent thought a difficult task. Not to mention she couldn't keep drooling over Nick. Maybe once she got some food into her empty stomach she could think more rationally. Uncertain as to how her queasy stomach would react, Laura took a small taste of the soup. Swallowing proved the hardest step in the process. Finally, she managed.

"I hope that look on your face has nothing to do with the palatability of the cuisine."

With a wavering smile, Laura swallowed again, then shook her head. "It's wonderful. I'm just not as hungry as I first thought." Her stomach roiled in protest of that tiny taste.

Nick's concerned expression tugged at her raw emotions. "You need to eat, Laura."

She sipped her water, trying her level best not to rush from the table and purge her body of that single sip. "I know." How could she eat when she didn't know if her child had been fed? Laura froze, the glass of water halfway to her mouth. The glass plunked back to the table, her hand no longer able to support its weight. She couldn't.

Nick was suddenly at her side asking her if she was all right. Laura turned to him and stared into those green eyes that looked so much like Robby's. Don't lose it, Laura. She drew in an agitated breath. If you lose it he'll believe James Ed and the hospital report, and then you'll never find Robby. Laura blinked at the flash of fear she saw in Nick's eyes. He still cared, but would that be enough?

"I'm okay," Laura said stiffly. She clenched her hands into tight fists beneath the table. "I'm just not hungry that's all." She manufactured a dim smile for his benefit. "I'm sure it's just the medicine affecting my appetite."

Nick moved back to his own chair then. "You'll probably wake up in the middle of the night starved," he suggested warmly.

Laura nodded, struggling to keep her smile in place. He had gone to all this trouble for her, the least she could do was try to force down a few bites.

Nick folded his napkin carefully and laid it aside before

meeting her gaze again. Laura moistened her lips in anxious anticipation of what was coming next. Did he know something that he hadn't wanted to tell her? Her heart butted against her rib cage. Something about Robby?

"We need to talk, Laura," he said quietly.

Laura's heart stilled in her chest. Adrenaline surged then, urging her heart back into a panicked rhythm.

That penetrating gaze bored into hers. "I need you to start at the beginning and tell me everything." He pressed her with that intense gaze. "And I mean everything. I can't help you if you hold anything back."

This wasn't about Robby. Relief, so profound, shook her that Laura trembled in its aftermath. "You're right, Nick," she said wearily. "There's a lot we need to talk about." She shrugged halfheartedly. "But I'm still not thinking clearly. Is it all right if we wait until morning when my head is a bit clearer?" Please let him say yes! Her emotions were far too raw right now, and she still felt groggy. She had to be in better control of herself before answering any questions. She might make a mistake. Laura couldn't risk saying the wrong thing while under the lingering influence of the medication.

"Tomorrow then," Nick relented.

Laura stood, intent on getting back to her room before he changed his mind. "I think I'll have a bath and crawl back into bed." She turned and headed for the door, concentrating on putting one foot in front of the other without swaying.

"Laura."

She paused. Laura closed her eyes and took a fortifying breath before she turned back to him. "Yes."

Nick sipped his water, then licked his lips. She shivered. "Don't lock the door in case I need to check on you," he told her.

Irritation roared through Laura's veins at his blatant reminder that he didn't completely trust her. "Sure," she said tightly.

Her movements still spasmodic and somewhat sluggish, Laura stormed back to her room. She jerked off her clothes and threw them on the unmade bed. Once in the bathroom, she not only slammed the door, but locked it for spite. She was an adult. She could certainly bathe herself without incident, she fumed, as she adjusted the faucet to a temperature as hot as her body would tolerate. The warm water would relax her aching muscles. Laura grabbed a towel and tossed it onto the chair next to the tub. Her reflection in the mirror suddenly caught her attention. The shallow half-moon slash on her upper chest zoomed into vivid focus.

The memory of the intruder who tried to kill her shattered all other thought. Image after image flooded her mind. Glittering pinkish eyes. The oddest color she had ever seen. The black ski mask. The glint of light on the wide blade of the knife. Her blood. *Time to die, princess.* Laura grasped the cool porcelain of the sink basin. She clenched her teeth to prevent the scream that twisted in her throat.

You're okay, you're okay, she told herself over and over. *You're safe. Nick is here now. He'll keep you safe.* Laura drew in a long, harsh breath. She had to stay calm. *You can't find Robby if you're hysterical all the time.*

The sound of the water filling the expansive garden tub behind her finally invaded Laura's consciousness. She relaxed her white-knuckled grip on the basin and turned slowly toward the brimming bath. Cool night air caressed her heated skin. Laura closed her eyes and savored the coolness. Nick must have opened a window. She inhaled deeply of the fresh air. She would feel better tomorrow, be more clearheaded. And maybe tomorrow would bring news of Robby. Hope shimmered through Laura as she stepped into the tub. The sooner she took her bath and got into bed, the sooner she would go to sleep and tomorrow would come.

Please, God, please let me find my baby.

Laura turned off the water and settled into its warm depths. She closed her eyes and allowed the heat to do its work. Absolute quiet surrounded her, except for the occasional drip of the faucet. Each tiny droplet echoed as it splashed into the steaming water, the sound magnified by the utter silence. Laura softly moaned her surrender as complete calm overtook her. Tension and pain slipped away. Fear and anxiety evaporated as the warmth lulled her toward a tranquil state just this side of sleep. She was so very tired. So sleepy…

She was under the water.

Laura struggled upward, but powerful hands held her down. Strong fingers gouged into her shoulders. She opened her eyes to see but inky blackness greeted her. Who turned out the lights? Her lungs burned with the need for oxygen. She wanted to scream. Laura flailed her arms, reaching, searching, grasping at thin air. Mental darkness threatened. *Don't pass out! Fight!* Her nails made contact with bare skin. She dug in deep. The grip on her loosened. She plunged upward. Blessed air filled her lungs.

Laura screamed long and loud before her head was forced beneath the water once more.

Chapter Six

Nick loaded the soiled dinnerware and utensils into the dishwasher and closed the door. He braced his hands on the counter and stared into the darkness beyond the kitchen window. Tomorrow he would have to make sure Laura ate something. She wouldn't regain her strength without food, and she would need all her energy to get through the next few days.

She was going to have to make a believer out of Nick. Laura would have to prove to him that someone had tried to kill her and that a child did exist...somewhere.

Laura's child.

Nick frowned at that thought. The idea had niggled at him for a while now. He and Laura had only made love once. If she did have a child, and if...he were the father—an unfamiliar emotion stirred inside him—that would make the baby...about fifteen months old. He would simply ask her the child's age. He shook his head in denial. That wasn't possible. If Laura had been pregnant with his child, surely she would have come to him for help rather than...

Nick cut off that line of thinking. There was no point in running scenarios when he still didn't know exactly what had happened two years ago. Nor did he know the real story about the events that led up to Laura's disappearance. As soon as Laura was up to it, he intended to find out every detail. He would give her the benefit of the doubt on the kid. If she said she had a son, maybe she did. He couldn't imagine what purpose that particular lie served.

Unless, he considered reluctantly, she was suffering from the mental condition listed in the report from the hospital. Nick rubbed at the ache starting right between his eyes. And if she were in the hospital all that time, did that negate the possibility that there was a child? No point in working that angle until he had some word from Ian. In the meantime, Nick would just have to concentrate on getting some answers from Laura. He wasn't going to bring up the medication either—unless she asked for it. He had an uneasy feeling about those damned pills. Besides, he needed her head clear if he planned to ascertain any reliable answers.

Just another job, he told himself for the hundredth time. Nothing else. Laura Proctor was his assignment, and he damned sure intended to get the job done right this time. Getting to the bottom of this tangled mystery once and for all was the only thing that kept Nick here. That and his damned sense of justice. If there was any chance Laura was right and James Ed had set all this up...

Who was he kidding? Nick had spent more than twenty-four hours monitoring James Ed's house because he couldn't bear to leave Laura under those circumstances. Fool that he was, he still wanted to protect her. Poised to push the dishwasher's cycle button, a muffled sound made Nick hesitate. He quickly analyzed the auditory sensation. A scream? Dread pooled in his gut.

Laura.

Nick bolted from the kitchen, shouting her name. Dodging family heirlooms as he flew down the hall, Nick ticked off a mental checklist of items in a bathroom with which one could hurt oneself. Razor topped the accounting. Nick cursed himself for not checking the room first. Why the hell had he allowed her even this much free rein? His heart pounded with the fear mushrooming inside him.

He skidded to a stop outside the closed door and twisted the knob. Locked. "Laura!" he banged hard on the door. "Laura, answer me, dammit!"

Water sloshed and something clattered to the floor. He could hear Laura's frantic gasps for air between coughing jags. "Laura!" Nick clenched his jaw and slammed his shoulder into the door, once, twice. The lock gave way and he shoved into the dark, humid room. He flipped on the overhead light.

Naked and dripping wet, Laura was on her hands and knees next to the tub. She struggled to catch her breath, water pooled on the tiled floor around her. An assortment of scented candles and a silver tray were scattered about near the end of the tub. No blood anywhere that he could see. Relief rushed through Nick. He grabbed the towel draped across a chair and, ignoring the pain roaring in his knee, knelt next to Laura. Gently, he wrapped the towel around her trembling body and drew her into his arms.

Nick sat down on the edge of the tub and pulled Laura onto his lap. "It's okay," he murmured against her damp hair. "I've got you." Nick swiped back the wet strands clinging to her face. "What happened, honey, did you fall asleep in the water?" Nick called himself every kind of fool for not considering that the drugs still in her system might make her drowsy again. His gut clenched at the idea of what could have happened.

Still gulping in uneven breaths, Laura lifted her face to his. "He…he tried to drown me. I…" She sucked in another shaky breath. "I screamed…" Her eyes were huge with fear. "The window." Laura lifted one trembling hand and pointed to the window. "He went out the window."

Frowning, Nick followed her gesture. He stared at the half-open window and the curtain shifting in the cold night air. "Why did you open the window? It's freezing outside."

Laura drew back and searched his gaze, confusion cluttering her sweet face. "I didn't," she said slowly. "I thought you did." She frowned. "He must have come—"

"Now why the hell would I do something as stupid as leaving the window open?" he demanded, disbelief coloring his tone.

One blond brow arched, accenting the irritation that captured her features. "But you thought I did *something that stupid?*"

Nick shook his head. "I didn't mean it like that," he defended.

"Sure you did." Laura struggled out of his grasp, jerked to her feet, and promptly slipped on the wet tile.

He steadied her, his grasp firm on her damp arms. Nick stood then, and glared down at her. He refused to acknowledge all the naked flesh available for admiration. He couldn't think about that right now. "I only meant," he ground out impatiently, "that *someone* opened the window and it wasn't me."

She smiled saccharinely. "So, of course, it was me."

"Well, there doesn't seem to be anyone else around," he said hotly. A muscle jumped in his tightly clenched jaw, adding another degree of tension to the annoyance already building inside him.

Laura shrugged out of his grasp. "No joke, Sherlock." She adjusted the towel so that it covered more of her upper chest, including the healing injuries from her last encounter with...who or whatever.

Nick forced away the unreasonable fear that accompanied that memory. There was no evidence that anyone else was in the damned room but Laura that time either. The image of her naked body slammed into his brain, reminding him of what he had seen with his own eyes. Nick had memorized every perfect inch of her two years ago, tonight's refresher had only made bad matters worse. She was still as beautiful, as vulnerable as she had been then.

Focusing on the task to counter his other emotions, Nick stepped to the window, closed and locked it before turning back to a fuming Laura. "I'll have to check the security system to find out why the alarm didn't go off when the window was opened. In the meantime, why don't you tell me exactly what happened," he suggested as calmly as possible.

"We're wasting time," she snapped. "Whoever tried to hold my head under the water—" she shuddered visibly, then stiffened "—is getting away." Laura fanned back a drying tendril of blond silk. "You're the one with the gun. Are you going to help me or what?"

Nick released a disgusted breath. "Laura, there is no one else here."

"Fine." She pivoted and stamped determinedly toward the door, slipping again in her haste.

Nick reached for her but she quickly regained her balance and stormed out the door. His arm dropped back to his side. Now this, he mused, was the Laura he remembered. Sassy and determined. Grimacing with each step, Nick stalked into the bedroom after her. He snapped to attention at the sight of Laura shimmying into her jeans, the tight denim catching on the damp skin of her shapely backside. Apparently deciding time was of the essence, she had foregone panties.

"What—" Nick cleared his throat. "What the hell do you think you're doing?"

Laura yanked an oversized T-shirt over her head and

turned to face him just as the soft cotton fell over her breasts. "I'm going after him."

Nick choked out a sound of disbelief. He braced his hands at his waist and shook his head. "No you're not."

Laura stepped into her sneakers, plopped down onto the end of the bed and tied first one and then the other, her fiercely determined gaze never leaving his. If this was a war of wills, she need not waste her time. Nick could out-wait Job himself when he set his mind to it.

"Just try and stop me," she challenged as she shot back to her feet. Laura flipped her still damp hair over her shoulders. "I'm tired of being treated like I'm a few bricks shy of a load. And I'm sick of no one believing anything I say." She walked right up to him. "Someone took my son. The same someone that's trying to kill me." She glowered at Nick, her eyes glittering with the rage mounting inside her. "You can either help me or get out of my way."

One second turned to five as Nick met her glower with lead in his own. When it was clear she had no intention of backing down, Nick's mouth slid into a slow smile. What the hell? He could use a walk in the cold air after this little encounter. The image of her naked, shapely rear flashed through his mind and sent a jolt of desire straight to his groin. "All right. We do it your way." Hope flashed in her eyes. "This time," he added firmly. Nick stepped aside and Laura darted past him.

"We need a flashlight," he called out as she disappeared around a corner.

"It's in the kitchen. I'll get it!" she shouted determinedly.

Nick moved his head slowly from side to side. He had to be crazier than she was supposed to be to do this. It was late. Laura should be in bed. His knee hurt like hell, and he could damned sure use a little shut-eye. He had hardly slept at all the last three nights. But he couldn't bring himself to deny her this. She was so sure…a part of him wanted to believe her. That same part that had fallen for a sassy, innocently seductive Laura two years ago.

"Got it." Laura almost hit him head-on when she barreled through the kitchen doorway.

"Good," he muttered. Nick followed Laura to the den but stopped her when she would have thrown the patio door open and burst out into the November darkness. "Hold on there, hotshot." She cast him a withering look. "I'm the one with the gun, remember?"

Laura blinked. "Right." She stepped back, yielding to Nick's lead.

More for her benefit than anything else, Nick drew his weapon from its position at the small of his back. "Stay behind me," he instructed. She bobbed her head up and down in adamant agreement. "And don't turn the flashlight on unless I tell you."

Nick flipped the latch and slid the door open. Instantly, the cold air slapped him in the face, escalating his senses to a higher state of alert. He surveyed the backyard for a full thirty seconds before stepping onto the patio. Slowly, with as much stealth as possible with Laura right behind him, he made his way down the back of the house until he reached the window outside the bathroom that connected to Laura's bedroom.

"Give me the light." Nick took the yellow plastic instrument and slid the switch to the on position. As thoroughly as possible with nothing but a small circle of illumination, Nick examined the area around the window. The window itself, the ledge, the portion of brick wall from the ledge to the ground, then the ground. Nothing. The window showed no signs of forced entry. With the ground frozen, there wouldn't be any tracks, and the nearby shrubbery appeared undisturbed. Nick crouched down and examined the dormant-for-the-winter grass a little closer just to be sure. He saw absolutely no indication that anyone had been there, but with the current weather conditions that determination would not be conclusive.

"Did you find anything?" Laura chafed her bare arms with her hands for warmth.

"Let's go back inside," Nick urged. "It's freezing out here."

Laura dug in her heels when he would have ushered her toward the patio. She lifted her chin defiantly. "You still don't believe me."

"Look." Nick tucked his weapon back into his waistband. "It's not a matter of whether or not I believe you." His grip tightened on the smooth plastic of the flashlight, its beam lighting the ground around their feet. "The fact of the matter is there's nothing to go on—either way."

Nick caught her by one arm when she would have walked away. "*If* anyone was here, there's no one here now and—"

"Go to hell, Foster," she said from between clenched teeth.

His fingers tightened around her smooth flesh. "And," he repeated, "there is no indication that anyone climbed in or out this window."

"He was here," she insisted, her voice low and fierce with anger. "He tried to drown me. And you know what?" She jerked with emotion. "I think he's going to keep trying to kill me until he succeeds. Will you believe me then, Nick?"

This time Nick released her. He watched until she disappeared through the patio door. He closed his eyes and fought the need to run after her. To assure her that he would never let that happen. What was he supposed to believe?

All the facts pointed to Laura as being mentally unstable, suicidal even. Nick flinched at the idea. Not one single shred of evidence existed to support her claims, except the knife wounds James Ed wanted him to believe were self-inflicted. James Ed didn't appear to have any reason to lie. Nick opened his eyes and shook his head. Then why the hell did he want—need—to believe her so badly?

Disgusted with himself as well as the situation, Nick strode slowly toward the still-open door. Maybe he was the wrong man for this job. Apparently he couldn't maintain a proper perspective in Laura's presence. ''Big surprise,'' he muttered.

Nick's gut suddenly clenched. The hair on the back of his neck stood on end. He stopped stock-still. Someone was watching. He felt it as strongly as he felt his own heart beating in his chest. Nick turned around ever so slowly and surveyed the yard once more. Taking his time, he studied each dark corner, watching, waiting for any movement whatsoever.

Nothing.

Nick scrubbed a hand over his beard-roughened face and considered the possibility that maybe he couldn't trust his own instincts anymore. Maybe paranoia was like hysteria, contagious.

One thing was certain, time would tell the tale. In Nick's experience, given time all things became clear.

Nick just hoped that time would be on their side.

''HARDHEADED JERK,'' Laura muttered as she flung another dresser drawer open. She rifled through the contents, then slammed it shut. She needed a change of clothes. Her own clothes. Surely there would be something here she could wear.

Laura paused in her search and tried to remember the

last time she had been here and what she had brought with her. Two years ago. The final barbecue bash of the summer. She remembered. James Ed had insisted she come along. He had invited Rafe. It was Labor Day weekend. Only two months before…

Closing her eyes, Laura fought the memories that tugged at her ability to stay focused. Two months before she met Nick, fell in love with his self-assurance and intensity. Ten years older than her, he seemed to know everything, to be able to do anything. He was so strong, yet so tender. The way he had made love to her changed something deep inside her forever. And he had given her Robby. Tears threatened her flimsy composure. Laura clutched the edge of the dresser when emotion kicked her hard in the stomach. How was she supposed to go on when she didn't know if her baby was safe or not. Had he eaten? Was someone bathing him and keeping his diapers changed? Pain slashed through her, making her knees weak.

No! Laura straightened with a jerk. No. Robby was fine and she was going to find him. She refused to believe anything else. Somehow she would get away and find him. Somehow…

Laura jerked the next drawer open and forced herself to continue her search. The next drawer contained some underclothes and socks, the one after that an old pink sweater. Laura exhaled a puff of relief. At least it was a start. All she had to do was get away from Nick, then she would go back to Doc's clinic and look for clues—

"Laura."

Startled from her plans, she met his gaze in the mirror above the dresser. He stood in the doorway, looking too concerned and too damned good. Laura willed away her heart's reaction to the father of her child. She didn't want to feel this way about Nick. She didn't want to love him.

He would never believe her. Never help her the way she needed him to. Laura clenched her teeth and blinked away the emotion shining in her eyes. She didn't need Nick. She could take care of herself and her son...

...if she could just find him.

"What are you doing?" His gaze strayed to the items she had stacked on top of the dresser.

To lie was her first thought, but Nick was too smart for that. He would see through her in about two seconds. "I'm packing myself a bag." Laura turned to face him. She gripped the edge of the dresser's polished wood surface for extra support. "Because the first chance I get I'm out of here."

Nick took two steps in her direction. He paused then and slowly looked the room over as if seeing her childhood summer sanctuary for the first time, and wanting to commit what he saw to memory. Finally, his gaze moved back to hers, dark, intense. Laura shivered with awareness. Heat stirred inside her. She wanted to touch him, to have him touch her. She swallowed.

"And you think I'm going to allow you to do that."

It wasn't a question, she knew. She leveled her gaze on his, and poured every ounce of determination she possessed into that unsettling eye contact. "You have to sleep sometime."

Two more steps disappeared behind him. "Is that a threat?"

"Yes." Laura's heart rate accelerated. "It is."

"Just for the moment, let's say you were successful in your plan." He paused, cocked his handsome head and assessed her thoroughly. Laura stiffened to prevent her body's need to tremble beneath his blatant act of intimidation. Did he have any idea how he still affected her? "What will you do?"

She held her spine rigid when her body wanted to sag with despair as her harsh reality momentarily pushed aside all else. "I'll find my baby," she told him.

He moved closer. The smooth movement of denim-encased muscle dragged her attention to those long legs and the limp that had first endeared him to her. Nick had gotten that limp by taking a bullet intended for a client he had been assigned to protect the year before Laura met him. He had taken a bullet for her, too. Because that's the kind of man he was. And despite his distrust of her, he had still come back to get her. To protect her. Laura's breathing grew shallow and irregular as renewed need twisted inside her. Giving herself a mental shake, Laura jerked her gaze back to his intense, analyzing one. She had to focus. But she was exhausted, mentally and physically. She needed so much for Nick to hold her right now. But at the same time, Laura needed to escape his watch.

"And the man who's trying to kill you?"

Laura's lips trembled then tightened with the blast of outrage that raced through her at his words. He didn't fully believe her. Why the hell was he asking? "I've been out-maneuvering him for two years. I can do it again."

"Until recently you mean," he suggested quietly. Another half yard of carpet disappeared between them.

"He would never have caught up with me and my son if it hadn't been for you," she told him tautly. Bottom line, Nick was one of the bad guys now. Why didn't he just leave her alone? Why had he come back for her? A tiny seed of hope sprouted in her heart despite her efforts to resist that very emotion.

"So you consider this to be my fault?"

"That's right." Laura pressed back against the dresser as he came closer still. "I hope you can live with it," she added bitterly.

He stopped two steps away. "Oh, I can live with it," he said with complete certainty. "If you can live with this."

Before Laura could fathom what he intended, Nick jerked his shirt from his waistband and pulled it over his head in one fluid motion. Laura's heart slammed mercilessly against her sternum. Her gaze riveted to his bare chest. Broad, tanned, muscled and sprinkled with dark hair. The memory of touching him, making love with him, swirled inside her. Then she saw it. The single jagged scar that marred that amazing terrain just beneath his heart. Laura's own heart dropped to her stomach then. A little higher and Nick would certainly have died.

"But I almost didn't live with it," he said, his voice dangerously low. A muscle flexed in that square jaw of his. "So while we're on the subject of blame, why don't you tell me about the guy you watched put this bullet hole in me. The one you disappeared with while I was bleeding to death." His fingers moved gently over the scar, but there was nothing gentle about his voice or his expression.

Fear, regret, pain churned inside her, but Laura fought to maintain her composure. She had to do this, had to say what needed to be said—for the good it would do. How could he think she had willingly left him to die? "It was my fault that you got shot," she said in a rush. Surprise flickered in Nick's gaze. "Not one day has gone by since that I haven't wished I could go back and somehow prevent what happened. But I swear to you, Nick, I didn't go anywhere with him. He tried to kill me, too."

Wariness slipped into his expression. "But you recognized him, Laura. I saw it in your eyes."

Laura raked her fingers through her wet hair. Her hands trembled so she clenched them into tight fists. God, how could she ever explain everything? "Look," she began wearily. "I admit that I got into some trouble in college."

She met Nick's guarded gaze. "Just like James Ed said. But I know now that I was just desperate for his attention." Laura closed her eyes and forced away the bitter memories twisting inside her brain. "I needed him and he was never there for me. He just wanted me away from him." She stared at the floor for a while before she continued. "When I came home after graduation, he tried to marry me off to Rafe Manning." Laura didn't miss Nick's reaction to Rafe's name. She tamped down the renewed burst of hope that maybe he did feel something for her.

"But you refused," he prompted.

Laura nodded. "James Ed wasn't very happy. And I pretty much made a fool of myself about it," she admitted. "But the car accident and all that other stuff was not my fault." She leveled her gaze on Nick's, hoping to convey the depth of her sincerity. "I tried to tell James Ed that the brakes failed, but he wouldn't listen to anything I had to say."

Nick snagged her hand. His thumb glided across the scar marking her wrist. "And this?"

Laura lifted her free hand and stared at the white slash of a scar. "All I know is that I came home from a party one night." She licked her dry lips. "James Ed and I had argued before I left. So I had a little too much to drink I guess. I came home and crashed on the bed. I woke up the next day in a hospital under suicide watch."

"You don't know for sure what happened then," Nick clarified.

She sucked in a weary breath. "I know I didn't do it. I was passed out. Besides, I had no reason to want to die."

Nick considered her words for a moment, then said, "Now, tell me about the man who shot me."

Laura tried without success to read Nick's closed expression. Did he believe anything she said? Would he believe what she was about to tell him now? Well, it was the truth. That's all she could do was give him the truth. "I saw him in James Ed's private office at the house a couple of times."

Nick's hands fisted at his sides, something fierce flashed in his eyes. "So you do know him?"

"I don't know him. I only saw him—"

"Be careful what you say next, Laura." There was no mistaking the emotion in his voice or his gaze then. Rage. Vengeance. "I know more than you think."

Laura shook her head in confused denial. "Why would you believe that? I did not know him. I still don't."

"I heard everything," Nick ground out.

"Everything?" She shook her head. "I don't understand what you mean." Laura had no idea what Nick was talking about.

Nick smiled, it was far from pleasant. "Oh you're good, Laura. Too good."

"What the hell are you talking about?"

"Before I blacked out completely, he told you that you didn't need me anymore, that it was just you and him now," Nick said coldly. "I heard him say it. You didn't deny it then, don't even think about denying it now."

Laura frowned, trying to remember. She allowed the painful memory to play out in her mind. She had screamed something like "why did you hurt him?" at the man after he shot Nick. Then he had said—oh God, she remembered. Laura met Nick's accusing glare. "He didn't mean it the way you think," she explained. "He meant that he had me where he wanted me—without protection."

"You expect me to believe that?"

Laura nodded. "I swear, Nick, it's the truth. I had never seen the man before in my life except the times I saw him in James Ed's office. That's what this is all about," she argued vehemently. "My brother wants me dead!"

"So you didn't leave willingly with the shooter?"

Astonishment struck her hard. Why wouldn't he believe her? "How could you think I left with him? That I left you hurt? He dragged me out to the riverbank and tried to kill me. He wanted it to look like a murder-suicide." Laura shook her head at Nick's still wary expression. How could she make him believe her? "The storm was still going strong. He lost his balance, and we both went over the edge. He hit his head on a rock on the way down. He never resurfaced, then I got swept away. I woke up the next day several miles down river. I was lost. It took me two days to find my way out of the woods."

"But you never came back, never let anyone know you were alive," Nick reminded her bitterly.

Laura slumped in defeat. "I thought you were dead. I knew my brother was trying to kill me. I didn't think coming back would be too bright."

"What about after you found out I was alive. Why not then? You could have come to me for help."

Uncertainty seized her. She had to tread carefully here. Laura couldn't risk allowing him to discover the truth about Robby. "You worked for James Ed. I knew you would take me back to him. And that's just exactly what you did," she reminded him curtly.

Nick hesitated, his green eyes bored relentlessly into hers. Something she couldn't read flickered in that fierce gaze. "Even after what we had shared, you didn't trust me?"

"Did you trust me? Our whole relationship stemmed from proximity and your desire to protect me. I..." Laura swallowed tightly. "I needed you so desperately. But how could I know that it was safe to trust you completely?"

The seconds turned to minutes before Nick responded. "You couldn't have," he offered flatly. "It's late. You should get some rest," he said, effectively changing the subject. "I'll check all the doors and windows, then I'll reset the alarm. Somehow it failed," he added. He picked up his shirt and started for the door.

Laura wasn't sure whether to be relieved or disappointed that he had left their discussion at a standoff of sorts. He had admitted what she knew as well. Two years ago everything had happened so fast there was no time to learn each other. What happened then hadn't been their fault. Just like now. Circumstances had brought them together, then torn them apart. She closed her eyes and took a slow, deep breath. She was tired. Sleep would come easily. Laura shivered. What if someone came into the house again? Maybe sleep wouldn't come so easily, she decided. The alarm system was obviously no deterrent. And Nick couldn't be everywhere at once.

At the door Nick turned back to her. "One more question," he said offhandedly.

Laura's gaze connected with his. "What's that?"

"How old is your baby?"

Laura's breath fled from her lungs. "Why do you ask?" she managed, her voice devoid of all inflection, her body paralyzed by uncertainty.

"Is there anything I should know about your child?"

She knew exactly what he meant. *Is the child mine?* Laura swallowed the words that wanted to spill out of her. "No," she said instead. Something in his expression changed. "There's nothing you need to know." She blinked back the tears that burned behind her eyes. "Except that I have to find him." She clamped down on her lower lip for a moment to hold her emotions at bay. "I'll die if anything happens to him."

He looked away. "Sleep. We'll talk more in the morning."

Laura watched him leave. Oh God. Why didn't she just tell him the truth?

Because she couldn't live without her son. And if Nick knew the truth, he would take Robby away. After all, Laura was considered unstable. And she couldn't prove any differently. Hadn't tonight's little episode added fuel to the fire? Laura shuddered at the memory of how those strong hands had held her beneath the water.

How would she ever be able to close her eyes now? Knowing her killer was near?

Panic slithering up her spine, Laura ran to first one window, then the next to make sure they were locked. She crawled into the bed and hugged her pillow to her chest.

No way would she be able to let her guard down tonight, even though Nick would be right next door.

All she had to do was stay awake....

Chapter Seven

Elsa smiled as she spooned another taste of strained carrots into the little boy's mouth. He was such a good child. How could anyone believe that this child had been neglected in any way? Elsa frowned. And the only way a mother would abandon a baby this healthy and sweet would be if she were dead.

She stalled, the spoon halfway to the baby's open mouth. If the mother and father were dead, why the abandonment story? The baby gurgled and swung his little fists about in protest. Elsa scolded herself for allowing her mind to drift.

"Okay, little one, be patient." She popped the next bite into his waiting mouth. "I'm just an old woman, and too slow for the lively likes of you," she cooed. The little boy loudly chanted his agreement in baby talk.

Elsa frowned again. This wasn't right. She had worked here for a very long time and nothing like this had ever happened before. Maybe she should slip and take a look at the child's file. There would be a perfect opportunity day after tomorrow with the director away.

Elsa nodded resolutely. Yes, she would see what she could find out. Not that it would really do any good, but it would put her mind at ease.

LAURA JERKED AWAKE. Sunlight streamed in through the partially opened blinds. She rubbed her eyes and tried to gather her thoughts. She had finally given in and fallen asleep a few hours ago. Laura stilled. She had been dreaming. The image of Robby smiling and playing with his food filled her mind's eye. Laura closed her eyes and allowed the dream to warm her. She prayed that it was a good sign. Robby had to be all right.

Two loud raps echoed from the door. "Laura, are you up in there? In about three seconds I'm coming in," he warned.

So that's what woke her. Laura bounded off the bed and hurried to the door. Today she would find a way to prove to Nick that Robby was real. Then maybe he would put some serious effort into helping her. If not, she would set out on her own. She reached the door just as Nick opened it.

The grim expression on his face loudly proclaimed his thoughts without his having to open his mouth. For at least a moment he must have thought she had made good on her threat to make a run for it. The realization that he had even considered her capable of giving him the slip lightened Laura's mood considerably.

"Good morning," she said with exaggerated cheer. God, why did he have to look so good? Her pulse reacted the moment her eyes lit on him.

He took stock of the room and then settled his searching gaze on hers. "Really, what's good about it?"

Laura studied his chiseled features as she shoved her unbrushed hair back from her face. She cringed inwardly when she considered how she must look. Her hair a mess, her clothes slept in, no makeup. But not Nick. He always looked picture-perfect. Never a hair out of place. He looked as if he had taken great pains with every aspect of his appearance. But Laura knew that wasn't the case. Perfection came naturally to Nick. It was the same with his love-making. Slow, thorough. Laura's mouth went unbearably dry.

"We're alive," she offered in answer to his question, and directing her mind away from his expertise between the sheets. "That's definitely good. And maybe today I'll find my son."

"There's coffee in the kitchen," he said impassively. He ignored her comment about Robby. "We should finish last night's discussion."

"Okay," Laura replied just as impassively. "Give me five minutes to change." Today was his last chance, she reminded that part of her that wanted so to believe in him. If he didn't help her today...

Nick's gaze traveled down the length of her and back. She didn't miss the glint of male appreciation, but his gaze was hard when he met hers once more. "Five minutes. I've got a lot of questions that need answers." Without another word, he turned and walked away.

Laura shoved the door closed behind him. She blew out a breath of annoyance. *Men.* She would never understand them. She was the victim here! Laura railed silently. Why did he make her feel like the villain? Someone tried to kill her last night. *Again.* Why wouldn't Nick believe her?

James Ed. Laura crossed her arms over her chest and considered her loving brother. He had done this to her. Taken her life away, taken her child and the man she loved. And for what? Laura shook her head in aversion. Money. It was all about the money.

To hell with the money.

Maybe it was time Laura got down on his level. James Ed wasn't the only one who could play dirty. Laura clenched her teeth until her jaws hurt. Whatever it takes, she promised herself. One way or another she would get her son back.

SEVEN MINUTES LATER, Nick noted impatiently, Laura breezed into the kitchen looking for all the world like a little girl. Jeans hugged her shapely legs while an oversized pink sweater engulfed the rest of her. Her hair was pulled back high on her head in a ponytail. Her sweet face was freshly scrubbed and bright with hope. Nick's chest constricted. He swallowed that damned burning need to take her in his arms and just hold her. He couldn't do that. It would jeopardize his perspective even further. He had a job to do. He shifted in his chair. Damn. Three seconds in her presence and his body was already reacting.

Things between them had always been like this—fast and furious. But neither was to blame. Their circumstances were equally fast and furious. Despite that fact, something drew Nick to her, made him want to believe her. To trust her. Whether Laura was telling the complete truth or not, something was wrong here. His instincts warned him that Laura was in real danger. Evidence or no, things just didn't add up.

Laura popped a slice of bread into the toaster. Nick sipped his coffee and watched her graceful, confident movements. The drug had worn off completely now, he decided. Good. That would make things a lot easier, unless, of course, she became overwrought. Nick set his cup on the table and started to speak but speech eluded him when Laura bent over and poked around in the fridge.

He averted his gaze from her heart-shaped rear and passed a hand over his face. ''I'm glad to see your appetite is back.''

''I just realized I was starving.'' Milk in one hand, jam in the other, Laura shoved the fridge door closed with one slender hip. "I have no idea when I ate last." She smiled as if knowing some secret he wasn't privy to. Nick almost groaned at the angelic gesture. "But I'm about to make up for at least part of it."

"The man," Nick began, drawing her attention from spreading strawberry jam on her toast to him. "Did he actually tell you that James Ed hired him to kill you?" Nick had replayed their conversation a dozen times during the night. He kept coming up with the same questions. Questions he needed answered. And only Laura could answer them. Half the night had been spent running scenarios, the other half fighting the need to go to her bed. Nick tensed. That couldn't happen—even if she were to invite him, which was highly unlikely. This go-around Nick had to remain as personally detached as possible. It was the only way to really protect Laura, and to get to the bottom of whatever was going on.

Laura placed the butter knife on the counter. She frowned thoughtfully. "No, not in so many words. But when I asked him why he was doing this, he said 'for the money, of course'." Laura shrugged. "Who would stand to gain from my death?" She met Nick's gaze then, hers certain in her conclusion. "James Ed."

"I checked his financial standing forward and backward. His assets were a bit shaky prior to the election two years ago, but he recovered. Most politicians barely skate through the election process without financial crisis. James Ed didn't seem to need your trust badly enough to kill for it, in my opinion." Nick pushed his now cold coffee aside. "He appeared to have enough money already."

Laura deposited her skimpy breakfast on the table and dropped into a chair. "Then why would that man have wanted to kill me if he weren't working for my brother?"

Nick lifted one shoulder in a semblance of a shrug. "It

could have been a kidnap-ransom plot gone awry,'' he suggested. That had been the police's theory two years ago.

Laura shook her head. ''No. He intended to kill me, then and there. What good's a ransom if the sacrificial lamb is already dead?''

She definitely had a point there. If only Nick had remembered more details about the man's physical features, maybe they could have nailed down his intent and his associates two years ago. But Nick had barely survived the gunshot and ensuing surgery. The entire event was forever a blur in his mind—except for the snatch of conversation he had heard. Nick would never forget that. The guy was dead according to Laura. Whatever had motivated him, he had gotten his in the end.

Nick took a deep breath and forced the old rage to retreat. ''Maybe he was just a nutcase who wanted to get back at James Ed,'' he suggested.

Laura laughed humorlessly. ''You just don't want to believe that James Ed is behind this little soap opera.'' She leveled her determined gaze on Nick's. ''He tried to marry me off, then he tried to prove me mentally unstable. And when all that failed, he got desperate and hired someone to kill me. Think about it,'' she urged fiercely. ''Ten million dollars is a lot of motivation. If I married, was pronounced mentally incompetent or dead before my twenty-fifth birthday, big brother gained control of the money. No matter what your investigation turned up, he wanted that money.'' Laura leaned back in her chair. ''He still does.'' Laura blinked. ''If he hasn't gotten it already.''

Nick shook his head, still denying her assertion. ''But why? He had enough of his own.''

''Is there ever enough?''

Nick just couldn't reconcile the picture Laura painted with the man he knew. James Ed had truly grieved after

Laura's disappearance. His happiness at having her back home was so clear a blind man could have seen it. "It just doesn't feel right," he countered.

Laura sighed. "I don't know anything to say that will convince you, but I know I'm right. And somehow he found out about my son and took him to get at me. He knows I won't go far as long as there's any chance my child is here somewhere." Her gaze grew distant. "How can I run from James Ed when he holds my heart in his hands?"

Laura's words touched Nick so deeply that he couldn't speak for a time. If Laura had a child, he would definitely help her find him. And if he discovered that James Ed was behind the threat to Laura, the man would not live to regret it. Finally, Nick looked from her untouched toast to her. "You should eat," he said quietly. No one was going to hurt Laura again. *But what about the hospital report?* his more logical side argued.

She shook her head. "No. You have something else to say." She pressed him with her gaze, reading him like an open book. "Say it."

"All right. How do you explain the hospital report? I read it myself." *Give me an answer I can live with,* Nick urged silently.

Laura pressed her lips together and blinked rapidly to fight the fresh tears shining in her eyes. "You know I've even considered that maybe I am crazy. Maybe I imagined the last two years." She shrugged one thin shoulder. "Maybe Robby isn't real." Laura flattened her palms on the table and slowly shook her head from side to side. "But I can't even imagine that. He is real, Nick. As real as you and me. And I have to find him, no matter what it takes." She drew in a bolstering breath. "There's no way I can live without him. He's all I have in this world. Can you understand that?''

Long minutes passed with nothing but silence and a kind of tension that only old lovers could feel between them. Emotions he knew he shouldn't feel battled with his need to stick with the facts. ''Prove it,'' he demanded softly. ''I need hard evidence, Laura.''

''Okay.'' Laura licked her trembling lips. ''Take me to the clinic where he was born. They have records. Would that be proof enough?'' she asked sarcastically.

''Absolutely,'' he said gently.

''Fine.'' Laura stood. ''We should get started then. The clinic is a good half-day drive from here.''

''First,'' Nick ordered, ''you'll eat. Then we'll go.'' Nick held her gaze with his until she relented and settled back into her chair. A single tear trekked down one soft cheek. Every cell that made him who he was reacted to her pain, ached to reach out to her. The strength and determination radiating beneath all that vulnerability played havoc with his defenses. ''You show me one slip of evidence and I swear I'll move heaven and earth to find your child,'' he vowed.

WELCOME TO PLEASANT RIDGE the sign read.

Laura's heart rate accelerated. She suppressed the excitement bubbling inside her at finally reaching the small Alabama town where Robby was born. In just a few short minutes she would have the proof she needed. Then Nick would help her find her baby. Laura brushed back the tears of relief. *Hold on, girl,* she told herself. *You'll find him. Nick won't let you down. He promised.*

Laura glanced at the strong profile of the man behind the wheel. He was so good-looking. She had fallen hard and fast for him two years ago, and had loved him ever since.

A tiny smile tugged at Laura's lips. Confusion had reigned supreme in her life back then with the insanity revolving around the election and James Ed's strange behavior. Laura's smile dipped into a frown. And the attempts on her life. Nick had charged in and taken control of everything, including her heart. She had rebelled at first. Just another man trying to tell her what to do, and who would believe nothing she said, Laura had assumed. But Nick proved her wrong on that score. He reached out to her, made her want to trust him.

But nothing had prepared her for the way he made love to her. Only her second sexual experience, Laura's un-skilled enthusiasm couldn't hold a candle to Nick's complete mastery of the art. She trembled inside at the memory of how easily he had coaxed the woman in her to bloom with just his touch, his kiss. Then when he had been inside her, all else had ceased to exist. There was only Nick and the way he loved her.

Hours had melted away as they had loved each other that one night. Then that murderous thief had barged in unimpeded and stolen the life she could have had with Nick. Laura clutched the car door's armrest and closed her eyes as the painful pictures flashed through her mind. Her heart pounded harder and harder with each passing frame of memory. Nick had pushed her behind him to protect her. Unarmed, he had looked death square in the eye without hesitation.

The sound of the gun firing echoed in Laura's ears. Nick had fallen at her feet, but the other man had grabbed her before she could help Nick. He had forced the small hand-gun into her hand, closed her fingers around it, then pitched it to the floor a few feet away from where Nick lay bleeding to death. Laura hadn't understood then that he was setting her up as Nick's killer.

Laura shivered and forced the memories away. Nick was alive. Somehow he had managed to find his cell phone in the tangled sheet on the floor. The call to 9-1-1 before he had lost consciousness was all that had saved him. Laura had read the story in the newspaper. She had been listed as missing, possibly dead. She swallowed, but not dead enough to suit her brother. If the world thought she was dead, why hadn't James Ed left it at that? She was out of his hair. He could have the money. Why had he hunted her down and dragged her back home?

Maybe, Laura thought with a frown, he hadn't been able to access the trust fund without producing a body. Or maybe he was afraid she would show up when she turned twenty-five and demand *her* money. She considered her brother's obvious determination. He wanted her dead, whatever the reason. Laura turned her attention back to the driver. Unless she could convince Nick that she was right very soon, she was as good as dead. Eventually he would have to turn her over to James Ed.

And where would that leave Robby?

"Is this the place?"

Laura jerked from her disturbing reverie. Nick had parked and was watching her closely, too closely. Laura quickly surveyed the one-story building in front of them. She nodded. "Yeah, this is it." Pleasant Ridge Medical Clinic was lettered on the plate glass window. Not much had changed as far as Laura could see. Thankfully the clinic still opened on Saturdays. There were several other cars in the parking lot, but that was the norm. People came from all over the county for low-cost and, in some cases, free medical care. The cost was based on income, but the service was as good as anyplace else. Laura had been extremely pleased with her care, as well as Robby's, here.

"What name did you use?"

Laura turned to Nick, but hesitated. Would he find her choice of aliases suspicious? There was no other way. She needed those records. "Forester," she said quickly before she lost her nerve. "Rhonda Forester for me, Robert—" Laura's heart skidded to a halt in her chest. Her son's full name was Robert Nicholas Forester. Oh God. "I named my son Robert."

"Just follow my lead," Nick told her as he opened the car door. "Don't say anything unless I ask you a question."

Laura nodded and scooted out after him. She followed Nick toward the entrance. She clenched and unclenched her hands, then smoothed the damp palms over the fuzzy material of her bulky sweater. There was no other alternative. She had to do this. Laura would deal with Nick's suspicions later. Right now she had to do what she had to do. Proving Robby existed was her primary goal. Without proof Nick wouldn't help her. Laura shivered and hugged herself. She had forgotten her jacket in her rush this morning.

Nick pulled the door open and waited for Laura to enter first. She met his gaze one last time before going inside. Okay, Laura, you can do this. Laura forced a smile for the numerous patients who glanced her way as she crossed the waiting room. Nick followed close behind her. She stopped in front of the receptionist's window and waited for the young blond woman to look up from her work.

"May I help you?"

She was new, Laura noted. The receptionist before was blond as well, but a little older.

"I certainly hope so," Nick said with a charming smile. The receptionist warmed to him immediately.

"What can I do for you, sir?"

Laura looked away. She didn't need to see this interaction, and she sure didn't need to feel what she was feeling as a result. Women probably responded to Nick this way all the time.

Nick displayed his Colby Agency ID. ''My name is Foster. I'm a private investigator from Chicago.''

The woman was impressed, Laura noticed when she allowed herself a peek in her direction.

''I'm working on a child abduction case.''

''Oh my,'' the receptionist named Jill, according to her name tag, said on a little gasp. ''How can I help you?''

''The child, a boy, was born here last…'' Nick looked to Laura.

''August sixth,'' she finished, praying that Nick wouldn't do the math. Jill looked doubtfully from Laura to Nick.

''Records you might have to corroborate that birth would be of tremendous assistance,'' he added.

''Well, our records are private,'' Jill said slowly, caution finally outweighing Nick's charm.

Nick smiled reassuringly at her. ''I don't need to see your records. I just need you to verify the birth, and that the child was a boy and left this clinic alive and well. His name was Robert Forester, the mother was Rhonda.''

Jill looked uncertain. ''I don't see any harm in that.''

''It's perfectly legal for you to answer that question,'' Nick offered placatingly. ''I'm sure you would much rather answer that simple question than to be subpoenaed to court.''

Jill's eyes widened. ''It'll take just a minute to locate the file.''

''Take your time.''

Nick openly studied Laura then. What was he thinking? she wondered anxiously. Was he doing the mental calculations to determine Robby's date of conception? Laura swallowed hard and forced her attention to Jill's search at the file cabinets. Now Nick would know that Robby was real. That Laura had a child. That James Ed was lying. That the hospital report from Louisiana was a fake.

Frowning, Jill glanced back in their direction. "You're sure of the name?"

Nick looked to Laura for confirmation. She nodded stiffly. Ice filled her veins. No. The records had to be here.

Jill shook her head and stepped back to the window. "I'm sorry, but we have no record of a Forester, Robert or Rhonda. Are you certain that's the right name?"

"That can't be," Laura argued, a mixture of anger and fear gripping her heart. "Dr. Nader was the doctor on call. The records have to be here."

"I'm sorry. I looked twice. There is no Forester."

Laura leveled her gaze on the other woman's. "Where can I find Dr. Nader then?" she demanded.

Jill looked to Nick then back to Laura. "I've only worked here for six months. Dr. Nader left before I came. I think he moved somewhere out west."

Laura shook her head in denial. "That can't be. The records have to be here," she repeated.

"Ma'am, I'm sorry. I can't give you something I don't have," the receptionist offered apologetically. "All births are registered at the state office. You could check there."

"But—"

"Let's go, Laura." Nick was next to her now, ushering her away from the window. "Thank you," he said glancing back at the receptionist.

"No, Nick." Laura pulled out of his grasp. "She has to be wrong." Confusion added to the emotions already knotting inside her.

Nick leveled his steady gaze on hers. "Let's go."

Trembling with reaction to the multitude of emotions clutching at her, Laura surrendered to Nick's orders. What choice did she have? She sagged with defeat. How would she ever prove her case now?

"Wait!"

Nick turned back to the receptionist, pulling Laura around with him. "Yes."

How could he be so damned calm? Laura wanted to scream. She wanted to run hard and fast—somewhere, anywhere.

"I almost forgot," Jill explained. "Right after I came to work here there was a break-in. Some files were stolen."

"Some?" Nick pressed.

"I can't say for sure what files." Jill frowned. "It was the strangest thing. The files were stolen and our computer's database was wiped clean. But nothing else."

"No drugs were taken?"

Jill shook her head. "Not a one."

NICK SWORE silently as he watched Laura storm across the parking lot. He followed more slowly, taking the time to study her. He wasn't at all sure how much more she could take. The cool wind shifted all that long blond hair around her shoulders as she slumped against the locked car door. His instincts told him that whatever happened at this clinic it definitely wasn't a coincidence. The robbery was a blatant cover-up. If Laura had a child why would anyone want to conceal that fact? If James Ed was somehow involved in all this as Laura thought, what difference would the kid make? But something was all wrong.

He hoped like hell that Ian would call soon. Nick needed a break in this case. He needed something—anything—to go on. There was no way he could cover Laura and do the kind of research required to solve this enigma. But Ian Michaels was as good as they came at ferreting out the truth.

And right now, Nick needed the truth desperately. He

couldn't help Laura until he knew what was fact and what was fiction. One thing was certain, someone was trying to push Laura over the edge. Nick had no intention of allowing that to happen. He paused in front of her. "We should be getting back," he suggested quietly.

"He did this. I don't know how, but he did." Laura lifted her chin defiantly, but her eyes gave her away.

Nick couldn't bear to see that much hurt in her eyes. He tried to take a breath, but his chest was too heavy. How could he watch this happen and do nothing? But what could he do? He had no proof.

"Laura, we'll get to the bottom of this," he told her with as much assurance as he could impart.

She shook her head and blinked back her tears. "He's won," she admitted on a sob. "Look." She swallowed convulsively and swiped at her damp cheeks. "I've made a decision, I want you to take me back to Jackson...to my brother. Maybe if he gets what he wants he won't hurt Robby." She searched Nick's eyes for a time before she continued. "I just need you to promise me one thing." She trembled with the effort of maintaining her flimsy hold on composure.

Nick waited silently for her to finish, but his entire being screamed in agony. The need to touch her, to hold her was overwhelming.

"No matter how the chips fall, no matter what anyone tells you, find my son and take care of him for me, would you?"

His resolve crumbled. Nick took her in his arms and pulled her close. There were no words he could say because he didn't have any answers, the only thing he could do was hold her. Laura's arms went around his neck. Nick closed his eyes and savored the feel of her, the scent of her. He would gladly give his life right now to make her happy again.

"Nick."

Nick opened his eyes and drew back to find her looking up at him. That sweet face so filled with sadness.

"Promise me," she whispered. "Promise me you'll find him."

His gaze riveted to those full, pink lips. So soft, so sad, and so very close. Nick shook his head slowly, in answer to her question or in denial of what he wanted more than anything to do, he couldn't be sure. "I'm not taking you back until I know it's safe." His voice was rough with emotion. Emotions he could no longer hold at bay.

Challenge rose in her eyes. "You're going to let them put me in that hospital, aren't you?"

He had to touch her. He lifted one hand to her cheek and allowed his fingers to trace the hot, salty path of her tears. He swallowed hard. "No one is going to touch you until I have some answers."

She searched his gaze, something besides the sorrow flickered in her own. "You're touching me," she murmured.

His fingers stilled at the base of her throat. "Do you want me to stop?" It was his turn to do the searching this time. He wanted to see the same desire that was wreaking havoc with his senses mirrored in her eyes.

She moistened her lips and gifted him with a shaky smile. "No, I don't want you to stop."

Nick lowered his head when he saw that answering spark of desire in her blue eyes. Slowly, as if an eternity yawned between them, his lips descended to hers. How could he have survived the past two years without her? She tasted of that same sweet heat that had burned in his memory every waking moment of every day for those two long years. His body hardened at the rush of bittersweet need that saturated his being. Nick threaded his fingers into her silky hair, loosening it from its constraints, and deepened the kiss. Her lips opened slightly and Nick delved inside. The traffic on the nearby street, the cold November wind all ceased to exist.

Laura tiptoed to press her soft body more firmly against him. Nick groaned his approval. His left arm tightened around her waist, pulling her into his arousal. Laura whimpered her own response. The need to make love to her was staggering in its intensity.

He had to stop. To get back in control. Nick pulled back. His breath ragged, his loins screaming for release. Laura's lids fluttered open. Her swollen lips beckoned his.

He clenched his jaw and stepped away from her. "We should get back."

Laura nodded, the sadness rushing back into those big blue eyes.

Nick reached to insert the key into the lock but she stayed his hand. "Wait," she said breathlessly.

His gaze collided with hers. "What?"

"There's one more possibility," she said quickly, hope filling her gaze once more. "I can't believe I didn't think of her already."

"Laura, you're not making sense." Reality had just crashed in on Nick. He had allowed himself to fall into that same old trap. Dammit. How had he let that happen again? Yes, he had reason to believe her now. But he wasn't supposed to allow himself to cross the line this time. Hadn't he learned his lesson two years ago? Obviously not or he wouldn't have kissed her.

Laura snagged the keys and hurriedly unlocked her door. She pitched them back to him then. "Come on!"

He was a Class-A fool. Nick cursed himself repeatedly

as he rounded the hood and unlocked his own door. He slid behind the wheel and shot his passenger, the bane of his pathetic existence, a heated glower. "Where are we going?"

She smiled, a wide, genuine smile and pointed to his left. "That direction. I'll explain on the way."

Chapter Eight

Laura stared in disbelief at the vacant house. The For Sale sign creaked as the wind shifted it, the sound heralding yet another failure. Jane Mallory had been Laura's last hope. Defeat weighed heavy on her shoulders. Laura closed her eyes and fought the sting of tears. It was as if destiny had determined her fate already. Now there was no one she could turn to. She and Robby had moved so often and stayed so much to themselves that few people would be able to verify Laura's story. And Jane Mallory had been the last one on the list.

"Do you mind telling me why we're standing on the front walk of an empty house?" Nick inquired in that non-chalant tone Laura hated.

She turned on him, a bolt of anger sending a burst of adrenaline through her. Even the memory of his kiss couldn't assuage her anger. Laura admitted to herself then and there that she was falling in love with the man all over again, but did he have to be so damned logical? *Because he's an honorable man, you idiot,* she scolded herself. Nick was only trying to be objective. To do what's right. Laura took a deep breath and summoned her patience.

"This is where Jane Mallory lived. She was the attending nurse at my son's delivery." Laura shot him an irritated look. "Robby and I stayed with her for a couple of weeks while I recovered."

Nick looked from Laura to the empty house. He tucked his hands into his pockets. "Looks like another dead end."

"You know, Foster, your perceptiveness amazes me."

Irritation flickered in his green eyes. "What do you want from me, Laura?" He raked the fingers of one hand through his hair. "I'm following up on every lead you toss my way. I've got one of the Agency's finest investigating your brother, your sister-in-law, and anybody else that has anything to gain by offing you. What else do you expect me to do?"

Laura leveled her gaze on his. "I want you to tell me that you believe me." Laura stepped closer to him. "Tell me that all these dead ends don't mean that all is lost." Laura stabbed his chest with her index finger as anger banished all else. "Tell me that my son is safe and that I'm going to find him—if not today, for sure tomorrow." A sob twisted in her throat, challenging her newfound bravado. "That's what I want from you, Nick."

The cold wind whipped around them, adding another layer of agony to her suffocating misery. How would she live without her son? She couldn't.

"Answer me, dammit," she demanded. Laura wilted when she saw the truth in his eyes. He couldn't make those kind of promises.

"I can't give you what you want, Laura. Not today, maybe not even tomorrow. But I will keep trying to find the answers you need until I've exhausted every possibility."

Laura looked up at the darkening sky. Why was this happening to her? What had she done to deserve this? She hugged herself to fight the chill coming more from the inside than the outside. What could she do now? *She needed a gun.* Nick's gun, she decided grimly. She would make James Ed tell her where her son was. Laura blinked at the irrational thought. With sudden clarity, she realized that she was now beyond simply desperate, and extreme measures might be the only way.

Next door an elderly woman shuffled onto her porch and retrieved the evening paper. She pulled her sweater more tightly around her as she surveyed the deserted street. She smiled when her gaze lit on Laura. Her movements slow with age, she turned and started back across the porch.

Nick was saying something but Laura ignored him. This was a small town. Neighbors kept up with neighbors in a place like this. Hope rushed through Laura, urging her to act. She put one foot in front of the other even before her brain made the decision to move. This woman would know where Mrs. Mallory had moved.

"Ma'am," Laura shouted before the old woman could disappear inside her house. "Ma'am!" She took the porch steps two at a time.

A welcoming smile greeted Laura. "Hello. Is there something I can help you with?" The woman shook her gray head. "I don't know a thing about what the real estate agent is asking for the house, but I can tell you it's a fine old place."

Laura returned her smile. "Hi, my name is Laura Proctor. Mrs. Mallory is a friend of mine. I was wondering where she had moved to."

The woman frowned. "Oh my." She clutched her newspaper to her chest. "I thought everyone knew."

A chunk of ice formed in Laura's stomach. "Knew what?" she asked faintly. Laura felt Nick's gaze heavy on her from his position on the steps.

"I'm sorry, dear, Jane passed away a few months back."
Laura's knees buckled but Nick was at her side now,

supporting her. "But I was here, with her, in August of last year. She was fine," Laura insisted.

The old woman nodded. "It was very sudden. A heart attack." She pointed to the neighboring yard. "She was always in that yard since she retired this spring, weeding and planting. Just got herself too hot, I reckon. It was a real shame. We had been neighbors for more than forty years."

Laura clamped her hand over her mouth for a moment to hold back the sob that wanted to break loose. When she had composed herself, she struggled with her next words, "Thank you for telling me." Laura closed her eyes and shook her head, exhaustion and anxiety sucking her toward panic. "I didn't know."

The old woman smiled kindly. "If you're not from around here, how could you have known? Jane never did marry and she didn't have any folks except one estranged brother." The woman shook her head. "A real shame that was. He didn't even come to her funeral. Course I'm not sure he even knew." She frowned. "Come to think of it, he probably didn't. At least his son hadn't known. Did you know Jane had a brother?"

Laura moistened her painfully dry lips. "No, I'm sorry I didn't know any of her family."

"Far as I knew that's all there was, but about four months ago, not long after Jane died, a fella showed up asking about her. A long-lost nephew it seems. Odd sort if you ask me."

A chill raced up Laura's spine. "Odd? What do you mean?"

The old woman rocked back on her heels. "Well I hate to speak poorly of Jane's folks, but he didn't look a thing like her or her brother. I'd never seen the brother, mind you, but I had seen his picture. Jane was a big woman, brawny even. So was that brother of hers. But this nephew, he was kinda short and stubby like. I suppose he took after his mama's side of the family. Strange fella,'' she added thoughtfully. ''Wore long sleeves even in the July heat.''

''What color were his eyes?'' The question came out of nowhere, but the image of those eerie pink-colored eyes flickered in Laura's mind.

''Can't rightly say. He wore them dark glasses. And gloves.'' She chuckled a rusty sound. ''I thought that was mighty strange myself.'' She tapped her chin with one finger. ''Maybe it was because he had such pale skin. Like a corpse.'' She frowned as if working hard to conjure the stranger's image. ''And the whitest hair I've ever seen on a young man.''

Nick's grip tightened on Laura's waist. Only then did she realize that she was leaning fully against him. Her legs had gone boneless. White hair, pink eyes, pale skin. *Albino.*

Laura turned in Nick's arms. ''It's him,'' she murmured. ''He's the one who broke into my room at James Ed's.'' Oh God. Laura closed her eyes and tried to slow the spinning inside her head. *The files were stolen and our computer's database was wiped clean. Jane passed away a few months back.*

The next thing Laura knew she was on the porch swing. She could hear Nick's deep voice as he questioned the woman about the strange nephew, but the words didn't quite register. *Time to die, princess.* Laura jerked at the memory. Why was this man trying to kill her? Why was he erasing all traces of Robby's existence? She swallowed. Laura didn't want to consider the reasons.

A wave of nausea washed over her. What did her sweet, innocent child have to do with any of this? *Nothing.* Laura trembled with the rage rising swiftly inside her.

Her child had nothing to do with any of this. And if

James Ed harmed one hair on her son's head, he was a dead man. Laura's breath raged in and out of her lungs. For the first time in her life the thought of someone's death brought a sense of comfort to her. Death would not be a harsh enough punishment for him if her child was hurt. Not nearly bad enough.

Laura's gaze moved to Nick. She had to get away from him. He would only hold her back. He would never allow her to do what she wanted to do. Nick was too honorable and straightforward to resort to what Laura had in mind. James Ed held all the answers.

And Laura intended to get them out of him one way or another.

"HE USED THE NAME Dirk Mallory." Nick paused while Ian made a note of the alias the albino guy had used. "He may or may not be connected to James Ed or the man who shot me, but it's worth checking into." Nick knew Laura was convinced that this was the man. He had no more to go on now in the way of hard evidence than he'd had three days ago, but his instincts told him to trust Laura on this one. Too many strange little coincidences and events added up to just one thing—a cover-up. "What do you have for me?"

"Governor Proctor has performed some pretty amazing financial acrobatics the past two years," Ian told him. "And he has definitely accessed Laura's trust fund. That would hardly be considered illegal since he had every right to do so with her sudden disappearance, and the assumption that she was dead. "

Nick swore under his breath. Maybe Laura was right. But, like Ian said, James Ed's use of the trust fund the last couple of years was strictly on the up-and-up. It still didn't prove that he tried to kill his own sister to get it.

"I also uncovered some rather strange details in Sandra's background."

Nick's attention jerked back to the conversation. "Good, anything is better than nothing."

"You already knew that she was adopted at the age of thirteen after spending one year in a state-run orphanage in Louisiana," Ian suggested.

Nick frowned in concentration. "Yeah, I remember that. The little wife was as clean as a whistle though. I remember that, too."

"Maybe, maybe not," Ian countered. "Her biological mother was one Sharon Spencer from a rural community just outside Bay Break."

"And?"

"And," Ian continued, "Sharon was involved with James Ed's father before he went off to college. There was a pretty big scandal before the Proctors enforced a gag order of sorts, and then sent their straying heir off to Harvard."

Rutherford's words echoed in Nick's head. "Damn," he breathed. The old man knew something, that's why he had innocently dropped that ancient gossip.

"Anything on what became of her?" Nick inquired hopefully.

"According to my source, she married the town drunk who died two years after Sandra's birth. Ten years after that, Sharon went off the deep end and the county took the child."

Nick passed a hand over his face. "So Sandra grew up, until the age of twelve at least, in a household where the Proctor name was mud. And her mother was a fruitcake."

"That would be my analysis," Ian agreed.

"I want to know everything you can find on Sandra Proctor, her first steps, her first kiss—everything."

"No problem," Ian assured him. "I should be able to get back to you later tomorrow on that. I have an excellent source."

Nick blew out a breath and plowed his fingers through his hair. "What about the report from the psychiatric hospital, Serenity Sanitarium?"

"That one's a bit more tricky."

"I need to know if that report's legit," Nick insisted. "That's the biggest fly in the ointment. I have to know if there's any chance Laura was really a patient there."

"Would you care to hazard a guess as to who one of the long-term residents of that facility is?" Ian inquired in a cocky tone.

Nick considered the question, then smiled with satisfaction. "One Sharon Spencer."

"Bingo."

"Excellent work, Ian," Nick praised. That gave Sandra a connection to the hospital. Maybe she or James Ed knew someone employed there who was willing to forge reports.

"Actually, it wasn't that difficult. I found a great source right up front."

Nick raised a speculative brow. "Who is your source?"

"Carl Rutherford."

"Son of a bitch," Nick hissed. "Why didn't that old geezer tell me all this?"

"He was afraid you were one of James Ed's bought-and-paid-for strong arms. He said more than he intended on the day the two of you met."

Nick didn't miss the amusement in Ian's tone. "Well, I guess you can't blame a guy for being cautious."

"That's it for now," Ian said. "I'll check in with you again within twenty-four hours."

"One more thing," Nick added before Ian could hang up. "Find out if the birth of a baby named Robert Forester was registered in the state of Alabama sometime in August last year.''

''No problem,'' Ian assured him.

''Thanks, Ian.'' Nick ended the call. He stood for a long moment and allowed the information to absorb more fully into his consciousness. He had no proof that Laura had a child or where she had actually been for the past two years. Despite Laura's claims, James Ed still surfaced from all this smelling pretty much like a rose in Nick's opinion. But then, there was this new light on Sandra. Nick massaged his chin as he considered the kind and demure first lady of Mississippi.

Sandra appeared as elated as anyone to have Laura back home. Sandra's school and college records indicated a disciplined, well-adjusted student. As first lady she was involved with numerous charities and a devoted churchgoer. The perfect wife to James Ed and surrogate mother to her young sister-in-law. No children of her own though. She and James Ed couldn't have children, Nick remembered. He wasn't sure of the reason, but he had found no indication that the problem was an issue. Sandra seemed to accept Laura as a substitute for a child of her own.

But how was that possible considering this new information? Sandra had grown up dirt-poor in a home with a drunk for a father and a mother who was mentally unstable. And where the Proctors represented everything she didn't have.

Uneasiness stole over Nick. That combination spelled trouble with a capital *T*. Nick exhaled heavily and passed a hand over his face. But why would Sandra go to such lengths to get Laura's money when James Ed would be in control of the trust fund, not her. Or did she have that much power over her husband? Nick wondered briefly. It just didn't ring true. James Ed was doing well on his own merit.

Is there ever enough? Laura's words filtered through his mind. Why would Sandra kidnap Laura's child if James Ed already had access to the trust fund? Maybe it was simply a matter of not wanting to have to pay it back. Even with Laura considered unstable, her child would be heir to her trust fund unless the will specified otherwise. That could be a distinct possibility, Nick decided.

The missing files, the knife wounds on Laura's throat and chest. The events in the cabin when he was shot. Laura's explanation of how the man had tried to kill her on that riverbank two years ago. Nick suppressed a shudder. He had lost his heart that night, and very nearly his life. That one incident might not have anything to do with the rest. The police labeled the case as a kidnapping gone sour. According to Laura, the man who shot Nick and tried to kill her died in the river that night. And she had seen him in James Ed's office more than once.

Anyone or thing that could provide hard evidence that Laura had a child had conveniently disappeared. Nick wondered again about the strange nephew who had shown up at Jane Mallory's neighbor's house. Nick supposed he could have been the real thing. And what about the hospital report? How convenient that Sandra's mother was a long-term resident of the very facility which provided the only hard evidence that existed as to Laura's whereabouts during the past months.

None of it actually added up to anything conclusive. And he doubted it would until he knew more facts. The only thing Nick knew for certain was that he had to protect Laura. He thought again about the way kissing her had made him feel, and the realization that he still cared deeply for her hit him hard. A weary breath slipped past Nick's lips. It was late. He couldn't deal with any of this right now. He glanced at the clock on the mantel above the fireplace. Midnight. He should check on Laura and get some sleep. Maybe Ian would come up with something more on Sandra tomorrow.

Rain pattered quietly on the roof. A storm had been threatening the entire drive home. Nick was glad the wet stuff had held off until they got back to Bay Break. The door to Laura's room was open. Nick slipped in soundlessly. The light from the bedside table cast a golden glow on her sweet face and silky hair. Laura had been so exhausted and overwhelmed, she had hardly spoken a word during the return trip. She had gone straight to bed as soon as they got home.

She was tired. Nick moved to her bedside and crouched down next to her. Tired or not, Laura was beautiful. Her bare shoulders made Nick wonder if she were naked beneath that sheet and thin cotton blanket. His mouth parched instantly at the thought. His eyes feasted on the perfection of the satiny skin revealed before him. Rage stirred inside him when his gaze traced the small slash mark, then flitted back to the tiny puncture wounds on her throat. Forcing the anger away, Nick shifted his slow perusal to her sweet face. All emotion melted, leaving him weak with want. Her lashes, a few shades darker than her blond hair, shadowed her soft cheeks. Those full, pink lips were parted slightly as if she were waiting for his kiss.

Cursing himself as a glutton for punishment, Nick allowed his gaze to trace her tempting jawline, then down the curve of her delicate throat to the pulse beating rhythmically there. He licked his lips hungrily and resisted the urge to touch her slender shoulder, to feel the warm smoothness of her skin. His body turned rock hard with desire.

Something snagged his attention. He frowned. Nick jerked his gaze back to her shoulder, near her neck. He moved closer to get a better look. The bottom fell out of Nick's stomach when his brain assimilated what his eyes found there.

Bruises. Small, oblong, barely visible marks that discolored her otherwise perfect, creamy skin.

He…he tried to drown me.

No way could Laura have made those bruises on herself. The position and size of which could only be labeled as finger marks. A churning mixture of rage and fear rising inside him, Nick eased down onto the side of the bed next to her. This, Nick seethed, was hard evidence.

"Laura." He shook her gently. "Laura, honey, wake up. We need to talk."

She moaned a protest and hugged her pillow. Nick's body ached with the need to hold her that way. "Laura." He shook her again. "We have to talk."

Laura sat up with a start. The sheet fell, exposing one high, firm breast briefly before she covered herself. "What?" she demanded irritably.

Nick leveled his determined gaze on her bleary one. "I want you to start at the beginning and tell me everything. Again."

LAURA WATCHED Nick pace back and forth across the room. She stood in the middle of the room, the sheet hugged close around her. She wished he had given her time to put some clothes on before he started this inquisition. After her long cry in the shower where Nick wouldn't hear or see her, she hadn't had the energy or the desire to dig up anything to sleep in. She had wanted to escape into sleep. She didn't want to think about the missing files or Mrs. Mallory's death.

Or the nephew.

Laura shivered. She blocked the memory of the man with

the strange eyes who had tried to kill her twice already. The bathroom had been dark and she hadn't actually seen his eyes that time. But she knew. Deep in her heart, Laura knew it was him. And with that instinct came the realization that he had probably been the one to take her son. James Ed would never have bothered himself with that part. Her heart shuddered at that thought.

"Does that about sum it up?"

Nick's question jerked Laura to attention. "What?" she asked as she forced herself to focus on him once more.

"Dammit, Laura," he growled. He jammed his hands at his waist and moved in her direction. "I need your full attention here."

"I'm sorry." She pushed the hair back from her face. "You're going to have to start over."

Nick swore under his breath. Those green eyes flashed with barely checked fury. What had him all worked up? Laura wondered, her own irritation kindling. Certainly nothing they had learned today. Though she knew with a measure of certainty that the nephew was the man after her, she couldn't prove that to Nick. She had proven *nothing* today.

The emptiness of that one word echoed around her. The only glimmer of hope in all this was that Nick was beginning to believe her.

"You came home that summer from college, and things were tense you said."

Laura nodded. "At first I thought it was because I hadn't put as much into school as James Ed had. He wanted me to be the perfect student, the perfect sister." She frowned, remembering her brother's disappointment. "But it didn't take long for me to figure out that it had nothing to do with me. It was the campaign for the Governor's office."

"And then Rafe Manning came on the scene."

Again Laura noted that change in Nick's eyes, in his posture, when he spoke of Rafe. "Right," she replied. "I dated him a few times because I was bored, but we didn't hit it off. James Ed tried to push the issue. Apparently he and Rafe's father were tight." Laura shrugged. "You know the rest."

Nick folded his arms over his chest and massaged his chin with his thumb and forefinger. The movement drew Laura's eyes to that sexy cleft in his chin. Emotion stirred inside her. Robby had a cleft just like that.

"Not once during all of this did you ever suspect Sandra of being involved?"

Taken aback by his question, Laura stared at him in amazement. "Sandra?" Laura shook her head slowly from side to side. "That's ridiculous. Sandra has never been anything but kind to me."

"What would you say if I told you that Sandra might not be who you think she is," Nick offered, his gaze intent on hers, watching, analyzing.

Laura frowned. "What does that mean?"

"Sandra's mother was involved with your father."

"That's not possible. Sandra's mother is dead."

"Did Sandra tell you that?"

Laura nodded, feeling as if another rug was about to be snatched from under her feet.

"Sandra's mother is a permanent ward at Serenity Sanitarium."

Laura stilled as her brain absorbed the impact of his words. That was the hospital James Ed claimed she had been committed to for the past eighteen months. Sandra's mother was alive? And a patient there? "Why would Sandra lie?" The question echoed in the room, only then did Laura realize she had said it aloud.

Nick placed a reassuring hand on her arm, his fingers

caressed her bare skin. That simple touch sent heat spearing through her. "I don't know, but we're damned sure going to find out."

Laura's gaze connected with his. "Why the sudden change of heart, Nick?" Laura examined his now impassive gaze closely. "Are you trying to tell me that you really do believe me now?"

He lifted those long fingers to her throat and touched her gingerly. He swallowed hard, the play of muscle beneath tanned skin made Laura ache to touch him there, the same way he was touching her.

"Believing you wasn't the problem, Laura. Let's just say I finally got that hard evidence." His gaze followed the movements of his fingers.

Laura stumbled away from him. She pivoted and hurried to the dresser, then stared at her reflection in the mirror. Several long, thin bruises marked her skin where strong fingers had held her beneath the water's surface.

Nick came up behind her, watching her in the mirror. "Laura, I'm sorry I let this happen. I should have believed you sooner." He touched her elbow. Laura flinched. "I won't let anyone hurt you again. I swear," he added softly.

Laura shunned his touch. "It took this," she gestured to the bruises, "to make you believe that someone was trying to kill me." Fury rose in Laura then. "What about my child? Do you believe in him yet?"

Nick's gaze wavered. "Of course I believe you, but we have to have proof."

"You bastard. You still don't really believe me."

Nick let go a heavy breath. "That's not true," he argued.

"Then look me in the eye and tell me that you believe I have a son. That his name is Robby and he's the most important thing in my life," she ground out, a sob knotting her chest.

Nick's concerned gaze collided with hers.

"Say it, damn you!" Laura trembled with the intensity of her fury. "Say it," she demanded when his response didn't come quickly enough.

Nick blinked. "It's not a matter of making me believe you—we have to be able to prove it to James Ed." He added quickly, "And the police."

She shoved at his chest with one hand and held the sheet to her breast with the other. "Get away from me! I don't give a damn about your proof!"

"Laura." Nick dodged her next attempt at doing him bodily harm. He grabbed her by both arms and held her still. "Laura, listen to me."

"I don't want to hear anything you have to say." Laura trembled, his long fingers splayed on her flesh and urged her closer.

"Laura." He breathed her name, the feel of his warm breath soft on her face. "I have to operate on facts, not assumptions. I can't go back to Jackson and demand to know where your son is when I have no physical proof that he exists."

Laura knew he was right. Deep in her heart, she knew. But that didn't stop the ache tearing at her insides. She needed to find her son more than she needed to take her next breath.

"I have to find him," she murmured. How many days had it been now? Laura squeezed her eyes shut. God, she didn't want to think about that.

"Please trust me, Laura," Nick pleaded. He angled his head down to look into her eyes when she opened them. "I won't let you down if you'll just trust me."

Laura met that intense green gaze and found herself drowning in the emotions reflected there. Desire, need... The same emotions she felt detonating inside her. She did trust Nick. He would never do anything to hurt her. She knew that. And she needed him so much. To hold her, to make her forget for just a little while. She needed him to love her the way he had before. She needed to reaffirm this thing between them, to feel his strong arms around her. Nick would help her, she knew he would. His strength was all that kept her sane right now.

"Hold me, Nick." Laura went into his arms. She slid her own arms around his lean waist and held him tightly. His scent, something spicy and male, enveloped her. And then his strong arms were around her, holding her, protecting her.

Nick pressed a tender kiss to her hair. "I just need you to trust me, honey, that's all." His lips found her temple and brushed another of those gentle kisses there. "Please trust me."

Laura closed her eyes and allowed instinct to take over. She needed Nick to take her away from this painful reality. To hold her and promise her that everything would be all right. Her hands moved over his strong back, feeling, caressing. She could feel the muscled landscape of his broad chest pressing against her breasts. Her nipples pebbled at the thought of how his warm skin would feel against hers.

His fingers threaded into her hair and pulled her face up to his. "You should get some rest," he said thickly, his gaze never left her mouth. "I won't be far away."

Laura shook her head, drawing his gaze to hers. "Don't leave me," she said in the barest of whispers. Laura tiptoed and quickly kissed his full lips. Nick sucked in a sharp breath. "I want you, Nick. I want you now."

He drew back slightly. "You're not thinking clearly, Laura." He searched her gaze, her face, then licked his lips, yearning clear in his eyes. "I don't want you to regret anything."

Determined to show him just how badly she wanted him, Laura stepped back and allowed the sheet to fall to the floor. "I do want," she told him. "I want you."

Nick's gaze moved slowly over her body. Laura felt its caress as surely as if he were touching her with those skilled hands.

"I want you, too," he admitted quietly. "But you're vulnerable right now and I don't want to take advantage of that." His eyes contradicted his words. He did want to do just that. He wanted it as badly as she did.

"The decision isn't yours," Laura concluded. "It's mine." She recovered the step she had retreated. Her eyes steady on his, Laura reached up and slowly began to unbutton his shirt. His gaze dropped to her hands and he watched as she bared his chest. The knowledge that he was watching her and responding sent a surge of power pulsing through her veins, heating her already too warm body.

Laura held out her hand. "Your weapon, sir."

Nick looked from her hand to her. Laura saw the flicker of hesitation in his eyes. She stepped back and opened the drawer to the night table. "I'm only going to put it away," she explained.

He nodded, then reached behind his back and retrieved the weapon. Nick's gaze held hers as he placed the ominous looking weapon in Laura's open palm.

She smiled, her lips trembling with the effort. "Thank you." Nick would never know how much that gesture meant to her. He could have put the gun away himself, but he hadn't. He trusted her at least a little.

Laura closed the drawer and turned to find him right behind her, she looked up into those sea green eyes and melted at what she saw. Savage need, overwhelming desire. Nick took her hand in his and pressed a kiss against her palm, then placed it over his heart. Laura felt weak with emotion. Knotting her hands in his shirt, she pulled it from his jeans, then pushed it off his broad shoulders until it dropped to the floor.

For a time Laura simply admired the exquisite terrain of his muscled chest. She touched the scar and electricity charged through her. Leaning forward, she kissed that place and thanked God once more that Nick was alive. Laura flattened her hands against his hair-roughened chest and allowed her palms to mold to the contours of that awesome torso. She closed her eyes and committed each ripple and ridge to memory. Desire sizzled inside her, making her bold, making her need. Her fingers slipped into the waistband of his jeans and circled his lean waist.

Nick groaned low in his throat. ''Laura,'' he rasped. ''How long do you plan to torture me this way?''

She released the button to his fly, then slowly lowered the zipper, the sound echoing around them. ''As long as it takes,'' she assured him, her voice low and husky.

Laura knelt in front of him. The immense pleasure in his eyes added to her own. She pulled one boot off, then the other. The socks were rolled off next. Slowly, she tugged his jeans down those long, muscled legs. Each inch of flesh she revealed made breathing that much more difficult. When his jeans had been disposed of, Laura sat back on her heels and admired his amazing body. Wide, wide shoulders that narrowed into a lean waist and hips, then long, muscled legs. She studied the scarred right knee momentarily, remembering the life he had saved by taking a bullet. Laura closed her eyes and forced away the possibility that he might get caught in the crossfire of all this madness again. She couldn't bear the thought of Nick being hurt again. The realization that his getting hurt or worse was a very distinct possibility hit her hard. She had to make sure that didn't happen. Everyone around her that she cared about was being hurt or worse.

Suppressing the thought, Laura's gaze moved back up those long, powerful legs. Black briefs concealed the part of him that made her wet and achy. Nick had taught her what it was to be a woman in the purest, most primitive sense of the word. Not one day had gone by in the past two years that her body had not yearned for his. Now, at last, she would know that pleasure once more.

One last time.

With painstaking slowness, Laura slid his briefs down and off. Nick groaned loudly when she pressed a kiss to one lean hip. His arousal nudged her shoulder sending a shard of desire slicing through her. She wanted him inside her. Now.

Laura stood, braced her hands against his chest and tiptoed to kiss his firm lips. His eyes opened and the savage fire burning there seared her from the inside out.

"No more," he growled. Nick lifted her into his arms as if she weighed nothing at all. Three steps later and they were on the bed.

"My turn now," he warned.

Laura bit down on her lower lip to hold back her cry of need as he kissed his way down her body. He paused to love her breasts. Taking his time, he laved and suckled each until Laura thought she would die of it. He gave the same attention to her belly button, licking, sucking, arousing.

Nick suddenly stilled. His fingers traced her side. "What's this?" he murmured.

Trying to make sense of his question through her haze of lust, Laura stared down at where his fingers touched her. *Stretch marks.* Few and faint, but there just the same. Why hadn't she thought of that before?

"Stretch marks," she answered. "From my pregnancy. Everyone gets them."

Nick traced the pale marks hesitantly.

"Your evidence," Laura added when he remained silent.

Nick smiled at her then. "Absolutely," he concurred. A predatory gleam brightened his beautiful green eyes. "And my pleasure as well." His tongue followed the same path his fingers had taken.

Laura moaned her approval.

His fingers trailed down her skin until they found that part of her which throbbed for his touch. Laura arched upward when one long finger slipped inside her. His thumb made tiny circles around her most intimate place of desire.

"Nick," she murmured. Instinctively her hips moved against his hand. A second finger slipped inside and Laura cried out.

His mouth captured hers. Slowly, thoroughly he kissed her, his tongue mimicking the rhythm of his fingers. The feel of his lips, soft, yet firm and commanding, commanding her with devastating precision. His tongue touched all the sensitive places in her mouth, a sweet torture to which she gladly surrendered. Laura writhed with the tension coiling tighter and tighter inside her. She gasped for air when his mouth finally lifted from hers. His ragged breath fanned her lips, igniting another fire in her soul. Nick moved between her thighs. Those magic fingers, hot and moist from her body, slid over her hip and beneath her to lift her toward him. Release crashed down on Laura the moment he entered her, stretching, filling, completing.

Nick covered her mouth with his and took her scream just as she took him inside her. His fingers entwined with hers, pulling her hands above her head. Slowly, drawing out the exquisite pleasure, Nick thrust fully inside her again and again. Her tension building even faster than the first time, Laura met his thrusts, urging him to hurry. Her heart pounding, her breath trapped in her lungs, Laura spiraled toward release once more. One last thrust and Nick followed her to that special place of pure sensation.

His breathing as jagged and labored as hers, Nick pressed his forehead to Laura's. "Are you all right?"

Laura nodded once, unable to speak.

"Rest now. We'll talk later," he told her as he rolled over and pulled her into his protective embrace.

Laura closed her eyes against the tears. How she loved this man. But they would never be able to be a family. No matter how he felt about her at this moment, when he discovered the truth, he would despise her for keeping his son from him for so long.

Laura had to find a way to get away from Nick. He had been hurt by her too much already. Nick had taken a bullet and almost died for her. She had kept his son from him all this time. He deserved better. She could not risk him being hurt by James Ed's men again. If something happened to her Robby would need his father. Nick only had to take one look at Robby to know that the child belonged to him. And she knew in her heart that Nick would not stop looking for him now no matter what happened. He had urged James Ed to give him this time with Laura. Nick had stuck his neck out for her too many times already. Decision behind her, Laura considered her best course of action. Too much time had been wasted already. Doc's office might hold some clue to where he had gone. And maybe even some proof of her child's existence. Something she could take to the police.

Laura had to find her baby. But she had to make sure Nick stayed out of the line of fire this time.

This was between her and James Ed.

Chapter Nine

The scent of an angel tantalized him. Nick snuggled more deeply into his pillow. *Laura.* He smiled and opened his eyes to the bright morning light spilling into the room. He reached for the woman who had turned his world upside down once more.

"Good morning," she murmured.

Nick kissed the tip of her nose. "Morning," he rasped. "Did you know that you look like an angel when you wake up?"

Laura giggled. God, how good it felt to hear that. But Nick wanted more than a glimpse of the woman he had fallen in love with. He wanted her to laugh out loud. To drive him crazy like she did two years ago. While he watched, sadness filled her gaze once more, and Nick knew she had remembered that her son was still missing.

"Hungry?" he inquired, trying to keep the mood light. "I could eat a horse."

She smiled. "You're always hungry." Laura searched his gaze for what seemed like forever, as if she were afraid it might be the last time she could look at him this way. "You go take care of breakfast. I want a long, hot bath," she said suggestively. "Maybe you can even come join me."

"Maybe I'm not as hungry as I thought." Nick nuzzled her neck, then nipped the lobe of her ear.

Laura gasped and pulled away from his exploring mouth. "For once I am," she murmured.

Nick bowed his head. "Your wish is my command, madam."

Laura giggled again as she scurried from the room. Nick watched her departure in rapt appreciation. He loved every square inch of her petite little body.

"Don't lock the door," he called out after her. "I'll be there in fifteen minutes."

"I'll be waiting," she called from the bathroom. The sound of water rushing into the tub obliterated any possibility of further conversation.

Nick threw back the sheet and got out of bed. He stretched, feeling better than he had in a very long time. He pulled on his jeans, tucked his weapon into his waistband and started toward the kitchen. This was the way it should be, the two of them together making love, sharing moments like this morning.

But there was Laura's child. Nick slowed in his progress toward the kitchen. He scrubbed a hand over his stomach. The notion of a child would take some getting used to. Nick certainly wanted children of his own. He paused at the kitchen doorway. Did it matter to him that this child belonged to another man? A slow smile claimed Nick's mouth. Hell no. Nick would love Laura's child just like his own.

Feeling like a tremendous weight had been lifted from his shoulders, Nick set to the task of making breakfast. He whistled as he worked. Nothing like great sex with the woman you love to make a man happy, he decided. All he had to do now was sort all this insanity out.

Twenty minutes later and Nick was ready to join Laura.

At this point he might only get to dry her back. He grinned. But that was fine with him. Nick sauntered down the hall, anticipation pounding through his veins. He could make love to Laura for the rest of his life and never stop wanting more of her. He tapped on the closed bathroom door.

"Ready or not here I come," he teased. Nick turned the knob and pushed the door open. Steam billowed out to engulf him. Nick frowned. What the hell? He stepped into the bathroom and water pooled around his feet. His heart rate blasted into overdrive, pumping fear and adrenaline through his tense body. He fanned his arms to part the steam. Water was pouring over the side of the tub. Where was Laura? Fear hurdled through Nick's veins. He peered down at the tub. No Laura. Thank God. He swallowed hard as he leaned down and turned the swiftly flowing water off, then opened the drain.

Nick straightened and took a breath. His next thought sent anger rushing through him, neutralizing the fear he had felt. He crossed the wet floor to the window, parted the curtain and cleared a spot of fog from the glass. Peering out, his suspicion was confirmed. His rental car was gone.

Nick swore hotly.

Laura was gone.

His fury burning off the last of the fear lingering in his chest, Nick stamped into Laura's bedroom. Pain roared up his leg, and his knee almost buckled in protest. He closed his eyes and gritted his teeth until the pain subsided to a more tolerable level. Taking a bit more care, he tugged on his shirt and socks and stepped into his boots.

How the hell had he let last night happen? Nick cursed himself again. It was two years ago all over again, only this time he wasn't bleeding. At least not on the outside, he amended. With all that had happened, how could he still feel this way about Laura?

He was a fool, that's why.

He had sworn that he wouldn't get sucked into the Proctor family saga this time. He headed to the door, pulling his jacket on and automatically checking the weapon at the small of his back as he went. Damn it, damn it. Here he was, heart deep in tangled emotions and deadly deceptions.

He had really screwed up this time. He should have known Laura was up to something. She had given in to his plan of action last night all too easily. She was desperate to find her son. And desperate people did desperate things. Nick knew that all too well. He should have reassured her rather than pushing for answers about her pregnancy. She had ended up unwilling to discuss the issue. Nick cursed himself again. Making love to Laura again had only served to reinforce the feeling that she was his and his alone. The thought that she had been with another man, even once, still tore at his heart. He shouldn't have pressured her about the child's father. He should have insisted they do things his way and his way only. He should have realized that something was up this morning.

Damn it, he was a complete idiot.

Nick followed the driveway until it intersected the highway. He glanced left. That direction would take her to Jackson. He didn't think Laura would head that way, not alone and unarmed. His gaze shifted right. It was only five miles to town. That was the direction he needed to take. His knee complained sharply at the thought. Nick shifted his weight to the other leg. Why would Laura go into town?

Nick swore when he considered that she may have gone back to the old woman's house. That's all he needed was for the old hag to call the police and get Laura thrown into jail. James Ed would…

He didn't want to consider that his instincts had gone that far south where James Ed was concerned. Protecting

James Ed's interests, including Laura, was the job Nick had signed on to do. But solving the puzzle that was Laura Proctor's predicament was Nick's ultimate goal. Nick's gut instinct just wouldn't permit him to believe that James Ed was the villain here.

And neither was Laura. She had definitely been attacked. There was no question in his mind about that. And she had obviously been pregnant. The stretch marks were there and Nick had noticed other subtle changes to her body. Her breasts were fuller. However, making love to her had proven the same—mind-blowing. The scent of her still clung to his skin, the memory of her tight, hot body was tattooed across his brain, easily arousing him even now.

Nick shook himself from the memory. He didn't have time for that right now. He had to find Laura. His attention jerked to the road when an old truck slowed as it approached him. He squinted to identify the driver.

Rutherford.

Headed in the direction of Jackson, the old man passed slowly, did a precarious U-turn, then stopped on the edge of the road right in front of Nick.

"Need a ride young fella?"

Nick braced his hands on the door and leaned into the open window. "I suppose that depends upon where you're headed, old man," Nick said tersely. He was still annoyed that Rutherford had spilled his guts to Ian and not him. Maybe Nick had gotten too close to all this. Whatever the case, he didn't like being jerked around or bypassed.

The old man eyed him suspiciously for one long minute, then one side of his mouth hitched up in a smile. He pushed his John Deere cap up and scratched his forehead. "I'm headed to the same place you're headed, I reckon," he replied cryptically.

Nick eyed him with mounting skepticism. "Is that a fact?"

Rutherford settled his cap back into place and adopted a knowing look. "It is if it's an angel you're looking for."

"You know where Laura is?"

The old man grinned widely. "I sure do. I was out to the barn for a ladder." He nodded toward the large barn right off the pages of a New England calendar that sat behind and to one side of the Proctor house. "Planned on cleaning out the gutters today. That rain last night pretty much cleared the rest of the leaves from the trees."

"You saw her leave," Nick prodded impatiently.

"She come running outta that house like the devil himself was on her heels." Rutherford cocked a bushy gray brow. "But you never did come out."

Nick tamped down the response that immediately came to mind. "Which way did she go?" he said instead.

"She jumped into that car of yours and took off toward town." He frowned. "I figured something was up so I followed her. She drove straight to Doc Holland's office. Didn't appear to be nobody there though, but she went on around back like she knowed what she was about. Then I got to thinking that maybe I should come back and get you. Seeing as you're supposed to be keeping an eye on her and all."

Nick jerked the door open and climbed in. "Thanks," he snapped. The fact that the man was right didn't help Nick's disposition.

Rutherford pulled back out onto the highway. He cast Nick a conspiratorial wink. "You have to watch those angels, young fella, they got themselves wings. They can fly away before you know they're gone."

Nick manufactured a caustic smile. "Thanks, I'll remember that.'' When he caught up with Laura, he fully intended to clip those wings.

In no time at all Mr. Rutherford chugged into the driveway leading to Doc Holland's place. Nick's black rental car was parked at an odd angle next to the porch. He opened his door before Rutherford braked to a full stop. Nick slid out and closed the door behind him.

''Thanks for the ride,'' he said, taking another look at the old man behind the wheel. ''And thanks for your help with Laura's situation,'' he added contritely. Hell, the man had done him a favor. Nick should be considerably more grateful.

Carl Rutherford's expression turned serious. ''You just make sure that little girl don't do no permanent disappearing act.''

Nick nodded and backed up a step as the old truck lurched forward. When Mr. Rutherford had exited the other end of the horseshoe-shaped drive, Nick turned his attention to the house-cum-clinic before him. What the hell was she doing here? Nick shook his head. Looking for more evidence to support her case, he felt sure. Or for the Doc, whichever she could find. Nick frowned. The place was awfully quiet for there to be anyone home—he glanced around the property—and no other vehicles besides his rental car were in the vicinity. Nick trudged slowly toward the house, the wet leaves made little sound beneath his feet as he crossed the tree-lined yard.

Not taking any chances on the possibility of anyone else having followed her, Nick withdrew his weapon. If ''Pinkie'' showed his ghostly mug, Nick would give him something to remember him by. The thought that the bastard had hurt Laura again and maybe taken her son burned in Nick's gut.

Nick moved cautiously across the porch to the front door.

It was locked. The sign officially proclaiming the doctor's absence still hung in a nearby window. He obviously hadn't returned. Surveying the quiet street, Nick moved down the side of the house. A couple of blocks off the small town square and lined by trees and shrubbery, the place was fairly secluded. The back of the house looked much like the front with a wide porch spanning the length of it. The back door stood open. Good. Nick preferred an avenue of access that didn't require breaking a window. An open door was invitation enough to skirt the boundaries of breaking and entering.

Not that a minor technicality would have kept him from going in, Nick mused. Upon reaching the door, he saw that Laura had beat him to it anyway. One glass pane in the door had been shattered. A handy rock lay on the painted porch floor. Nick swore under his breath. What the hell was she thinking? The police surely patrolled the area. Nick eased inside, scanning left to right as his eyes adjusted to the natural early morning interior light. The large old-fashioned kitchen looked homey and quite empty. Silently, Nick weaved between the massive oak furnishings and made his way to the dimly lit hall.

A sound reached him. He frowned in concentration. *Crying*. Laura! Hard as it proved, Nick remained absolutely still until he got a fix on the direction of the heartrending weeping. Farther down the hall and to the right. Nick moved soundlessly toward the door he had estimated would lead him to Laura. The soft sound of her tears echoed in the silent house. If anyone had hurt her...

Rage twisting inside him, Nick paused next to the open doorway and listened for any other sound coming from the room. Nothing. Taking a deep breath and firming his grip on his weapon, Nick swung into position in front of the door. He scanned what appeared to be an office for any threat. The place had been tossed. It looked as if a tornado had ripped through it. Maintaining his fire-ready stance, Nick dropped his gaze to the floor where Laura huddled...

...over what was obviously a very dead man.

BLOOD.

Laura stared at her hands. The warm, sticky red stuff oozed between her fingers. She had tried to help Doc but it was too late.

Too late.

Dizziness washed over her, making her want to give in to the darkness that threatened her consciousness. Who would do this to Doc? Laura's gaze riveted once more to the large kitchen knife protruding from his chest. She swallowed back the bitter bile rising in her throat.

She had done this. Laura moaned a sob. She had come back to Bay Break and brought nothing but pain, loss and death to those she loved most.

Robby...

Doc...

And Nick.

Laura closed her eyes and surrendered to the flood of emotion pressing against the back of her throat. She was responsible for this senseless violence.

''Oh, God,'' she murmured as she rocked back and forth. ''I killed him. I killed him,'' she chanted.

''Laura.''

Slowly, Laura looked up into the stony features of Nick's grim face. ''Doc's dead,'' she told him weakly.

Nick knelt next to her then and checked Doc's pulse.

''It's too late,'' she whispered. ''He's gone. Robby's gone, too.'' A heart-wrenching sob tore from her lips. Laura slumped in defeat. *Too late. Too late. Too late,* her mind screamed.

"Come on, Laura, we have to get you out of here."

Nick was moving her. She could feel his strong arms around her as he lifted her. Laura's head dropped onto his shoulder.

Doc was dead.

Robby was lost.

And it was all her fault.

Laura's stomach churned violently. The room spun wildly when Nick settled her back onto her feet near the kitchen sink. Laura moaned a protest when he began washing the blood from her hands. *No, no, no,* her mind chanted.

"Oh, God." Laura dropped her head into the sink and vomited violently. The image of Doc's blood pooling around his dead body was forever imprinted in her memory. The sound of Robby's cries for mommy rang in her ears.

"It's okay, baby, it's okay," Nick murmured softly as he held her hair back from her face. He turned on the tap to wash away the pungent bile.

When the urge to heave passed, Laura cupped her hand and cooled her mouth and throat with as much water as she dared drink with her stomach still quivering inside her. She splashed the liquid relief on her face, then swiped the excess moisture away with her hand. *Doc was dead.*

Nick lifted her onto the counter and inspected her closely, a mixture of fear and concern etched on his face. "You're not hurt?" He brushed the damp hair back from her face.

Laura shook her head. Nausea threatened at even that simple movement. *Doc was dead.*

She squeezed her eyes shut to block the horrifying images. "This is my fault. I shouldn't have come here."

"You have to tell me what happened," Nick urged gently. "Why did you run away from me?"

She swallowed, then shuddered, more from grief than the

bitter taste still clinging to the back of her throat. "I didn't run away," she told him. "I thought if I could find my file, that maybe Doc had made some sort of notations regarding Robby. Then James Ed couldn't pretend my son doesn't exist." Laura closed her eyes and suppressed the mental replay of the scene she had found. She opened her eyes to him then. "I want to do this alone, Nick. I don't want you to help me anymore. It's not safe. I won't risk you getting hurt again."

"There was no one else here when you arrived?" Nick seemed to ignore all that she had just said.

Laura shook her head. "Just…just…" She gestured vaguely toward the hall. "Doc," she finished weakly.

"Laura, I need you to think very carefully. Was the door open when you arrived?"

"I…I broke the glass and unlocked the door," she told him. Laura allowed her frantic gaze to meet his now unreadable one. Those piercing green eyes bored into hers, searching, analyzing.

"Did you touch anything besides the door?"

"What?"

"Did you touch anything at all, Laura, anything besides the door?" he demanded impatiently.

She thought hard. What did she touch? Nothing… everything, maybe. "I can't remember." What was he thinking?

His fingers, like steel bands, curled around her arms, he gave her a little shake. "Listen to me," he ground out. "The blood hasn't congealed yet. Do you know what that means?"

Laura's stomach roiled at the mental picture Nick's words evoked. "I don't want to hear this…." She tried to escape his firm hold. "Just let me go, Nick."

"Dammit, Laura," he growled. "Whoever killed Doc

hasn't been gone long. Doc was out of town, remember? He probably arrived back in town and surprised someone in his office. Think! Think about what you saw first when you came inside. What did you hear?''

Laura concentrated hard. She heard…silence. Her gaze connected to Nick's. "Nothing. There was silence." She swallowed. "But I could smell the blood." A sob snatched at Laura's flimsy hold on composure. "The moment I walked in I could smell it."

Nick swore under his breath. "You're sure," he repeated slowly, "that you didn't touch anything."

"I don't think so." Laura let go a shaky breath. "But I can't be sure. I was…I was hysterical." A kind of numbness had set in now, Laura realized. She didn't really feel anything at all, just tired. So very tired.

"Don't move," Nick instructed harshly.

Laura nodded. She clamped her hand over her mouth and fought the urge to scream. She felt her eyes go round with remembered horror. Doc was dead. Robby was lost. Oh, God. Oh, God. She had to do something.

But what?

Minutes or hours passed before Nick came back. Laura couldn't be sure which. He swiped the faucet and the area around the sink with a hand towel. Laura frowned. What was he doing?

"Can you stand?" he asked, his expression closed.

"Yes," she murmured.

Nick lifted her off the counter and settled Laura on her feet. "Don't move, don't touch anything," he ordered.

Laura blinked, confused. Nick swiped the counter, then ushered her toward the back door. Once they were on the porch, he gave the doorknob, the door, and its surrounding casing the same treatment. Still too dazed to marshal the strength to question his actions, Laura watched as he threw the rock she had used to break the glass deep into the woods at the back of the yard. She tried to think what all this meant, but her mind kept going back to the image of Doc lying dead on the floor. Laura shuddered and forced the images away.

Nick took her hand and led her back to the car. He pitched the towel he had used into the back seat. As if she were as fragile as glass, he settled Laura into the passenger seat and buckled her seat belt. Laura watched him move to the other side of the car and slide behind the wheel. Memories of their lovemaking suddenly filled her, warmed her. Laura closed her eyes and savored the remembered heat of Nick's skin against hers. His lips on her body, his kiss. The last time they had made love Robby had been conceived.

And now he was lost. Laura's heart shuddered in her chest. Her baby. She had to find her baby.

"Nick, we have to find my baby," she urged. Laura shifted in the seat. "Don't you see. They're erasing every trace of my baby's existence." She shook her head. "It's as if he has disappeared into thin air. Never existed."

Nick cast her an understanding look as he pulled the car out onto the street. "I'm calling Ian when we get back to the house." He glanced back at her then. "I'm making arrangements to take you some place safe. Too much I don't understand is going on around here. I'm not taking any chances."

Fear rolled over Laura in suffocating waves. "No! I can't leave without Robby."

"The point is not negotiable."

Laura caught a glimpse of Vine Street as Nick crossed town. Desperation like she had never known before slammed into Laura. She had left Robby with Mrs. Leeton. She had to know where he was. She wasn't the fragile old woman she pretended to be. She knew. She had to know.

"Take me to Mrs. Leeton's house." The quiet force in those few words surprised even Laura. She had to go back.

Nick cast a glance in her direction. "All right," he agreed without hesitation and to her complete surprise.

Laura closed her eyes and prayed that Mrs. Leeton would tell the truth…and that it wouldn't be too late.

NICK BANGED on the door again, louder this time. The old woman would have to be deaf not to hear him. Laura stood next to him, impatiently shifting her weight from one foot to the other.

"She's not going to answer because she knows you're on to her now," Laura insisted.

He glanced at his watch. "Give her a minute. It's early and she's old. Maybe she's still in bed."

Laura huffed a breath and crossed her arms over her chest.

Nick released a long, slow breath of his own. *I killed him. I killed him,* kept echoing in his brain. He passed a weary hand over his face. She couldn't have, of course. But someone had intended to make it look as though she had. Her file had been lying right next to the Doc's body, the contents missing.

Nick shook his head at his own stupidity. In his irrational desire to protect Laura, he had tampered with evidence by wiping down the place, including any prints the real killer might have left behind. He was a bigger fool than even he had imagined.

"She isn't coming to the door," Laura prodded.

Nick cut her a look. He reached into his pocket and retrieved his all-purpose key. Laura watched in silent amazement as he quickly and efficiently "unlocked" the door.

Laura rushed past him before he could step aside. Nick

surveyed the quiet parlor while Laura rushed from one room to the next calling the old woman's name.

Mrs. Leeton was history.

Nick scanned the parlor.

She had either gotten out of Dodge or she was pushing up daisies somewhere like the Doc. Laura rushed back into the room.

"She's not here," she said wearily.

Nick picked up a picture frame and studied the smiling couple inside. "She's gone."

"But her things are still here," Laura argued. "Her clothes, her pictures." She gestured to the frame in his hand.

Nick turned the silver frame so that Laura could see it. "Lovely couple," he noted. "But they came with the frame."

Laura frowned, then quickly scanned the two frames hanging on the far wall. "Why would she take the pictures and leave the frames hanging?"

Nick placed the frame back on the table. "She doesn't want anyone to know she's gone." He crossed the room, stared out the window at nothing in particular, then looked back to Laura. "Can you tell if any of her clothes are gone?"

Laura shrugged. "It's hard to tell. There are clothes in the closets and in the dresser drawers, but I can't be sure if they're all there."

"I'll bet they're not," he assured her. "Where's the kitchen?"

Laura led him to the small immaculate kitchen. The woman was definitely obsessive-compulsive about house-cleaning, he noted. He glanced at the shiny tile floors and sparkling white countertops. Nick walked to the refrigerator and opened the door. He leaned down and peered inside for a moment or two.

"She's been gone at least three days," he said when he had straightened and closed the door.

"How do you know that?"

"The milk expired day before yesterday," he explained. Nick nodded toward the calendar hanging from a magnet on the appliance door.

Laura stepped closer to see what had caught Nick's eyes. Mrs. Leeton had meticulously marked off each day until day before yesterday. "Oh, God," she murmured.

Laura swayed. Nick caught her. "Come on, Laura, there's nothing else we can do here."

Nick locked the door and led Laura to the car. He watched her for signs of shock or panic. She had seen too much today. He didn't see how she could tolerate much more defeat. It was a miracle she hadn't fallen completely apart.

Once they were back at the house, Nick would insist that Laura lie down. Then he would call Ian and set up a new location to take Laura. Things were definitely getting too hot around here. One way or another, he intended to get to the bottom of this mess. But first he had to make sure Laura was safe. It wouldn't be long before Dr. Holland's body was discovered. Time was running out for Laura's freedom. If James Ed suspected Laura was in any way involved with Doc's murder, he would insist that she be sent away now.

Maybe, Nick decided, he would tilt the odds in their favor. A quick call to his old friend Ray would set things in motion.

NICK PULLED the afghan over Laura. He hoped she would sleep for a while. She had been so despondent over the Doc's death that Nick had been worried out of his mind.

Shortly after finally lying down, she had fallen asleep on the couch and Nick was immensely thankful. He didn't think he could bear one more moment of her self-deprecation. She blamed herself for Doc's death. If she hadn't come back here, she kept saying. But her baby had been sick. With no insurance and no money, she hadn't known who else to turn to. Now Doc was dead.

Nick blew out a breath. He wished he could find one single shred of real proof that Laura did, in fact, have a child. The stretch marks indicated a pregnancy, but proved nothing as to her having had a live birth. He had to have solid evidence.

Shaking his head in disgust, Nick walked to the kitchen and numbly went through the motions of brewing coffee. Hell, he hadn't even had a cup of coffee today. He glanced at the clock on the wall, two o'clock. He had a feeling that this was going to be one hell of a long day. He had busied himself earlier with cleaning up the water in the bathroom, but now he felt that old restless feeling. They were getting closer to the truth now. He could feel it.

With a cup of strong coffee in his hand, Nick sat down at the table and pulled out his cellular phone. He hadn't wanted to make this call until he was certain Laura wouldn't hear. He punched in the number for information, then requested Ray's home number. Less than two minutes later he was holding for his old friend, Detective Ray Ingle.

"Hey buddyro, what's up?" Ray quipped, sounding a great deal more relaxed than the last time Nick had spoken to him.

"The easier question would be what's not," Nick told him with humor in his tone though he felt none at all.

"I hear you're hanging out in Mississippi for a week or two."

"Yeah, I just can't seem to learn my lesson right the first

time.'' Nick compressed his lips into a thin line. Beating around the bush wasn't going to make telling Ray what he had to tell him any easier.

"Hell." Ray laughed. "If you hang around down here long enough, maybe we'll make a real Southern gentleman out of you yet."

Nick smiled in spite of himself. "Thanks, but I think I'll stick with what I know best."

Silence waited between them for several long seconds.

"What's really up, man?" Ray ventured solemnly.

Nick stretched his neck in an effort to chase away the tension building there. "There's been a murder here in Bay Break."

"I see," Ray answered much more calmly than Nick had anticipated.

"Dr. Holland. Sometime this morning I think. His office has been trashed."

"Do the locals know yet?"

"Not yet."

"Is there anything else I should know?" Ray asked pointedly. "I won't even ask how you know all this."

"You may find Laura's prints in there," Nick admitted. "Hell, you'll probably find mine, too."

"Anything else?"

Nick hesitated only a second. "No."

Another long beat of silence passed.

"What is it you want me to do?" Ray asked finally.

"I know the locals will request a detective from your office to conduct the investigation." Nick moistened his lips. "I need you to make sure we're clean on this one."

"Are you?"

"I wouldn't ask if we weren't."

"Does the Governor know about this?"

"No," Nick said quickly. "And I'd appreciate it if you didn't tell him."

"What's going on, Nick?"

Nick heard the tension in Ray's voice. "I just need some more time to figure this out. I don't want Laura connected to anything that might muddy the waters."

"All right," Ray agreed. "I'll take care of it."

"Thanks, man," Nick said. "You know if you ever need anything at all, I'll be there for you."

"Don't think I'll forget it, slick," Ray said frankly.

"Let me know if you come up with any suspects," Nick added before he could hang up.

"Hey," Ray blurted before the connection was cut.

Nick pressed the phone back to his ear. "Yeah, Ray, I'm still here."

"What's the deal with the kid?"

Nick froze. Had James Ed told Ray about Laura's claims of having a child. Maybe James Ed had Ray looking into the possibility. Nick shook his head. No way. Ray would have told him right up front.

"What kid?" Nick asked slowly, reserving reaction.

Ray made a sound of disbelief. "Hell man, the kid Laura had with her when I spotted her down there. What kid did you think I meant?"

Nick's chest constricted. "Laura had a child with her when you saw her?"

"Yeah," Ray said, confusion coloring his tone. "A baby, maybe a year or so old. You couldn't miss him, he—"

"Her child is missing," Nick interrupted.

"Missing? What do—"

"Thanks, Ray," Nick said quickly, cutting him off. "Gotta go. I'll explain later." Nick closed the phone and tossed it onto the table.

He stood, the chair scraping across the floor in protest of his abrupt move. James Ed had definitely lied about Laura being in the hospital for the past eighteen months. She had been telling the truth all along. There really was a child.

Laura's child.

And now Nick had the evidence he needed to prove it.

Chapter Ten

Laura woke with a start. It was dark outside. She had slept the afternoon away again. She licked her dry lips and swallowed, the effort required to do so seeming monumental. How could she have slept so long? The medication was no longer in her system. Exhaustion, she supposed. Sleep had brought blessed relief. She had been able to leave reality behind. To escape...

Doc was dead.

The memory hit like a tidal wave. Laura squeezed her eyes shut and resisted the urge to cry. She refused to cry. Crying would accomplish nothing. She had to do something.

Doc was dead.

The files were missing.

Mrs. Mallory was gone.

Mrs. Leeton had disappeared.

Anyone who knew anything about Robby's birth was no longer available to help Laura. There was no one. Desperation crashed in on her all over again.

She would just have to help herself.

She could do it.

Nick would help her, but she wasn't going to allow him to take that risk. Doc had tried to help her and he was dead.

Laura clenched her teeth and forced her weary, grief-stricken mind to concentrate on forming a plan. If she could get her hands on a gun…

Nick would need his gun to protect himself.

Doc had a gun. She remembered seeing it on her first visit with Doc when she returned to Bay Break with Robby. Doc had shown her that he kept it loaded and in the drawer by his bed. If anyone showed up to cause trouble for Laura he knew how to use it, too, he had said. Doc loved her. When this nightmare started she had hoped that maybe he had Robby with him, hiding out somewhere.

Another wave of fierce grief tore at Laura's heart. But he was dead. Gone forever. The albino had killed him. James Ed's henchman. Laura knew it as surely as she knew her own name. He would kill Nick, too, if he got in James Ed's way. Laura would not permit that to happen.

A sense of calm settled over Laura with the decision. It would be simple. All she had to do was take the car like she did this morning, drop by the clinic to get the gun, and head to Jackson. She would get the truth out of James Ed one way or another. Nick would never suspect that she would go back to her brother's house. At least not until it was too late. But first, she had to escape Nick's watchful eye. He would be monitoring her even more closely now.

Throwing back the afghan, Laura sat up and pushed the hair from her face. She looked around the den. No Nick. Maybe he had decided to take a shower. She listened. Nothing. She didn't smell food cooking either, so he probably wasn't in the kitchen. But he wouldn't be far away that was for sure.

Laura pushed to her feet. She closed her eyes and waited for the dizziness to pass. She needed to eat, but couldn't bring herself to even think of food. Her body was so weak. Laura took slow, deep breaths. When the walls had stopped spinning around her, she moved toward the kitchen. Though she rarely drank it, coffee would be good now. Laura shuffled into the hall and bumped straight into Nick. It was as if he had some sort of sixth sense about her. She smiled a secret smile. Except for this morning. She had definitely thrown him off balance then. Or maybe it was the lovemaking the night before. Warmth flowed instantly through Laura at the thought of making love with Nick.

"Laura." He smiled and brushed her cheek with gentle fingers. "I've been waiting for you to wake up. We need to talk, sweetheart."

The desire to tell Nick the truth about his son almost overwhelmed all else. She looked into those caring green eyes and remembered every detail of the way he had made love to her. The tenderness, the heat. The same as two years ago when she had fallen in love with this special man in the first place. Nick was the most caring, giving person she had ever met. He was the only person since her parents had died who believed in her at all. He was nothing like her brother. He was unlike any man she had ever met. And she had to protect Nick. He would willingly die for her if it came down to it. Laura had to make sure that didn't happen.

Laura shook off the lingering doubts regarding what she was about to do. She had to do it for Nick. "What did you want to talk about," she asked casually. Talking would give her time to devise a plan. She stilled. As long as he didn't start pressuring her again about her baby's father. God, if he suspected the truth for one minute...

"Let's go back into the den and get comfortable," he suggested.

For two long beats Laura could only stare into those caring jade depths. She loved this man so. The truth was going to forever change how he felt about her. Could she bear that? Finally, she nodded. "Okay." She allowed Nick to usher her back into the den and to the sofa. She sat down obediently and sent up a silent prayer that he hadn't figured things out yet. Laura knew she had to tell him eventually. Just not now. She couldn't deal with anything else right now.

Nick paced in a kind of circle for a moment as if he couldn't decide how to begin. Laura swallowed hard. Surely he didn't have bad news that he feared passing on to her. Laura closed her eyes for a second to calm herself. No, she couldn't take more bad news at the moment. The image of Doc lying lifeless on the floor of his office flashed before her eyes.

"I spoke with Detective Ingle this afternoon," Nick began, jerking her splintered attention back to him.

"Robby?" Terror snaked around Laura's heart and she instantly slammed a mental door shut on her fears. She had to be strong. Otherwise she wouldn't be able to find Robby or to lead the albino away from Nick.

Nick paused a few feet away, his back turned to her he bowed his head. "I'm sorry, Laura, I should—"

Shattering glass interrupted Nick's words. Laura's startled gaze darted to the window across the room. A gust of wind blew the curtains outward, they fluttered briefly then fell back into place. Fragments of glass littered the carpet. Laura frowned. She stood—

Nick's arms went around her and they hurtled to the floor, overturning the sofa table in the process. The telephone and lamp crashed to the floor. The dial tone buzzed from the dislodged receiver.

Stunned, Laura lay against the carpet for a several seconds before she could think. Nick's body covered her own, protecting her. "Nick, what's going on?" she whispered hoarsely. The answer to her question struck her like a jolt of electricity. Her breath thinned in her lungs. Someone had shot through the window. Ice formed in Laura's stomach. *He* was out there. He was shooting at them.

"Nick!" Laura twisted her neck to an awkward angle to try and see his face. His eyes were closed, blood dripped down his forehead. She realized then that his full body weight was bearing down on her. Terror ignited within Laura. She pushed with all her might to roll herself and Nick over. She scrambled onto all fours and lowered her cheek to his face. He was breathing. Thank God. She quickly studied the injury that started an inch or so above his right eyebrow and disappeared into his hairline.

Please don't let him be hurt badly, she prayed.

Laura's hands shook as she traced the path the bullet had made with her fingers. Her lips trembled and she clamped down on her lower one to hold back the sobs twisting in her throat. Nick's warm blood stained her fingers. The vision of Doc lying in a pool of blood reeled past her eyes. Laura forced away the vivid memory. She had to help Nick. She frowned at the large bump rising on the left side of his forehead, near that temple. Laura glanced at the overturned table and broken lamp. He must have hit his head on the way down. The bullet appeared to have only grazed his head. She prayed she was right about that. He was still breathing but out cold. Could there be internal damage? Renewed terror zipped through her.

Laura shook him gently. "Nick. Nick, please wake up."

Laura's chest tightened with a rush of panic. She had to get help. She crawled to the other side of the table and snatched up the receiver and uprighted the telephone's base. Something cold and hard pressed to the back of her head.

"Hang it up," a coarse voice ordered.

It was him. She knew that voice. In her panic to help Nick, Laura had completely forgotten that he was somewhere outside. Now, he was here.

"Now," he commanded harshly. "Or I'll put another bullet in your boyfriend and finish him off."

Laura dropped the receiver onto its base and quickly stood. "He needs help," Laura pleaded. "Just let me call for help and then I'll do anything you want."

His weapon trained on her heart, the albino circled around her then glanced down at Nick. Laura gasped when he kicked Nick in the side.

"Stop!" she shrieked.

The albino grinned. "He'll live." He cocked one pale brow. "But he might not if you don't do exactly as I say."

Laura grabbed control of herself. She nodded adamantly. "What do you want me to do?"

He gestured toward the hall. "Outside, princess."

Laura led the way to the front door. She said one more silent prayer that Nick would be all right. Once outside, she turned to the man and asked, "What now?" Whatever it took to appease him and keep him away from Nick.

He glanced around the dark yard as if trying to decide. "The barn," he suggested. "Lots of imaginative possibilities in a barn."

Laura shuddered, but quickly composed herself. She needed calm. She needed to think. She had to think of a way to defend herself. If he killed her now, he might go back inside the house and kill Nick as well.

"Let's make this easy on the both of us," the man murmured next to her ear as he ushered her in the direction of the barn. "I'm going to kill you, and you're going to let me. Got that?"

Laura's eyes widened in fear, but she squashed the paralyzing emotion. She wracked her brain to remember what might be in the barn that could help her.

"Got that?" he demanded, the gun boring into her skull.

Laura nodded jerkily.

"Good," he acknowledged.

The scent of hay and stored fuels filled Laura's lungs as they entered the big double doors of the barn which stood partially open. No one ever bothered to close them, she remembered as if it mattered now. The albino made a half-hearted attempt at closing them. That effort would be to no avail Laura knew, the doors would only drift open again. They always did. But who would notice tonight?

Nick. Tears streamed down Laura's cheeks. She suddenly found herself praying that he didn't wake up and come to her rescue. Maybe if he stayed in the house, this bastard would just leave after he did what James Ed had paid him to do. Laura trembled. She didn't want to die. She wanted to be with her son, and she wanted to be with Nick.

But her life meant nothing if either of them was hurt by this. Laura closed her eyes against the painful possibility. Her captor flipped a switch and a long fluorescent light blinked to life overhead. Laura blinked quickly, her frantic gaze searched for anything that might aid her escape. The light's dim glow lit the center of the spacious barn, but the stalls remained in shadow. At one time, when she was a child, she remembered abruptly, there had been horses in this barn. But not anymore. Not in a long time. James Ed had gotten rid of what he had called an unnecessary nuisance.

The albino shoved her to the floor. "Don't move," he warned as he surveyed their surroundings. A smile lifted one side of his grim mouth when his gaze lit on something in particular. Laura shifted to see what it was that had captured his attention.

"Perfect," he muttered. Keeping the rifle aimed at her chest and his gaze trained on Laura, he walked to the row of hooks lining one wall and took down a sturdy-looking rope coiled there. Rope in hand, he moved back to tower over her. Laura committed every detail of his appearance to memory. Ghostly white hair and skin, and those eerie pink eyes. He wasn't very tall, but was solidly built. And strong, Laura remembered well. If she got away this time, she fully intended to be able to describe him to Nick.

"One peep out of you and I'll kill you now," he warned as he fiddled with the rope. "Then I'll kill lover boy just for the hell of it."

Not allowing his threat to frighten her further, Laura concentrated on his actions. Was he going to tie her up? She ordered the hysteria rising inside her to retreat, and her mind to focus. She had to escape. He was going to kill her this time, that was certain. The finality of that realization was oddly calming. Laura scanned her immediate surroundings for a weapon of some sort. A pitchfork stood on the wall farthest from her. She chewed her lip as she considered the distance. She would never be able to reach it before he shot her.

This was hopeless. There was nothing she could do.

Laura felt weak with regret. The thought that she would never see Nick or Robby again was a bone-deep ache.

No! she told herself. She had to do something. She couldn't just let him do this. She needed to get the albino talking. She had to stall him. At least it was some sort of plan. Maybe if she distracted him he would screw up somehow.

"Why did you have to kill Doc?" she demanded, her voice harsher than she had intended.

He cut his evil gaze to her and grinned. It was then that Laura noted the one thing about him that wasn't white—his teeth. They were a hideous yellow. She shivered.

"The old man was lucky once," he informed her haughtily. "When I came for him, he had left town. He had himself a sudden personal emergency." He laughed as if relishing Doc's troubles. "His only living relative, a sister out in Arkansas, had herself a heart attack and died."

"How do you know that?" Laura asked sharply, annoyed that he derived pleasure from Doc's loss.

"I was there at the clinic. One of the patients leaving that morning told me," he retorted. "If he hadn't left so quickly I would have taken care of him then and there." He shook his head with feigned regret. "But then he showed up this morning. Bad timing, too. I was taking your file." He frowned, his hands stilled on the rope. "Pissed me off that I couldn't get it the day he disappeared, but there were too many witnesses who saw me in his yard. I couldn't risk doing anything suspicious. So I left." That sick smile lifted his lips again. "People aren't likely to forget how I look."

Laura shivered. That was the truth if she had ever heard it. "You killed Doc just because he helped me?"

"I killed Doc because he knew too much."

Same difference, Laura thought with growing disgust.

"What about Mrs. Leeton, did you kill her, too, or was she working with you?" Laura clenched her teeth at the thought that the woman had betrayed her. Had helped someone steal her son. Laura's lips quivered with as much anger as fear.

"Not yet," he said casually. "The old bag disappeared. But I'll find her."

"Where's my son?" Laura held her breath. She feared the answer, but she had to know. Please, God, she prayed, don't let him have hurt my baby.

"You're not going to be needing him," he suggested as he tightened the strange knot in the rope. "Unless you want him buried with you."

Laura jumped to her feet, fury shot through her. "If you've hurt my son," she threatened.

"Don't worry, princess, he's worth too much alive." The albino recoiled the rope. "But you," he allowed that evil gaze to travel over her, "you're worth a whole lot more dead. And I'm tired of playing with you now. It's time to get down to business."

NICK ROUSED slowly to a piercing pain that knifed right through his skull. He touched his forehead and blood darkened his fingertips.

"What the hell happened?" he muttered.

He sat up, groaning with the pain pounding inside his head. He pushed to his feet and the room spun around him. Nick closed his eyes and fought the vertigo threatening his vertical position. He took a step and something crushed under his boot. Wiping the blood from his face, Nick stared down at the broken lamp and overturned table. The events that had taken place slammed into him with such force that he staggered.

"Laura." Nick scanned the room, then rushed into the hall. The front door stood open. The cold November wind had blown leaves into the hall. They skittered this way and that across the shiny hardwood like lost souls.

Nick hurried out onto the porch, his step still unsteady. The rental car was in the driveway where he had left it. He looked from left to right. Which way would the son of a bitch have taken her?

A shriek cut through the dark fabric of the night. Nick whirled in the direction of the sound. The barn. The barest glow of light filtered past the half-open doors. Nick ran like hell. He clenched his jaw against the resulting pain twisting in his knee and then shooting up his right thigh. He ignored the fierce throb still hammering inside his head. He had to get to her. Nick pushed harder despite the grinding pain and the vertigo still pulling at him. He stumbled, barely catching himself before he hit the ground. Nick swore and propelled himself toward the barn. He skidded to a stop near one wide door. Commanding his respiration to slow, he inched toward the crack where the door hinged to the doorway. He leaned forward and peered through the narrow opening.

Nick jerked back at what he saw. Laura was standing on a small stepladder. A length of rope had been strung over a rafter, its noose snug around her neck. Nick swallowed the terror that climbed into his throat. He carefully stepped back up to the narrow slit and forced himself to look again. The albino stood near her, talking to her, the barrel of his weapon jabbed into her stomach. Absolute fear held Laura's every feature captive. She clutched frantically at the rope as if it were too tight already.

A crimson rage engulfed Nick. The son of a bitch was a dead man. Nick remembered to breathe, breathe deeply and slowly. He needed to focus. He couldn't risk Laura getting hurt. But the albino was *dead*.

Nick moved soundlessly toward the open doorway. He needed to get as close as possible without being detected. Taking one last deep breath, Nick stepped into the reaching fingers of light and began the slow, careful journey toward his target. He moved to the far right, toward the shadows near the stalls. If he could circle around and come up directly behind the bastard, Nick would hopefully prevent any sudden or unexpected moves when he took him down.

"Go ahead," the albino sneered. "Don't be a wimp. Scream all you want. Nobody's going to hear you. Lover boy is out cold." He moved closer to Laura. "Sound effects always add to the pleasure."

"Just tell me where my son is," Laura demanded hoarsely.

"Now this isn't going to be so bad." The albino gestured

toward her precarious position with the barrel of his high-powered rifle. "It'll take about four minutes, depending on how long you can hold your breath, for you to pass out, and then it'll all be over. And everyone will live happily ever after. They'll all say, poor Laura, we did everything we could for her but she still committed suicide in the end."

"Swear to me that my son is safe," Laura spat vehemently.

Nick blocked the emotion that crowded his thinking at the sound of her desperation. She wasn't afraid to die, she was only afraid for her child. His throat constricted. The child no one had believed in, including him at first. Nick's lips compressed into a thin line, he barely restrained the roar of rage filling him now.

"Don't you worry about that baby boy of yours," the albino taunted. "He's going to make someone very happy. Happy enough to pay me all the money I'll ever need," he added in a sickeningly cocky voice.

Laura stiffened, the old, rickety stepladder rocked precariously beneath her.

"Don't move, princess," he warned. "I wouldn't want you to actually kill yourself." He stepped closer to her. "I want the pleasure of giving you that final little push myself. Then I'm going in the house and finish off your friend."

"You promised if I did what you said that you would leave Nick alone," she challenged.

The albino made a sound of approval in his throat. "I love it when you talk back."

Laura turned her face away from him. Nick stopped dead in his tracks when her terrified gaze flickered back to him. He shook his head but it was too late. Recognition and relief flared in her expression. Seeing the change, the albino whirled toward Nick. Nick took a bead right between his pink eyes.

"Drop it," Nick ordered.

The albino smiled. "Well, what do you know. That head of yours must be harder than I thought."

"Cut her down," Nick growled savagely. "Or you die where you stand."

The bastard stroked his cheek with his free hand, his weapon trained on Laura's face now. Nick tightened his grip on his Beretta in anticipation of the right opportunity to take this son of a bitch down.

"See here, wise guy," he smirked, "this is my little party and you weren't invited. Don't you know that two's company and three's a crowd?"

"Cut her down," Nick repeated coldly, the thought of killing the man making him feel decidedly calm. "And I'll let you live."

"What's to keep me from shooting her first?"

Nick heard the uncertainty in the albino's voice then. "Just one thing," Nick paused for effect, "the closed-casket funeral required since I'm about to take the top of your head off." Nick snugged his finger on the trigger.

"Wouldn't want that, now would we?" the albino relented.

His gaze locked with Nick's, the albino slowly began to lower his weapon. Nick took a step forward. And then everything lapsed into slow motion. The albino kicked his right foot outward. The stepladder clattered to the floor. A startled scream shattered the still air. Nick's horrified gaze riveted to Laura. Her arms stretched over her head, she struggled to grasp the rope and keep her weight from pulling her downward. Her legs dangled in thin air. Her face contorted with fear and desperation.

The albino kept his weapon trained on Laura as he

backed toward the door. Uncertainty flashed again in those strange eyes. "Are you going to waste precious seconds trying to decide if you can put a bullet in me before she asphyxiates? How long do you think she can hold her breath?" he added with a twisted smile.

Instantly, Nick found himself beneath Laura, supporting her weight to keep life-giving air flowing in and out of her lungs. His heart slammed mercilessly against his rib cage.

"Can you get the noose off?" he asked hoarsely. Nick felt himself tremble with delayed reaction. The vision of Laura dangling from the end of that damned rope swept through his brain.

Gasping for breath between sobs, Laura didn't answer for a while. "I think so," she rasped, then coughed.

Nick's gaze shot to the barn doors. The albino was gone.

But Laura was alive. Nick closed his eyes and held her lower body more tightly in his arms.

At the moment, nothing else mattered.

Chapter Eleven

"My baby's alive," Laura whispered. "He told me my baby was alive. I…" She shuddered. "You're still bleeding. I have to get you to a hospital."

"Shhh," Nick soothed. "I'm fine. The bullet didn't do as much damage as that damned table."

Laura caressed his cheek with trembling fingers, her worried gaze examining him closely. "But there's so much blood."

"I'm fine." He pressed a kiss to her forehead, then pulled her close against his chest. "Just let me hold you a minute." Nick sat on the cold dirt floor and held Laura in his arms. She trembled and he held her closer. He almost lost her tonight. He should have anticipated that the bastard would make a move after killing Doc. He was growing impatient.

Laura had been through so much already. Her missing child. Her son. Ray's words echoed inside Nick's head, *"A baby, maybe a year or so old."*

Laura's child.

Ray had seen her with the child. Ian would no doubt confirm tomorrow that the clinic Nick and Laura had visited had, indeed, registered the birth of a Robert Forester with the registrar's office in Montgomery. That would be more hard evidence. Laura had a child, and by noon tomorrow Nick would be able to prove it.

James Ed had lied. Nick couldn't believe he had been that wrong about the man. He had seemed genuinely overjoyed to have Laura back home. To know that she was alive and unharmed.

And Sandra. She might not even know her mother was alive. Her adoptive parents may have told her that the woman died years ago. What would Sandra stand to gain from Laura's death? Nothing, as far as Nick could see. It wasn't as if she and James Ed had needed the money that desperately. Of course, once it was available, they had apparently taken advantage of it. But Sandra wasn't in control of the money, James Ed was. All evidence pointed to James Ed.

Just like Laura said.

Nick frowned. Still, something about that scenario didn't quite fit. Didn't sit right with him. He blew out a disgusted breath. Nick closed his eyes and cursed himself for not believing her in the first place. He should have followed his instincts instead of allowing the past and his pride to get in the way. His eyes burned with regret. It shouldn't have taken him so long to come around.

He was a fool twice over.

Nick placed a soft kiss against Laura's hair. "Let me get you inside," he murmured. "We'll talk then."

"Okay," she said weakly. She stared into his eyes, her own bright with tears. "But first I want to get that wound cleaned up."

Nick nodded and they stood together. His grasp on her arms tightened to steady her when she swayed. She glanced around the dimly lit barn, her eyes wide with fear. Her body tensed as he slid his right arm around her waist.

"It's all right, honey, he's gone. I don't think he'll be

back,'' Nick assured her. He couldn't bear the fear in her eyes. If the bastard did come back he was a dead man.

Taking his time so as not to rush her, Nick ushered Laura in the direction of the house. Her skin felt as cold as ice. He had to get her inside and warmed up. He shuddered inwardly again at the thought of how close he had come to losing her tonight. Shock was a definite threat at the moment. A warm bath and hot coffee or cocoa would do the trick. He would call Ian and then Nick and Laura would talk. He wasn't sure she could tolerate any more surprises, good or bad right now. When she was up to it, he would tell Laura that she didn't have to worry anymore.

One way or another Nick would find her child. If he had to beat the truth out of James Ed with his bare hands.

Half an hour later Laura had cleaned and bandaged the wound on his forehead where the bullet had grazed him. Nick had a hell of a lump where the table had gotten in his way, but there was nothing to be done about that. Nick had settled Laura in the wide garden tub and then he'd put in a call to Ian while warming some milk for cocoa. Tracking down the identity of the albino probably wouldn't be difficult, Nick considered as he carried the steaming cocoa to the bathroom.

He paused inside the bathroom door just to look at Laura. Mounds of frothy bubbles enveloped her, hiding that exquisite feminine body. She had bundled all that silky blond hair atop her head in the sexiest heap Nick had ever seen. He loved every sweet, perfect thing about her. A fierce stab of desire sliced through him, making his groin tighten. How he wanted to touch her. But not tonight, he reminded the hungry beast inside him. Laura needed to rest tonight.

Relaxed within the warm depths, her eyes closed, Nick couldn't read what Laura's emotional state was now that the day's events had had time to absorb fully. His throat constricted at the thought of just how much she had endured over the past two years. Running for her life, and with a baby. How had he ever doubted her? If James Ed were behind all this—Nick shook his head slowly, resolutely—he would pay. He forced a deep, calming breath. Going off half-cocked wouldn't help, but there would definitely be a day of reckoning.

Nick's errant gaze moved back to Laura's face, then traveled down one soft cheek, past her delicate jaw, and over the fragile column of her throat. Anger unfurled inside him when his gaze traced the offensive marks caused by the rope. The abrasions, already shadowed with a purplish tinge, were stark against her creamy skin. The albino had better hope Nick didn't find him.

Adopting a calm he didn't feel, Nick crossed the quiet room and sat down on the edge of the luxurious tub. Laura's lids slowly fluttered open revealing those soft blue eyes. Nick smiled, then placed her cocoa near the elaborate gold faucet.

"It's warm," he told her. "You should drink it before it cools."

Laura moistened those full, pink lips. "I suppose it's safe to say that you believe me about James Ed now," she suggested with just a hint of bitterness.

Nick nodded. He deserved a good swift kick in the ass. "It would be safe to say that, yes. All the evidence seems to point to him."

Her expression solemn, those sweet lips trembled. "We have enough evidence to prove my son exists, too?"

Nick's gaze remained locked with hers for a long moment as he considered whether to tell her about the call to Ray. No, he decided, she'd had enough for one night. She needed to relax, not get all worked up again. "Yes. We can prove your child is real." He didn't want to think about another man touching Laura. She belonged to him....

Laura blinked away the moisture shining in those huge blue orbs. "You'll make James Ed tell the truth?"

Nick smiled then. It didn't matter who the father was. Nick would find Laura's child. "Absolutely."

"He said that someone is going to pay him a lot of money for my baby." She swallowed, then pulled her lower lip between her teeth as she composed herself. "I can't believe my own brother would sell my baby."

"We'll get him back, Laura."

Her arms folded over her breasts, Laura sat bolt upright. "I want you to take me to James Ed. I want you to take me right now, Nick," she demanded. "I don't want to waste any more time."

For a moment Nick couldn't speak. Suds slipped over her satiny shoulders and down her slender arms. Laura was a wonderful mother. The kind any child would want, he realized suddenly. The kind of mother he wanted for his own children. She was sweet and beautiful and kind. And all that sass buried beneath her worry for her child pulled at him like nothing else ever had. She was everything he wanted.

"First thing in the morning," he countered finally, a restless feeling stirring deep inside him. "We'll head for Jackson then."

She pressed Nick with her solemn gaze. "And you'll do whatever it takes to get the truth out of my brother?"

"You can count on it." He would have the truth out of James Ed...or else.

"Swear it, Nick," she insisted. "Swear to me that you'll do whatever it takes."

"I swear," he replied softly.

Laura nodded her satisfaction. Several tendrils of that

golden silk fell around her face, and clung to that soft neck. "That's all I can ask of you." A frown wrinkled her pretty forehead. "Does your head hurt much?"

"Not much," he whispered. The need to touch her overwhelmed all else. Slowly, while maintaining that intense eye contact, Nick allowed his fingertips to glide over one smooth cheek. Want gripped him with such ferocity that for a long moment he couldn't breathe. "You can ask anything you want of me," he murmured.

Laura took his hand in hers and pressed a soft kiss to his palm, her gaze never leaving his. "And would you give me anything I ask, Nick?" she whispered. A hot flash of desire kindled in her eyes.

He nodded, no longer capable of articulation.

"You're sure you're up to it?" she teased, a smile playing about the corners of her full mouth.

Nick hoped the grunt he uttered was sufficient response.

When Laura slid his hand down to her breast he knew it was. He squeezed. Her head lolled back and her eyes closed in sweet ecstasy. Nick watched as Laura guided his hand to all the places she wanted him to touch. Her other breast, then lower to her flat stomach, then lower still.

Nick groaned when she parted her thighs and opened for him. He slipped his middle finger inside her hot, moist body. A shudder wracked him as an instant climax threatened. Nick clenched his jaw and grabbed back control. Laura was the only woman who ever made him want to come with nothing more than a touch. Nick gripped the edge of the tub with his free hand as he moved that small part of himself rhythmically inside her. Her moans of pleasure urged him on. Her lips parted slightly as her breathing became labored. Nick used the pad of his thumb to massage her tiny nub of desire until it swelled beneath his touch. She reared back, thrusting her firm white breasts upward, as if begging for his attention. Determined to watch, Nick resisted the urge to taste her. Water and bubbles slipped over her smooth breasts. Her dusky nipples tightened and budded right before his eyes. Nick licked his lips. His arousal throbbed insistently, and he jerked with restraint.

Laura's fingers splayed on the sides of the tub, providing leverage as she arched against his hand. Nick growled with need when he felt the first tremors of her release. He moved more quickly, propelling her toward that peek. Laura cried out as her inner muscles tightened around Nick's finger. His own need for release roared inside him. Nick leaned forward and covered Laura's mouth with his own. She took him hungrily, sucking his tongue into her mouth. Nick groaned. His arms plunged into the water and around her. He pulled her to him savagely, his body needing to feel hers against him.

"I need to be inside you," he breathed against her lips.

"Now, Nick," she murmured greedily. "Hurry."

Holding her firmly against him, Nick lifted Laura from the tub. Water sloshed over the side. Wet heat and suds from her damp skin soaked into his shirtfront. Laura's legs wrapped instinctively around his waist. Nick stumbled toward the door, his mouth still plundering hers. Hot and sweet. She tasted so good. He had to get her to the bed. He couldn't hold out much longer. Nick backed into a wall, cursed—the word lost in the kiss—and groped for the door with one hand.

"No," Laura protested between kisses. "Here," she demanded.

Nick pivoted and pressed her back against the wall. His hips ground into her softness. Nick groaned deep in his throat. Squeezing Laura's thigh with one hand, he wrenched his jeans open.

Laura arched against him, her fingers dug into his shoulders. "Hurry, Nick," she moaned. "Hurry." Her breath came in fierce little spurts. She needed him as much as he needed her. The thought sent another jolt of desire raging through him, almost snapping his control.

Laura screamed at the first nudge of his arousal. Nick grunted, intent on plunging deep inside her. Breathtaking, gut-wrenching sensations washed over him when he finally pushed fully into Laura's hot, tight body. He sagged against her for the space of one beat as the powerful tide of pleasure almost took him over the edge. His heart pounded hard in time with Laura's. He gulped a much-needed breath.

Her arms tightened around his neck and she pulled him closer. "Nick," she murmured as her eyes closed in an expression of pleasure-pain. "Oh, Nick."

Capturing her sweet lips with his own, Nick began the slow, shallow thrusting that would bring Laura to the brink of release once more. He clenched his jaw and resisted the urge to swiftly drive into his own release. Her thighs tightened on his waist, urging him into a faster rhythm. The air raged in and out of Nick's lungs as he pushed ever closer to climax. The case and all its ugliness faded into insignificance, leaving only Laura behind. Her taste, her scent filled him, mind and body. The final, tense seconds before climax brought complete clarity to Nick's tortured soul.

And he knew in that crystal clear moment that his life would never be the same. He loved her. He had always loved her. She was part of him. She completed him.

The rocking explosion that followed left him weak-kneed and feeling totally helpless in her arms. Nick's gaze moved to hers, she smiled, and something near his heart shifted.

NICK'S NAKED FLESH felt hot against hers. Laura snuggled closer, then smiled. She wanted to feel all of him. To hold him closer still.

For as long as it lasted.

Laura's smile melted. She swallowed back the fear that crowded into her throat. The bandage on his forehead served as a reminder of just how close she had come to losing him tonight. Laura couldn't protect Nick anymore than she had protected Robby. Hurt twisted inside her.

And, dear God, what would Nick do when he discovered the truth? There would be no denying Robby's parentage when they found him. He looked so much like Nick. And Nick had promised her that they would definitely find her baby.

Blinking back the uncertainty, Laura redirected her focus to Nick's long, lean body pressed so intimately to hers. He had said they would talk. But he seemed content for the moment to simply lie next to her without words or questions of any sort. The cool sheets draped their heated skin. She glanced at the clock on the bedside table, 9:00 p.m. What was Robby doing now? she wondered. Her heart squeezed painfully. Was he sleeping soundly in a bed somewhere safe? If someone intended to pay a great deal of money for him, surely they were treating him well. Laura shivered at the thought of someone else cuddling and loving her sweet baby. The idea that he might call someone else mommy tore at her heart. She had to find him.

"You cold?" Nick asked, the words rumbling from his chest.

"I'm fine," Laura said quickly. She immediately regretted the shortness of her response.

Nick shifted onto one elbow and peered down at her. He frowned. The white bandage stark against his dark coloring. "We'll find him, Laura," he assured her. "Don't doubt that."

She essayed a faint smile. "I know." Nick was the kindest, most honorable man she knew. He deserved so much more than she had to give him.

Nick's frown deepened and he fell silent for a few moments. Laura's heart skipped into an erratic staccato. She recognized the precise instant that realization dawned. The air evacuated her lungs.

"You told the receptionist at the clinic that Robby was born on August sixth," he said slowly, thoughtfully.

Laura licked her lips. Ice rushed through her veins. "That's right."

Three seconds later the mental calculations were complete. Nick's gaze landed fully onto hers. "Forester. You used the name Forester."

Laura nodded. Speech wasn't an option.

Suspicion crept into his wary green eyes. "Robert?"

"Robert," she managed to agree.

"Robert what?" His tone held no inflection, his eyes were openly accusing now.

Laura drew in a deep breath. She met that accusing gaze. "Robert Nicholas Forester."

There was no way to describe the expression that claimed Nick's features then. Something between rage and wonder battled for control, but, in the end, the rage proved victorious.

Nick sat up, putting distance between them. "He's my son."

Laura knew it wasn't a question. She also knew with complete certainty that Nick would never forgive her for keeping his son from him.

"Yes," she said finally. Had it not been for the fierceness of his piercing gaze, uttering that solitary word would almost have been a relief. But there was no way to garner any good feelings from what she saw in Nick's eyes.

Nick shot out of bed. His back turned to her, he pulled

on his jeans. Laura sat up. She hugged the sheet to her chest and willed the emotions threatening to consume her to retreat.

He shifted back to face her, then raked those long, tanned fingers through his uncharacteristically mussed hair. A muscle flexed rhythmically in his tense jaw. "Why didn't you tell me?" His hands fisted at his sides. "Why didn't you come to me as soon as you knew you were pregnant?"

"You were one of them," she said quietly, defeatedly.

Slowly, but surely every nuance of emotion disappeared from Nick's eyes and expression. That cold, hard, unfeeling mask slipped firmly into place like the slamming of a door. His broad, muscled chest heaved with the rage no doubt building inside him.

"I was never one of them," he said coldly.

Tears stung her eyes, but Laura refused to cry. "You worked for James Ed. I couldn't be sure that I could trust you." She met his gaze with hope in hers. "When you first found me this time you didn't believe anything I told you. Then, later, I was going to tell you but so much happened."

"Believing you and trusting you are two entirely different things," he snapped. "Don't mistake the two."

Laura struggled to her feet, dragging the tangled sheet with her. They were back to the trust issue. "I couldn't tell you," she told him with as much force as she could summon. "I was afraid for my life, Nick! Don't you get it? James Ed was trying to kill me."

"What did that have to do with trusting me?" he demanded, his tone low and lethal.

Laura shook her head at his inability to see the obvious. "James Ed hired you. Your loyalty was to him."

"We made love, Laura," he ground out. "That didn't spell anything out for you?"

"I was afraid," she said wearily.

"You kept my son from me all this time and all you've got to say is that you were afraid?" Contempt edged his voice.

"I had to protect my child," Laura argued. The starch seeped out of her spine and standing proved difficult.

"Well you did a hell of a job, didn't you?"

The tears would not be contained then. The humiliating liquid emotion slipped down her cheeks. "I did the best I could considering the circumstances."

Nick stepped closer, his body rigid with fury. "But that wasn't good enough, was it? And it never once occurred to you to call on me for help?"

Anger surged, steeling her resolve. "Forget all that. The important thing now is finding him," Laura countered, her tone as lethal as his.

"I will find him," Nick promised. "And when I do, I'll make sure nothing like this ever happens to him again."

Stunned, Laura could only stare into those cold, emotionless eyes. This was her worst nightmare come true. Not only had she lost her son, but if she did find him he would still be lost even then. Nick's cell phone splintered the ensuing silence. His gaze still riveted to hers, he snatched the phone from the bedside table and snapped his greeting.

Blocking out all other thought, Nick listened carefully as Ian relayed his latest findings.

"The albino is a Rodney Canton, a dirty P.I. with a most impressive rap sheet. Kidnapping, assault with a deadly weapon, and worse."

Nick shifted his weight from his throbbing right knee. "Is there any connection between him and the Proctors?"

"No, not directly. But he worked with a Brock Redmond who owned and operated a P.I. office in Natchez for years. Funny thing is," Ian continued, "this Redmond fellow disappeared suddenly about two years ago. No one has seen him since.''

Nick frowned. ''Do you have a physical description?''

''Oh yes. He fits perfectly the description Laura provided of the man who shot you.''

Anticipation nudged at Nick. ''Any connection to James Ed?''

Ian laughed. ''A long and productive connection. James Ed hired Redmond on several occasions to provide the low-down on potential staff members.''

''Do you have anything that will stand up in a court of law to back that up?''

''I'm looking at the man's files.''

Nick shook his head. ''I'm not sure I want to know how you managed that.''

''It would seem that Redmond stiffed his secretary out of two months pay when he disappeared.'' Amusement colored Ian's tone. ''So she confiscated his files. She has been most helpful.''

''Nothing else on Sandra?''

''The jury is still out on the first lady,'' Ian told him. ''But the evidence against James Ed is undeniable. If Redmond is the man who shot you, and he appears to be, then James Ed is in this up to his politically incorrect neck.''

''Good work, Ian. I'll touch base with you tomorrow.''

Ian hesitated. ''You sound a little strange, Nick. Is there anything you're not telling me?''

''I'll fill you in tomorrow.'' Nick flipped the phone closed before Ian could say anything else.

Nick had a son.

And James Ed Proctor was about to discover that Nick was more than just a man of his word. He was a man of action. Only Nick wasn't sure James Ed was going to like the action Nick had in mind. He intended to find his son if he had to wring the child's location one syllable at a time out of James Ed's scrawny neck. Nick would not stop until he found his son.

Nick shot Laura a withering look. "Get dressed. We're going to Jackson.

A NARROW SLIT of moonlight sliced through the darkness of the room from the gap between the heavily lined drapes. Propelled by her dreams, Elsa tossed restlessly beneath the thick covers. A cold sweat dampened her skin, making her nightgown stick to her in all the uncomfortable places.

It was wrong, it was wrong, her mind chanted.

Elsa sat up with a start. She blinked, then pushed her disheveled hair from her sweat-dampened face. She looked at the clock. Almost midnight. It seemed so much later. Elsa blew out a breath of weariness. The dreams. Oh, the dreams were so disturbing. She shook herself. But they were only dreams.

Soon it would be a new day.

The day.

Today the little boy's new family would come to take him away to their home. Elsa passed a hand over her face and tried to reconcile herself to that fact. She shook her head. It wasn't right. Deep inside, past all the indifference and looking the other way, she knew it wasn't right.

She swallowed. She had to do something.

Yes. A sense of calmness settled over her.

She had to do something.

Chapter Twelve

Uneasiness crawled up Nick's spine the moment he parked behind the Governor's home. The second floor of the house stood in darkness, a few lights glowed downstairs. Nick found it particularly odd that security had not already approached the car. He knew from experience how difficult it was to outmaneuver those guys.

"What are we waiting for?"

Nick shifted his attention to the woman seated next to him. It was the first time she had spoken since they left Bay Break. Renewed anger flooded Nick when he met her hesitant gaze. She had lied to him. Kept his son from him. Nick's fingers tightened on the steering wheel. No matter what her reasons, and no matter what that more foolish part of him wanted to feel, Nick wasn't sure he could ever forgive her for that.

"Something isn't right," Nick told her, emotion making his voice harsh in the hushed darkness that shrouded them.

"I don't care," Laura said with a shake of her head. "I have to find Robby."

Nick snagged her left arm. "You'll do exactly as I say, Laura," he ground out. "I'm going in and you're staying right here."

"No way," she argued. "I'm going in, too. You can't

stop me.'' The warning in her voice was that of a desperate mother's.

He blew out an impatient breath. ''All right, but stay right behind me. No wandering off on your own.''

Laura nodded her understanding.

Nick emerged from the car. He scanned the dark yard as he repositioned the Beretta beneath his jacket at the small of his back. Every instinct warned Nick that trouble awaited them inside. Finding his son and keeping Laura safe, no matter what she had done, were top priority. Laura climbed out behind him. They walked straight up to the back of the house without encountering anyone.

Where the hell was security? Nick wondered grimly. James Ed was too cautious a man to be caught with his pants down like this. Nick reached out and grasped Laura's arm as they stepped up to the verandah. No sense risking her making any sudden moves. Laura stalled at the French door leading to the rear entry hall.

''Promise me you won't let him talk his way out of this, Nick,'' she urged. ''No matter what James Ed says, you have to believe me. He tried to kill me and he took away my son.''

Nick met her fearful gaze in the darkness. ''No one is talking their way out of anything,'' he said pointedly. Including you, he didn't add. Nick set his jaw hard and reached for the doorbell. He paused. Maybe he didn't want to announce their arrival.

He turned back to Laura. ''Stay right behind me,'' he ordered tersely. When she nodded he reached for the brass handle on one French door and opened it. An eerie silence greeted them as they entered the dimly lit hall. Nick felt Laura move closer. He scanned the long, empty corridor with mounting tension. Something was definitely wrong. Very wrong.

The long hall extended the width of the house from back-door to front, with two ninety-degree turns in between. Nick paused and surveyed each room they passed. No Governor. No First Lady. No staff or security.

Every nerve ending had gone on full-scale alert by the time they reached the parlor. To Nick's relief, James Ed sat on the sofa, his head bowed over what appeared to be a photo album. Other photo albums were scattered on the sofa table. Wearing a robe and pajamas, James Ed appeared deeply involved in the pictures.

"Governor," Nick said, announcing their presence.

James Ed looked up, then quickly removed his glasses. "Nick?" He frowned. Something that resembled regret stole across his features when his gaze landed on his sister. "Laura?" James Ed pushed to his feet. "You're here."

Ignoring his comment, Nick crossed the room. Laura remained near the door. "There are a few questions I need to ask you," Nick told him quietly.

James Ed's gaze lingered on Laura. "You look as if you're feeling much better, Laura," he remarked with a sad smile.

Again, Nick couldn't shake the feeling that James Ed was serious in his concern for his much younger sister.

"Where's my son?" Laura demanded.

James Ed's expression turned distant. "I don't understand all this," he said, his tone remote.

"Laura does have a child," Nick ground out. It took every ounce of willpower he possessed not to grab the Governor by the throat. "I'm about to give you one last opportunity to redeem yourself here, James Ed. Why did you hire someone to kill Laura and where is the baby?"

"I would never do anything to hurt you, Laura," James Ed insisted. "You must believe that." His sincere gaze turned to Nick's. "I love her too much."

"Tell me about your associate, Brock Redmond," Nick suggested coolly.

Denial flickered across the Governor's features. "I didn't hire him to do this."

"So you admit that you do know him," Nick pressed.

James Ed hesitated, his expression distracted now. "What?"

"It's over, James Ed. We know what you did."

James Ed shook his head slowly. "I...I don't want to talk now. I'm not feeling well. Please go away."

"Redmond is the man who shot me, and left me for dead. He," Nick added bitterly, "is the man who tried to kill Laura on the riverbank that same night. And you hired him."

"You're wrong," James Ed argued wearily. "Brock Redmond is—"

"Was," Nick cut in. "He's dead."

James Ed seemed to shrink right before Nick's eyes. "I didn't know," he murmured. "I didn't know...."

Laura couldn't stand idly by and do nothing a moment longer. She had to find Robby. While Nick and James Ed were caught up in their discussion, Laura used the moment to slip back into the hall. They had already checked the downstairs rooms. Laura glanced at the wide staircase that flowed up to the second floor. He had to be upstairs. She frowned at the thought that Sandra was probably watching him. Why would Sandra go along with James Ed? She had never mentioned to Laura that she even wanted a child. Being the perfect political wife had always appeared to be enough for her.

Pushing the disturbing question aside, Laura rushed up the seemingly endless stairs. Once on the second-story landing she paused to listen. Laura strained with the effort to hear even the slightest noise. Something, some indistinguishable sound touched her ears. She turned to her right and followed the soft sound to the far end of the corridor. The room was on the right and across the hall from James Ed and Sandra's bedroom.

The closer Laura came to the door the louder and clearer the sound became. Music, she realized.

A lullaby.

Laura stopped dead in her tracks. A chill raced up her spine and spread across her scalp.

"Robby," she murmured. Laura ran the last few feet and burst into the room. She smoothed her hand over the wall until she found a light switch. A soft golden glow filled the bedroom when she flipped it to the on position. Blue walls embellished with white clouds, gold stars and moons wrapped the space in warmth. Beautiful cherry wood furniture, including a large rocking chair, filled the room. A lavish crib, adorned with a coverlet bearing those same moons, stars, and clouds stood near the open French doors. Blue, gauzy curtains fluttered in the cool night air. A windup mobile slowly turned, playing the familiar tune.

Her heart rising in her throat, Laura blindly walked the few steps that separated her from the crib. She braced her hands on the side rails and peered down at the fluffy coverlet and matching pillow and bumper pads.

The crib was empty save for linens.

No Robby.

Laura gasped, a pained, choking sort of half-sob sound.

"I've been expecting you."

Tears streaming down her cheeks, Laura turned slowly to face the cold, emotionless voice.

Sandra.

"Why?" The word struggled past the lump constricting Laura's throat. How could Sandra do this? Laura had trusted Sandra, loved her even. Had thought that Sandra loved her. How could this be?

Sandra laughed. She waved the gun Laura had only just noticed in the air. "Why not?"

"Where is my son?" Laura demanded more sharply.

"I wasn't finished with the first question," Sandra snapped. "In the beginning it was simply the money," she said boldly. She fixed Laura with an evil look. "It should have been mine anyway. If your meddling grandfather hadn't stepped in, my mother would have had the life she deserved. *I* would have had the life I deserved—your life."

Laura shook her head in confusion. "What are you talking about?"

Sandra smiled. "Oh, that's right you wouldn't know, would you?" She stepped closer to Laura, the gun pointed at her chest. "Your dear father was once in love with my mother. But she wasn't good enough for that blue blood that ran through his veins. So, your loving grandfather took care of the situation. He sent your father off to Harvard where he met your sweet, equally blue-blooded mother."

"What does this have to do with anything?" Laura didn't care about the past. The only thing she wanted was to find her son.

"Everything, my dear, everything." She used the barrel of the weapon to turn Laura's chin when she would have looked away. "You see, after your father deserted her, my mother married my sorry-excuse-for-a-father. He was a drunk and beat us both every chance he got."

Laura shook her head, fear and sympathy warred inside her. "I'm sorry, but what does that have to do with my son?" she murmured.

"I'm getting to that," Sandra snapped, her eyes sparkled with hatred. "Be patient. Not a day went by that my mother didn't remind me of what should have been ours." She poked Laura in the chest with the muzzle of the gun. "Money, position, power. Instead, we lived in poverty. Finally my mother had to be hospitalized and I was sent away."

Despite what Sandra had done, Laura's heart went out to the little girl who had suffered such injustices. Unlike James Ed, who was driven by greed, Sandra's evilness grew out of a horrible childhood. "But your adopted parents were good to you," Laura countered. "You told me so yourself."

"You can't make up for the past, Laura. What's done is done. And one way or another I intended to have what was mine." Another sinister smile spread across her face. "Of course I might never have been born had my mother not married the drunk who sired me. But, fate finally smiled on me. Your parents got themselves killed in that car accident and James Ed was all alone with a little sister to raise." Sandra drew in a pleased breath. "By then I was all grown-up, had a different name, and lived with parents who were socially acceptable."

Laura searched her mind for some way to get away from Sandra. The woman was deranged. Laura had to get to Nick and tell him about this room—she surveyed the beautiful nursery—and Sandra's crazy story.

"You like my baby's nursery?"

Laura blinked. Her gaze collided with Sandra's once more. "But you can't have children," she said before she thought.

Sandra's expression grew fierce. "Yes, well, that crazy old lady Leeton saw to that."

"What?" This just kept getting more confusing, more bizarre. Laura gripped the side rail more tightly. What did Mrs. Leeton have to do with Sandra's past? Mrs. Leeton had been Doc's nurse in Bay Break for as long as Laura could remember.

"I wanted to make sure I had James Ed right where I wanted him, so I got pregnant to seal our fate. But he didn't want children," she added with disgust. "He claimed he needed to get his political career off the ground and get you raised before he had children of his own." She sneered at Laura. "So I had to take care of that before he found out." She frowned. "Something went wrong. The stupid old nurse kept telling me that it wasn't her fault, that she had done the best she could. But I knew better. I could have killed her," Sandra said coldly. "But I decided I might need her in the future." She laughed then. "Guess I was right."

"Where is Robby?" Laura demanded, her anger suddenly overriding any misplaced sympathy she had felt.

"Why do you keep asking me that?" Sandra said haughtily. "You've been in a hospital for the past eighteen months. You have no proof that Robby even exists. I've seen to that. Who would ever believe you?"

"Nick believes me," Laura bit out.

Sandra shrugged. "Big deal. I can take care of Nick." Her lips compressed into a grim line. "I thought I had him out of the way once before. But Redmond screwed up. Oh well," she added with amusement. "He got his, didn't he, princess?"

Ice formed in Laura's stomach. "*You* sent Redmond to kill me?"

"Well, of course," she retorted unapologetically. "You didn't think James Ed had the balls to do it, did you?"

Laura shook her head. "I didn't have anything to do with what happened to your mother. How could you hate me so much?"

"I already told you," she intoned. "You had my life.

And now I intend to have it all. Everything that should have been mine all along. The name, the money, everything.''

''Where's my son?'' Laura stepped nearer, putting herself nose to nose with Sandra.

Sandra pressed the muzzle of her gun into Laura's stomach as a reminder of who was in charge. ''I knew you didn't die in that river with Redmond.'' Her eyes narrowed. ''I knew it. So I sent Redmond's partner to look for you. It took him almost a year, but he found you.'' Sandra's eyes lit with a glow that was not sane. ''And lo and behold what did he discover? You'd had yourself a baby.''

''Where's my son?'' Laura demanded again.

''With my dark hair and hazel eyes, he was perfect,'' Sandra continued as if Laura had said nothing. ''But, of course, with James Ed's career to consider, I had to make it all look legal. That wasn't so hard. Over the years I've gotten to know the hospital administrator at Serenity Sanitarium pretty well—'' she smiled that evil smile again ''—very well, in fact. So that part was easy. Canton, of course, was willing to do anything for enough money. Killing you and making it look like a suicide sounded like fun to him. All he had to do was find you.'' Sandra breathed a relieved sigh. ''When you showed up in Bay Break, it was like a gift from God. Doc had no way of knowing that his former nurse owed me such a huge favor. She called me the instant you showed up at her house.''

Rage rushed through Laura's veins. ''You had Doc murdered.''

''Unfortunately it was a necessary step in the process. He had a long and prosperous life, what's the big deal?''

''I want my son back,'' Laura said dangerously. At the moment she was prepared to kill Sandra with her bare hands if necessary.

"Enough," Sandra announced savagely. She gestured to the French doors. "Let's go onto the balcony. I wouldn't want to sully *my* son's new room."

She jabbed Laura with the gun when she hesitated. "I said move," she ordered.

Laura took one last look at the crib, then walked through the open doors. The barrel of the gun urging her forward, she walked straight across the wide balcony to the ornate railing. Laura stared into the darkness searching for some avenue of escape.

"Now jump."

Startled by her demand, Laura pivoted to face Sandra. "What?" She had expected the woman to simply shoot her.

Sandra stepped to the railing. "I said jump. I have to keep this on the up-and-up." She rolled her eyes. "Poor unstable Laura, she threw herself off the balcony after killing her lover and trying to kill her own brother. Not to mention poor old Doc."

Nick. Oh God. Frantic to stall her, Laura asked, "What makes you think James Ed will go along with you killing Nick?"

"James Ed will do whatever I tell him to." Sandra's smile widened. "Or else he'll have an accident, too." Her smile disappeared just as quickly. "Now jump."

Remembering her lesson in the barn well, Laura flicked a glance toward the open doors as if she had heard or seen something. Sandra followed her gaze. In that moment of distraction, Laura knocked Sandra's arm upward. The gun fired, momentarily deafening Laura. Laura kicked her in the shin and drove her fist into Sandra's wrist with all her strength. The gun flew from her grasp and slid across the floor.

"Die, damn you," Sandra hissed as she grabbed Laura

by the throat and slammed into her with her full body weight.

Laura stumbled back upon impact. She struggled to breathe and to pull Sandra's hands free of her throat. Laura pivoted, trying to shake Sandra loose, and lost her balance. Laura fell backwards. The rail cut into her back, breaking Laura's fall. Sandra leaned over her, her fingers cutting off the air to Laura's lungs. Determination contorted Sandra's features as she clamped down harder on Laura's throat.

"Die," Sandra shrieked.

Laura arched upward to throw her off. Sandra twisted, then went over the rail, pulling Laura with her.

THE LOUD REPORT of a weapon jerked Nick from the useless argument with James Ed. He turned to the door. Laura was gone. Damn. Nick ran into the hall.

"Laura!"

Nick took the stairs two at a time. He raced toward the one open door where light glowed. The room was empty. He frowned when his brain assimilated the visual assessment that it was a nursery. A shriek drew his gaze to the open balcony doors. Nick sprinted across the room and onto the balcony just in time to see Sandra and Laura go over the edge of the railing.

Outright panic slammed into him. Fear clawed at his chest as he rushed to the railing. Sandra lay on the concrete walk below. Laura was hanging on to one spindle. His heart hammering with fear, Nick leaned over the rail and reached for her.

"Give me your hand, Laura," he said quickly.

Straining with the effort to hang on, Laura reached one shaky hand toward his. The spindle she clung to snapped and Nick barely snagged her hand before she fell. Slowly, his hold on her slipping more than once, he pulled a trembling Laura over the rail and into his arms.

"Sandra stole my baby," Laura cried.

"It's okay," Nick assured her. "You're safe now."

"She sent security away, you know," James Ed remarked behind them as if nothing out of the ordinary had happened.

Nick turned to him, sensing a change in his tone. James Ed picked up the weapon on the floor, then stared at it a moment before lifting his gaze to Nick and Laura. His grip tightened around the weapon and Nick tensed for battle.

"I suppose it was for the best," he added.

"Put the gun down, James Ed," Nick told him calmly. He moved Laura behind him, but didn't reach for his own weapon. He didn't want to scare James Ed into doing something stupid. The man had just had his whole world turned upside down. He was obviously in shock.

"This is really all my fault," James Ed continued in a voice totally void of emotion. He shrugged halfheartedly. "I needed money to keep up appearances. I'm sure Sandra only thought she was helping me. She didn't mean to hurt anyone. I'm certain of that."

Nick felt Laura go rigid behind him.

James Ed shook his head in defeat. "I believed everything Sandra told me. I trusted her unconditionally."

Nick held Laura back when she would have rushed toward her brother. She wanted answers, now. Nick glanced over his shoulder and told her with his eyes to stay put. He took one cautious step toward James Ed. James Ed's gaze flickered to him.

"You do believe me, don't you?" James Ed looked past Nick and searched Laura's face as if looking for some sign of forgiveness. "I didn't know. You were so wild and unhappy it seemed. That's why I tried to marry you off to

Rafe. I hoped that he could do a better job of making you happy. I had so many responsibilities already. I just couldn't give you what you needed.''

Nick moved one more step closer. "So you didn't know about Sandra's scheme to kill Laura."

James Ed's expression filled with remorse. "I almost lost my mind when Laura disappeared." He waved the gun in frustration. "I had no idea that Sandra had hired Redmond behind my back,'' James Ed insisted. He shrugged wearily. "I truly thought Laura was unstable. Sandra had me convinced. Then Laura disappeared and I thought she was dead. Eventually I used the trust fund, but not until I felt sure Laura wasn't coming back,'' he added quickly. "I didn't want to but Sandra insisted that Laura would have wanted me to have the money.''

"But Sandra wasn't convinced that Laura was gone for good,'' Nick suggested. "She kept looking.'' More space disappeared between them.

James Ed nodded. "Apparently. I didn't know until tonight what she had done.'' He pressed Nick with his gaze, searching for understanding, beseeching him to believe. "That other man, Redmond's partner, showed up a few hours ago and told Sandra what happened.'' James Ed dropped his head in defeat. "I couldn't believe she had done it.'' A sob cracked his voice. "I couldn't believe that I had been so blind. I thought Laura was imagining the episodes, that she truly was unstable.'' His shoulders sagged in defeat. "I loved Sandra. I trusted her.''

"Give me the gun, James Ed,'' Nick told him again.

James Ed stared at the weapon for a long moment as if it held the answers to all his worries. "I don't deserve to live after what I've allowed to happen.''

Nick grabbed James Ed's arm when he would have lifted

the weapon. "That's not the issue right now," Nick argued. "Right now *we* have to find Laura's son."

James Ed relinquished the weapon. His gaze moved to Laura. "Can you ever forgive me, Laura? I'd give anything if this hadn't happened."

Laura was next to Nick then. She lifted her chin and glared at her brother with little or no sympathy. "Where is my son?" she demanded.

He shook his head slowly. "I'd give my life right now to be able to tell you. But, I swear, I don't know where your child is, Laura. We—" James Ed glanced at the room beyond the open doors, then at the balcony railing over which Sandra had disappeared. He winced. "—we were going to adopt a child. Sandra had made all the necessary arrangements. We were supposed to bring him home to-morrow."

"Him?" Nick echoed.

James Ed nodded. "A little boy just over a year old."

"Where is he?" Laura pressed.

"At the orphanage in Louisiana." James Ed looked thoughtful for a moment. "Sandra was there for a while when she was a child, and someone rescued her. She thought it only fitting…" His voice trailed off.

Laura tugged at Nick's sleeve. "Let's go!"

Nick pulled his cell phone from his pocket. "We have to get the police out here first." He glanced at James Ed who had wandered to a nearby chair and dropped into it. "We can't leave him like this."

"I'm not waiting," she argued.

Nick grasped her arm when she would have rushed away. "You will wait."

"I have to find my son," she cried, desperation in her voice.

Nick saw the pain and worry in her eyes, he hardened his heart to what he wanted to feel. "He's my son, too."

Chapter Thirteen

Laura awoke with a start. Shops, sidewalks and pedestrians lined the street. It was daylight now. Eight o'clock, according to the digital clock on the dash. Traffic moved at a snail's pace, morning rush hour apparently. Laura rubbed the back of her hand over her jaw, then massaged her stiff neck as she sat up straighter in the car seat. She wondered if this place was Careytown. She glanced at the driver's grim profile. Nick's beard-shadowed face was chiseled in stone, the white bandage stark against his dark skin and hair. He hadn't spoken a word to her since they left her brother's house. It had been almost four o'clock in the morning before the police had allowed them to leave.

A banner announcing Careytown's fifth annual Thanksgiving Festival draped from crossing light to crossing light over the busy street. Laura's heart skittered into overdrive. She was almost there. Very soon, possibly in just a few short minutes, she would be able to hold her son in her arms once more.

Laura closed her eyes briefly and summoned the memory of Robby's sweet baby scent. Her arms ached to hold him. But what kind of court battle lay before her? Laura blinked. Her gaze darted back to Nick's granite-like features. He was never going to forgive her for keeping Robby a secret.

In his opinion, she should have turned to him for help in the first place. But she just couldn't take the chance that he wouldn't turn her over to James Ed.

James Ed.

Regret trickled through Laura. She had blamed James Ed for everything all this time, when it had been Sandra all along. Laura still couldn't believe that Sandra had harbored such ill will toward her all those years. Had wanted her dead. Had wanted to steal her son.

Laura shook off the disturbing thoughts. Sandra was dead. She would never be able to harm Robby or Laura again. Canton was still at large, but hopefully the police would find him soon. She and James Ed would work things out eventually, she supposed. After all, he was her brother. The only thing that mattered now, Laura resolved, was getting her son back. She glanced at Nick again. She would just have to deal with his demands when the time came. No judge in his right mind would take her son away from her. But Nick was a good man....

Joint custody.

The phrase tore at Laura's heart. How would she be able to survive days or weeks without her son? Even if she knew he was safe in Nick's care. And what if Nick married someone else? Fear and hurt gripped Laura with such intensity that she thought she might be sick at her stomach. There could even be someone in his life right now. Nick was a very good-looking man.

But he had made love to her just last night. Laura swallowed tightly. It wasn't uncommon for people to cling to each other during or after near-death encounters. It had happened two years ago. Last night was probably no different. The time she had spent in Nick's arms obviously hadn't affected him as it had her. She loved him with all her heart. She would give most anything if they could be a family.

Laura closed her eyes and fought the tears brimming. She would not cry. She was about to be reunited with her child. If any tears were shed today, they would be tears of joy.

"This is it," Nick said quietly.

Laura jerked to attention. He guided the car into the parking lot of an old, but well-maintained two-story building. The parking lot wasn't large, but Laura could see a huge fenced-in play yard behind the building. Multi-colored playground equipment and numerous trees, bare for the winter, claimed the play yard landscape. The exterior of the building wasn't particularly bright, but it was clean and neat. If the staff took such good care of the property, surely they cared equally well for the children.

Nick was out of the car and opening her door before Laura realized they had parked. She shook off the distraction and emerged into the cool November morning.

Just a few more moments, she told herself. The first genuine smile in too many days to recall lifted her lips. *Thank you, God,* she prayed. Laura folded her arms over her chest and ignored the biting wind. Her son was in there somewhere and she was about to find him.

"Are you all right?" Nick's voice was gentle, laced with concern.

Laura looked up at him and mentally acknowledged the mistake she had made. She should have told Nick. She should have gone to him for help long ago. He was the father of her child. He was a good man. She should have trusted him. But she hadn't. And now she would pay dearly for that mistake.

The cost would be Nick's trust. If he had ever even considered trusting her, he wouldn't now. And there was no way he would ever love her the way she loved him.

"I'm fine," she managed past the lump in her throat. It

was a lie, she wanted to scream. She would never be fine again.

"Then let's go get our son."

Our son. The words echoed through her soul.

Nick's long fingers curled around Laura's elbow as he guided her up the long walk and through the double doors leading into the Careytown Home for Children. A wide, tiled corridor rolled out before them. Doors lined both walls. A sign proclaimed one as the main office.

A few moments later they entered the cheery office. A sunny yellow, the walls displayed hundreds of framed photographs. On closer inspection, Laura realized the pictures were of children of all ages. An older lady wearing a cartoon character T-shirt greeted them.

"May I help you?" She smiled kindly.

"I'm Nick Foster and this is Laura Proctor. I believe someone called to let you know we were coming."

The woman's smile immediately crumpled. "Yes. Our director received a call at home a couple of hours ago." She attempted another smile, which proved decidedly less enthusiastic than her previous one. She stood. "Follow me, please."

Uneasiness slid over Laura. Something was wrong. Her heart bumped into an erratic rhythm as a dozen possibilities flashed through her mind. They were too close now. Things just couldn't go wrong. Laura followed Nick and the receptionist into an inner office. Laura moistened her lips and squared her shoulders. Robby was safe. He was here and when Laura left, she would have her baby in her arms.

A woman of about forty waited for them inside the small office. Her hair was pulled back in a tight bun, revealing her attractive features. At present, those features were cluttered with what could only be labeled worry.

"Ms. Proctor. Mr. Foster." She shook first Laura's hand,

then Nick's. "I'm Mary Flannigan, the director. Please have a seat," she offered nervously.

"I'm sure you can understand that we're in somewhat of a hurry," Nick told her candidly.

With obvious effort, she produced a smile. "Of course." Mrs. Flannigan retrieved a file from her desk. "Before we go any further, I'll need you to identify the child."

Laura moved closer to the woman's desk. "Identify?"

Mrs. Flannigan opened the file. "We photograph all our children for our records."

The woman opened the folder and Laura's gaze latched onto the pictures of Robby. He smiled at the camera, those mischievous green eyes bright with happiness. "It's him," Laura breathed the words. Her fingers went instinctively to the photographs to caress her son's image. Tears rolled down her cheeks. "That's my baby," she murmured, awe in her voice.

Nick touched one of the pictures, his fingers tracing the image of his son. Laura watched the myriad emotions move across his handsome face.

"He's beautiful, isn't he?" Laura said softly.

Nick nodded. Laura knew that he couldn't possibly speak right now. He had just gotten the first glimpse of his son. A son he couldn't have denied even if he had been so inclined. Robby looked so very much like him.

Laura released the breath she had been holding and shifted her attention to Mrs. Flannigan. Maybe the lady was simply nervous over the mistake. She had placed a stolen child into adoption proceedings, unknowingly, of course.

"I'd like you to bring my son to me now," Laura said as calmly as she could.

Mrs. Flannigan looked first at Laura, then at Nick. As if somehow sensing that Nick would take the news better than Laura, she directed her words to him. "I am so sorry that this has happened.'' She shook her head. ''I've been the director at this home for ten years and nothing like this has ever happened. Our staff is thoroughly screened.''

''Get to the point, Mrs. Flannigan. Where is Robby?'' Nick insisted.

''I don't know.''

Laura's heart dropped to her feet. Her muscles went limp and passing out seemed a distinct possibility. ''What?''

''When I arrived this morning, the night nurse was in a panic. Your child—'' she moistened her lips ''—was missing. When the midnight rounds were made he was there, but at seven this morning he was gone.''

''Gone?'' Nick leaned forward slightly, his intimidating frame looming over the woman's desk. ''Don't you have security here?''

Mrs. Flannigan nodded. ''Excellent security. No one gets in or out without a key after hours. We believe that one of our staff members took your son.''

''No.'' Laura shook her head in denial. This couldn't be. She had only just found this place. He couldn't be gone.

''I thought you said you screen your staff,'' Nick countered hotly.

''We do, Mr. Foster. Elsa Benning is an excellent employee. I can't imagine why she has done this. She has worked here for more than twenty years. It doesn't make sense.''

''How do you know it was her?'' Nick demanded.

Mrs. Flannigan smoothed a hand over her hair. ''She hasn't reported for duty this morning. In twenty years she hasn't missed a day.'' The director blinked beneath Nick's ruthless gaze. ''She is the only employee who holds a key and who is unaccounted for this morning.''

''No.'' Laura backed away from the reality. ''No, this can't be.''

"I am so terribly sorry. The Louisiana State Police have issued an APB."

"Laura." Nick moved toward her.

"No." Laura shook her head adamantly. "He has to be here."

"Ms. Proctor." The director stepped to Nick's side. "If it's any consolation to you at all, Elsa is a good woman. I don't believe she would hurt your baby."

NICK SETTLED an almost catatonic Laura into the passenger seat. He reached across her and buckled her seat belt. He had put a call into Ian to bring him up to speed. Nick closed the door and braced his hands on the top of the rented car. He squeezed his eyes shut and called the image of his son to mind. Dark hair, green eyes, chubby cheeks. Nick clenched his teeth to hold back the rage that wanted to burst from him.

Okay, he told himself. *Pull it together, man. You can't lose it now. Not here. Not in front of Laura.* His whole body ached at the look of pain and defeat sucking the life out of her. Nick straightened. By God he was going to find his son. One way or another. As much as Nick wanted his son, he wanted even more to reunite him with his mother. He couldn't bear to watch Laura suffer a minute longer. He skirted the hood and jerked his own door open. Nick dropped behind the wheel and snapped his seat belt into place. Laura had been through enough. Robby had been through enough.

And someone was going to pay.

Nick slammed his fist against the steering wheel again and again until the pain finally penetrated the layers of anger and frustration consuming him. Laura only looked at him, too grief stricken to react.

The cell phone in his jacket pocket rang insistently. Nick

blew out a heavy breath. He reached inside his jacket and retrieved the damned thing. He couldn't ignore it, it might be Ian.

"Foster," he said tautly. He had to get back in control.

"Nick, it's Ray."

Nick frowned. Why would Ray be calling him? The murder investigation. Damn. Nick massaged his forehead. He didn't want to do this right now. "Yeah, Ray, what's up?"

"I called James Ed's house and a policeman told me to call this number."

Nick impatiently plowed his fingers through his hair. "What can I do for you?"

"I'm not sure. But you mentioned that Laura's baby was missing." Ray exhaled mightily. "Maybe it's nothing, but a woman showed up here first thing this morning with a baby that looks the right age and the hair color's right. I remember all that black hair. She says she thinks the kid was stolen or something. We're running a check on her now."

Adrenaline pumped through Nick's veins. "What's her name?"

"One Elsa Benning."

"We're on our way." Nick started the car, then frowned. "Ray," he said before disconnecting, "do me one favor."

"Sure, buddy, anything."

"Don't let that woman and child out of your sight."

TIRES SQUEALING, Nick turned the wheel sharply, guiding the car into the precinct parking lot. Laura jerked forward when he braked to an abrupt halt. They had made the trip to Natchez in record time. She was out of the car right behind Nick. Her son was in that police station.

Laura rushed up the walk and into the building, Nick right on her heels.

"Detective Ingle," Nick said to the first officer they met in the corridor.

"Down the hall, fifth door on the left."

Laura was on her way before Nick could thank the man. Her heart pounding, her skin stinging with adrenaline, she burst through the door the officer had indicated. A half dozen desks filled the large room. Laura scanned each one. Her gaze locked on the back of a gray-haired lady. She sat in a chair, facing a desk. A tall man stood behind it shuffling through files. Ignoring all else, Laura rushed to the woman. Her heart pounding so hard in her chest that she felt certain it would burst from her rib cage, Laura stepped around the woman's chair.

Robby sat in her lap, pulling at the large ornate buttons on her jacket. Relief so profound swamped her, that Laura thought she might die of it. She dropped to her knees at the stranger's side. Laura held out her arms. "How's mommy's baby?" she murmured softly.

Robby reacted instantly. He flung his chubby little arms and bounced in the woman's lap. The woman, Elsa, smiled down at Laura and shifted Robby into Laura's arms.

Laura held Robby close. She inhaled deeply of his sweet baby scent. "Oh, my baby," she whispered into his soft hair. Emotions flooded her being so quickly and with such force that Laura could not think clearly.

The old woman nodded knowingly, capturing Laura's overwhelmed attention. "I knew this was no abandoned baby. Today they were going to give him to the adoptive couple." She shook her head. "I knew it wasn't right. So I brought him back to the police station in the city where they said he had been found."

"Thank you," Laura choked out. Robby tugged at her hair and made baby sounds as if nothing had ever been amiss. "I know you took good care of him."

"I did at that," Elsa agreed. "That's my job."

Laura smiled at the woman, then struggled to her feet. She turned to Ray Ingle, Nick's detective friend. "Thank you, Detective Ingle."

His lopsided smile warmed her. "Just doing my job, ma'am."

Taking a deep breath for courage, Laura turned to Nick. She manufactured a watery smile. "This is your son, Robby."

Total and complete awe claimed Nick's features. He touched Robby's hand. Instinctively Robby curled chubby little fingers around Nick's finger. The smile on Nick's face made Laura weak in the knees. She wanted so to offer Nick the opportunity to hold his son, but she couldn't bring herself to let go of him just yet.

"Hey, man," Ray exclaimed. "You've been holding out on me."

Nick just grinned at Ray, his eyes barely leaving Robby for a second.

"Canton is still at large," Ray mentioned quietly.

Laura turned to him, then looked at Nick.

"That's not good. Laura and Robby aren't safe as long as he's on the street," Nick returned, his gaze still riveted on his son.

Laura's arms tightened around her baby. "What will we do?"

"Do you have some place you can lay low until he's caught?" Ray asked Laura.

She glanced at Nick, then back to Ray and shook her head. "I couldn't possibly go to my brother's house, or the house in Bay Break." Laura had no money she could access without lengthy legalities. For one fleeting second fear slipped back into her heart. She snuggled her baby's head. None of that mattered.

She had Robby now.

"Laura, you can stay—" Nick began.

She shook her head, cutting him off. "That's not a good idea right now."

"Ma'am," Ray interrupted. "You and your little boy are welcome to stay with me and my wife until you figure this thing out."

Laura kissed Robby's satiny forehead. "Oh, I couldn't impose like that. I'm sure we can find some place."

"Why you'd be doing us a favor." Ray smiled widely. "You see, we're about to have our first child. My wife was an only child and has never had to care for a little one. She could use the practice." Ray blushed to the roots of his hair. "That is if you wouldn't mind."

Relief bolstered Laura's sagging resolve. "Thank you, Detective, that would be wonderful."

"I'll call my wife," he suggested quickly.

"You take good care of that fine little boy," Elsa said quietly.

Laura's gaze connected with the dark brown eyes of the older woman who had brought Robby here. "Thank you. I'll do my best." Belatedly, Laura shifted her attention back to Detective Ingle. "Is she going to be in trouble?"

"Don't you worry none about me," Elsa argued.

Ray shot Elsa a smile then turned back to Laura. "Apparently since her instincts were on the money, no charges will be pressed. And she won't lose her job," he added quickly. "But she will be on probation with Mrs. Flannigan for a while."

Elsa poohed Ray's comment. "Mary Flannigan will consider herself lucky I'm back. She couldn't get along without me."

Laura smiled down at Elsa. "I'm sure she couldn't."

Knowing she couldn't avoid the inevitable any longer,

Laura turned back to Nick. She steeled herself. It was impossible to read what he was thinking at the moment. "I've been on the run for a long time, Nick. So much has happened." She hugged Robby to her heart. "I need some time to pull myself together, before you take any legal steps to share custody." When he hesitated, Laura added quickly, "I'm not asking for forever, just a few weeks to figure out what happens next in my life."

Nick's gaze was intent on hers for several seconds before he answered. "All right. I can live with that as long as you keep me posted of exactly where you are and how—" his gaze moved to Robby "—and how my son is doing."

Laura stiffly nodded her agreement.

It was over.

She had gotten Robby back safe and sound.

She was safe.

But she had lost Nick.

Chapter Fourteen

Two weeks had passed. Nick had not tried to see Robby or taken any legal action, giving selflessly the time Laura had requested. She knew it was difficult for him. He called every day. Each time he asked the same question, how was his son? And then, how was she? Did he really care? Laura wondered. The way she did about him. She couldn't blame him if he didn't. And she certainly couldn't expect him to put off being with his son much longer. She could hear the growing anticipation in his voice with each call. Laura gazed forlornly at the salad on her plate. Though she felt more rested than she had in years, she had no appetite. Laura looked at her baby seated happily in the Ingles' brand new high chair, where he played with his food. His smiles and excited baby words let her know that Robby, too, was happy and rested. Laura's gaze shifted to her very pregnant hostess. Joy Ingle watched every move that Robby made with glowing anticipation.

Ray had been right. This time with Robby had done his wife a world of good, and greatly boosted her caregiving confidence. Laura was glad she had come. If only she could find that kind of happiness in her own life.

The doorbell chimed.

Joy frowned. "Who can that be? It's too early for Ray

to be home for lunch,'' she said, glancing at the clock on
the wall.

''I'll get it.'' Laura pushed to her feet. ''I'm through
anyway.''

Joy smiled. ''Thank you. I'll just bask in your son's eat-
ing antics.''

Laura returned her smile, then headed for the front door.
She breathed a sigh of satisfaction as she moved through
the Ingle home. Ray and Joy were so much in love. When
their baby came, he would lack for nothing in that department. Laura lifted a skeptical brow. Or any other department for that matter. She only wished Robby were going
to grow up in a home filled with love and both his mother
and father. How on earth would they ever manage sharing
him? And if Nick married someone else?

Laura pushed the disturbing thoughts aside and paused
in front of the door. Still cautious, she peered through the
viewfinder. She didn't recognize the man waiting outside
the door. Tall and handsome, he had dark hair and wore an
impeccable black business suit.

Laura opened the door a crack, leaving the security chain
in place. ''May I help you?''

''Laura Proctor?''

Laura studied his steady gray gaze. ''Yes.''

''My name is Ian Michaels. I'm an associate of Nick's
at the Colby Agency.'' The European accent, coupled with
his dark good looks reminded Laura of James Bond.

She shook off the silly notion. Laura remembered the
name. Nick had called him frequently, but she had never
met the man. ''Do you have any ID?''

''Of course.'' With practiced grace, Mr. Michaels removed the case containing his picture ID and held it up for
Laura's inspection. ''I have some news regarding your
case.''

Laura frowned. "Why didn't Nick come?"

"He thought you would be more comfortable if I took care of the final details."

Laura moistened her lips instead of allowing the frown tugging at her mouth to surface. Nick didn't want to come. He didn't want to see her. She supposed she really couldn't blame him. Laura had done a lot of thinking in the past two weeks. She had made a serious error in judgment. She should have trusted Nick. It was wrong for her to keep his son from him. Now she would face the consequences.

She removed the chain and opened the door. "Come in, Mr. Michaels."

He smiled. "Call me Ian."

Laura nodded and closed the door. She led the way to the living room and sat down on the sofa. Ian settled into a chair facing her.

"Laura, is everything all right?"

Joy hovered near the door, her expression wary.

"Yes," Laura assured her. "This is Ian Michaels, a friend of Nick's."

Ian stood. "It's a pleasure to meet you, Mrs. Ingle."

Laura watched the wariness melt from Joy's expression, only to be replaced by pure feminine appreciation. James Bond, all right, Laura decided.

Joy backed away from the door. "I'll just get back to Robby." She smiled. "Nice to meet you, Mr. Michaels."

Ian nodded. After Joy had gone, he sat down again. He settled his gaze back on Laura. "Canton has been caught," he said quietly. "He's being held by the authorities in Georgia awaiting extradition to Mississippi to face murder charges related to Dr. Holland's death."

Relief rushed through Laura. "Good. I'll breathe a lot easier knowing he's behind bars." Canton represented the last hurdle to a normal life.

"Nick has taken the liberty of upgrading security at your family home near Bay Break. You may return there whenever you're ready. He also suggested that you acquire a dog. A large dog," Ian added with a slight smile.

Laura couldn't help the answering smile. "Robby would love a dog."

"Good," Ian said with obvious relief. "Because Nick has already taken that liberty as well. A Mr. Rutherford is caring for the animal until you return."

Laura's smile widened at the thought of Mr. Rutherford. She hadn't seen him in ages. The day he had stopped by and talked to Nick she had been sleeping. Maybe it was time to go home. She swallowed tightly. Of course, it would never be the same. Doc was gone. And she still wasn't sure if she could forgive James Ed. He had called twice to check on her through Ray. With all that had taken place, James Ed had resigned as governor. According to Ray, James Ed had decided to return to practicing law.

"Detective Ingle tells me that James Ed has been cleared of all suspicion."

"That's correct," Ian confirmed.

Laura nodded. "I guess we'll work things out someday." For the first time in her life, Laura felt truly alone. She forced the thought away. She had Robby. She didn't need anyone else. Nick's image sifted through her mind, making a liar out of her.

"Mrs. Leeton has also been located. She has confessed to her part in your son's kidnapping."

Laura blinked back the moisture. "That's good." How could people she had known and trusted all of her life be so evil?

"It appears that James Ed and Sandra did not go through your entire trust fund. There is some money left."

Laura frowned. "I assumed he used all the money."

''Most of it,'' Ian explained. ''But he has insisted on putting back all that he could. In fact, he plans to sell his private estate to add to that amount.''

''I'm glad that some of the money is still there,'' Laura said with relief. Though she had her education, the idea of leaving her son with anyone after all they had been through was unthinkable, though she knew mothers did so everyday. After losing him once, Laura wasn't sure she could take the chance of leaving him in anyone else's care. ''But I'd rather he didn't sell his home for me. If you would see that he gets that message I would appreciate it.''

''Certainly,'' Ian offered. He paused for a moment. ''Laura, the situation between you and Nick is none of my business, but I think you're both making a serious mistake.''

Laura lifted her chin and leveled her gaze on this handsome stranger who seemed to read her entirely too well. ''I don't know what else I can do. Nick doesn't appear to be interested in working anything out. Whenever he calls to check on Robby he never asks if I would like to talk about my plans. I have no idea what he wants. And, frankly, I'm tired of worrying about it.''

Ian considered her words for a time. ''Nick is suffering, too. He wants to do the right thing for his son. He's convinced that there is no hope for a relationship between the two of you, but he doesn't want to hurt you by taking legal steps.''

Laura sat very still. ''Did he tell you that?''

''Not in so many words. But I know him. He won't risk hurting you. But each day that passes knowing he can't be with his son, destroys another small part of him.''

Laura shot to her feet. ''Thank you very much, Mr. Michaels, for making me the bad guy.'' Suddenly restless, she paced back and forth in front of him.

Ian stood. "That's not my intent. I only wanted you to know that Nick—"

"Look." Laura's hands went to her hips. "I know I made a mistake, okay? I admit that. But it's done. I can't undo it. If Nick can't get past this, then what am I supposed to do?"

"You could start by telling him what you just told me," Ian suggested. "Nick doesn't want to take a wrong step where you and Robby are concerned. He's waiting for you to make the first move. He cares a great deal for you."

Laura's gaze connected with his. "And if you're wrong?"

Ian smiled, a lethal combination of confidence and masculinity. "I'm rarely wrong."

And somehow Laura knew he was right.

Laura locked the door behind Ian when he left. She sagged against it and heaved a beleaguered sigh. The first move. A knowing smile tilted Laura's lips. She had learned her lesson about not going out on a limb to trust the people she cared about. She would make a move all right.

All Nick Foster had to do was react.

NICK SHOVED the completed files into the out basket on his desk. Hell, it was Friday. If Mildred came up with any more paperwork for him today, her long-standing position at the Colby Agency would be in serious jeopardy. Nick smiled. The surface gesture felt strange on his lips after so long with nothing to smile about. The agency wouldn't be able to function without Mildred. She kept everyone straight, including Victoria.

Nick closed his eyes and allowed the images that usually haunted him free rein. Hell, it was late, he was tired. Why not add insult to injury? The memory of making love to Laura always surfaced first. Nick's fists clenched in reaction. The feel of her soft body beneath his. Her taste, her sweet smell. How would he live the rest of his life without being with her that way again? How would he live without her?

But he had ruined any chance of that with his arrogant pride. Nick had slowly, but surely come to terms with Laura's actions. She had been protecting her baby. Fear had kept her from coming to him. It still stung that she hadn't trusted him. But Nick had to remember that Laura had only been twenty-two at the time. Too young to make all the right decisions. Hell, he was thirty-four and he still screwed up regularly. Case in point, his handling of the situation with Laura.

Robby's chubby cheeks loomed as big as life in Nick's mind. His son. It still humbled him to think that he had a son. A son that wouldn't even know him at this rate. Nick had to do something. But what?

Laura apparently had no intention of ever speaking to him regarding her personal plans. He had given her every opportunity by always asking how she was when he called to check on Robby. What was he supposed to do? If he took steps to gain visitation rights he would only be making bad matters worse. How could he take Robby from his mother and bring him all the way to Chicago for weeks at a time? Nick knew he couldn't do that to Laura. There had to be a solution.

There had to be one, he repeated, as if the answer would come to him from his sheer determination.

But he had probably blown it with his unforgiving attitude.

A soft knock sounded at Nick's door. He looked up to find the subject of his reverie standing in his doorway. Stunned, Nick pushed to his feet.

"Laura." His first thought was that something was wrong.

"Hello, Nick." She smiled, Nick's breath caught. "May we come in?" She shifted Robby to her other hip.

The little boy looked as if he had grown considerably in the past two weeks. How could Nick allow one more day to go by without having his son in his life? He was not above begging at this point. But he wouldn't hurt Laura. The decision to work something out had to be hers. Her entire life had been spent with people manipulating her and telling her what to do. Nick wouldn't do that. He couldn't, no matter what it cost him personally.

Nick jerked himself to attention. "Yes, please, come in." He moved around to the front of his desk, his gaze riveted to the squirming baby in Laura's arms. A colorful diaper bag hung over one shoulder. Between the bulky coat, the diaper bag, and the baby, Laura was barely visible.

"Have a seat," Nick offered belatedly.

"No." Laura shook her head. "I need to say this right now before I lose my courage."

Nick's gaze connected with hers. Confusion formed a worry line between his brows. She had come all this way without calling first. "Is something wrong?"

Laura met his gaze head-on. "I've done a lot of thinking, Nick. And you're right. It was a mistake for me to keep Robby from you. I should have trusted you. I was wrong." She looked away for a moment. "But it's done and I can't take it back."

"Laura, I—"

She held up her free hand, halting his words. "Let me finish, please."

Nick relented with a nod. Anticipation stabbed at his chest. Could Laura possibly want to try again? Would she give him a second chance to prove that he loved her? And he did love her—with all his heart. He loved his son, too.

"I've decided that Robby needs to get to know his father. Enough time has been wasted already." Laura blinked, but not before Nick saw the uncertainty in her eyes.

She took the two steps that separated them and dropped the diaper bag at his feet. She thrust Robby at him. Surprised by her action, Nick put his arms around his son with the same uncertainty that he had seen in Laura's eyes. All else ceased to matter when Robby clung to Nick's chest. His little hands fisted in Nick's shirt. A foreign sensation seized Nick's heart. Nothing had ever felt like this before.

This was his child.

"So," Laura said, drawing Nick's awestruck attention back to her. "Here he is." She blinked again and backed toward the door a step. "Instructions are in the bag regarding what he likes to eat, and what he's allowed to drink. I'm at the Sheraton. Call me if you need anything, otherwise I'll pick Robby up on Monday." Moisture shining in her eyes, Laura whirled toward the door and started in that direction.

She was leaving.

Panic seized Nick. She couldn't do this—he didn't know the first thing about taking care of a baby. "Laura," Nick called to her swiftly retreating back. And, besides, he wanted her to stay. "Don't go," he added quietly. Robby bounced in Nick's arms, as if adding his agreement.

She paused at the door, then turned slowly to face him. Tears trekked down her cheeks. "Everything he needs is in the bag. You don't need me," she said, her voice quaking.

Nick swallowed with extreme difficulty. His arms tightened instinctively around the little boy in his arms. "Yes, I do. We do," he amended quickly. "I was wrong. You were afraid. You did what you thought was right. And I can't hold that against you.''

Laura crossed her arms over her chest. She swiped at the moisture dampening her cheeks. ''None of that matters. I just want to do what's right for Robby now.''

''So do I.'' Nick took a step in her direction. ''But I want us to do it together.''

Hope flashed in Laura's surprised gaze. ''You do?''

He smiled. ''I thought I made that pretty obvious a couple of times while we were in Bay Break.''

Laura pushed her hair back, her hand trembling visibly. ''I was afraid that it hadn't meant as much to you as it did to me. I can't be sure if you feel the same way I do.''

Nick reached out and touched one soft cheek. ''It meant the world to me—*you* mean the world to me.'' His heart ached at the worry etched across her beautiful face. ''It's been hell giving you the time and space you asked for. But this had to be your decision.''

Her expression grew suddenly solemn. ''I love you, Nick.''

''Could you put up with me for the rest of your life?'' he suggested softly.

''Are you asking me to marry you?'' Her eyes widened with anticipation.

''Absolutely.'' Nick leaned down and kissed those sweet lips. Her arms flew around his neck and she kissed him back. ''Is that a yes?'' he murmured when he could bear to break from her sweet kiss.

''Yes,'' she whispered.

Robby added his two cents worth in baby talk. Nick and Laura laughed. Nick stroked her cheek with the pad of his thumb. His fingers curled around her neck and pulled her closer. ''I love you so much, Laura,'' he told her softly.

"I've loved you since the day I first laid eyes on you." Robby squirmed between them. "And I love our son."

Nick gazed lovingly at his son.

Laura's child.

His gaze moved back to the woman he loved with all his heart. A frown creased Nick's brow. "You weren't really going to leave Robby here and me with no clue as to how to take care of him, were you?"

She grinned. "Are you kidding? If you hadn't stopped me before I got out the door, I was going to turn around and demand that you marry me."

"I suppose it's only right that you make an honest man out of me."

"It'll be my pleasure," Laura murmured, before kissing Nick soundly on the lips.

Nick held his child and the woman he loved against his heart as he planned to do for the rest of his life.

Epilogue

Victoria looked up from her desk when a knock sounded at her door. She smiled. "Ian, come in."

Ian Michaels crossed the room and paused before her desk. "You wanted to see me, Victoria?"

"Yes, have a seat, please."

Ian settled his tall frame into one of the chairs in front of her desk. As always, the man looked impeccable. Dressed in an expensive black suit, he presented himself in a manner very becoming to the Agency. His job performance remained at a superior level no matter how tough the assignment. He displayed numerous characteristics that Victoria admired. "I wanted to compliment you on your work here," she said finally. "You've done an outstanding job, Ian. The Colby Agency is very fortunate to have you."

"Thank you," he replied noncommittally.

Victoria almost smiled. Ian wasn't one to discuss his attributes, and he had many. He and Nick shared that particular characteristic. With Nick most likely not coming back, she needed to fill his position. Victoria had never seen Nick happier, and she couldn't be happier for him. Laura and Robby were just what he needed...what he deserved. But his absence left Victoria with a dilemma that required immediate action. Directing her attention back to the matter at hand, Victoria leveled her gaze on Ian's. "I'm sure you know that Nick has taken an indefinite leave of absence to be with his wife and child."

"Yes." That gray gaze remained steady on hers.

"That leaves me without a second in charge."

"There are several top investigators on staff. I'm sure you'll be able to find a proper temporary replacement."

Victoria did smile this time. "I already have."

"What can I do to assist in the transition?" he offered politely.

"You can direct Mildred to issue a memo announcing your promotion, effective immediately."

A hint of a smile touched Ian's lips. "Of course." He stood. "Is there anything else?"

"One more thing," Victoria said as she rose to match his stance. "I'd like you to personally handle this inquiry." She passed a thin red folder to Ian.

"Any specific instructions?" Ian glanced only briefly at the folder before meeting Victoria's gaze.

"The contact is Lucas Camp. He's a close personal friend. You have complete authority to handle whatever he needs."

"I'll keep you informed of my progress."

"That would have been my next request."

Ian smiled fully then, giving Victoria a tiny glimpse of just how much charm the man commanded. Without another word, he turned and walked to the door.

"Ian." Victoria halted his exit.

He turned back. "Yes."

"Don't let Lucas give you any flack. He can be a bit pushy at times."

Ian lifted one dark brow. "We'll get along fine."

"I'm sure you will."

Victoria watched with satisfaction as Ian Michaels walked away. She had made a wise choice.

Don't miss Ian's story in

PROTECTIVE CUSTODY

The next COLBY AGENCY
story by Debra Webb
on sale April 2001.

HARLEQUIN®

INTRIGUE®

your source for outstanding
romantic suspense!

Prologue

"Absolute trust is essential." Nicole Reed's solemn gaze settled heavily on Victoria. "Both our lives will depend on my being able to trust your investigator completely. I know Ian Michaels. I can trust him."

Victoria Colby considered that last statement for a time before she spoke. Not a single doubt existed in her mind that Ian would be the wisest choice. Not only was he the Colby Agency's most experienced investigator, he was a man of his word. With Nick Foster's retirement, Ian had transitioned into the position of second in command. Victoria employed only the finest in their fields at the Colby Agency. And Ian had proven no exception during his three years of service.

"Miss Reed, I understand your need for a civilian investigator. Obviously, you can't trust anyone in your own organization."

"I can't trust anyone even remotely connected to the Bureau or the Witness Security Program." Nicole sighed. "I wish that weren't the case, but it is. There have been two attempts on my life already. My director is dead, as well as another agent I've worked closely with in the past. Until I get to the bottom of what's going on, I need someone I can trust to watch my back. Your agency has an impeccable reputation, Mrs. Colby, and I *trust* Ian Michaels.''

Victoria relaxed into the soft leather of her chair and studied the client seated across the wide expanse of her oak desk. The woman's features were striking. She looked as if she had just stepped off the pages of *Vogue.* A navy silk jacket and trousers lent an air of professionalism as well as elegance to her image. Blond hair fell around her shoulders. Wide, assessing blue eyes highlighted a face that could only be called beautiful. So, Victoria noted, this woman was the reason Ian Michaels had walked away from a promising career as a U.S. Marshal.

Victoria arched a speculative brow. "Your history with Ian may be a problem, Miss Reed."

Nicole frowned. "I don't understand."

Victoria almost smiled at the look of innocence Nicole Reed could adopt. "Before I employ anyone at this agency, I research their background thoroughly. I evaluate their strong points as well as their weak points, and I familiarize myself with their past mistakes. You worked with Ian Michaels on a high profile case just over three years ago. The Solomon case, I believe."

Nicole's expression grew guarded. "That's right."

"I'm aware of your personal involvement with Ian, and the subsequent outcome of that involvement," Victoria added, leaving no question as to the point she intended.

"Raymond Solomon died, Mrs. Colby. We did our best to protect him, but he died anyway. End of story."

Between the suddenly blank look in the other woman's eyes and the emotionless tone of her voice, Victoria had her doubts as to whether the story had ended. But that wasn't the issue here. Nicole Reed needed help, and the Colby Agency had made its reputation by providing the kind of help she required. Victoria straightened, then pressed the intercom button. "Mildred, ask Ian if he's free. I'd like him to join this meeting."

Nicole blinked, then looked away. Asking for Ian's help couldn't be easy, Victoria imagined. After all, it was Nicole who helped end his former career. And if Victoria had Ian pegged right, which she likely did, Miss Nicole Reed had probably broken his fiercely guarded heart as well.

* * * * *

*And look for Debra Webb's debut
with Harlequin American Romance
next month!*

LONGWALKER'S CHILD

*Available February 2001 wherever
Harlequin books are sold.*

HARLEQUIN®
INTRIGUE

opens the case files on:

TOP SECRET
BABIES

Unwrap the mystery!

January 2001
#597 THE BODYGUARD'S BABY
Debra Webb

February 2001
#601 SAVING HIS SON
Rita Herron

March 2001
#605 THE HUNT FOR HAWKE'S DAUGHTER
Jean Barrett

April 2001
#609 UNDERCOVER BABY
Adrianne Lee

May 2001
#613 CONCEPTION COVER-UP
Karen Lawton Barrett

Follow the clues to your favorite retail outlet.

HARLEQUIN®
Makes any time special ™

Visit us at www.eHarlequin.com

HITSB

Spines will tingle…mysteries await…
and dangerous passion lurks in the night
as *Reader's Choice* presents

DREAM SCAPES!

Thrills and chills abound in these four romances
welcoming readers to the dark side of love.
Available January 2001 at your
favorite retail outlet:

THUNDER MOUNTAIN
by Rachel Lee

NIGHT MIST
by Helen R. Myers

DARK OBSESSION
by Amanda Stevens

HANGAR 13
by Lindsay McKenna

CELEBRATE VALENTINE'S DAY WITH HARLEQUIN®'S LATEST TITLE— *Stolen Memories*

Available in trade-size format, this collector's edition contains three full-length novels by *New York Times* bestselling authors Jayne Ann Krentz and Tess Gerritsen, along with national bestselling author Stella Cameron.

TEST OF TIME by Jayne Ann Krentz—
He married for the best reason.... She married for the only reason.... Did they stand a chance at making the only reason the real reason to share a lifetime?

THIEF OF HEARTS by Tess Gerritsen—
Their distrust of each other was only as strong as their desire. And Jordan began to fear that Diana was more than just a thief of hearts.

MOONTIDE by Stella Cameron—
For Andrew, Greer's return is a miracle. It had broken his heart to let her go. Now fate has brought them back together. And he won't lose her again...

Make this Valentine's Day one to remember!

Look for this exciting collector's edition
on sale January 2001 at your favorite retail outlet.

HARLEQUIN®
Makes any time special ™

Visit us at www.eHarlequin.com

PHSM

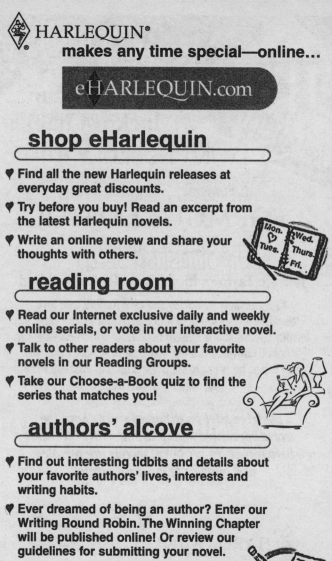

HARLEQUIN®
makes any time special—online...

eHARLEQUIN.com

shop eHarlequin

- ♥ Find all the new Harlequin releases at everyday great discounts.

- ♥ Try before you buy! Read an excerpt from the latest Harlequin novels.

- ♥ Write an online review and share your thoughts with others.

reading room

- ♥ Read our Internet exclusive daily and weekly online serials, or vote in our interactive novel.

- ♥ Talk to other readers about your favorite novels in our Reading Groups.

- ♥ Take our Choose-a-Book quiz to find the series that matches you!

authors' alcove

- ♥ Find out interesting tidbits and details about your favorite authors' lives, interests and writing habits.

- ♥ Ever dreamed of being an author? Enter our Writing Round Robin. The Winning Chapter will be published online! Or review our guidelines for submitting your novel.

#1 *New York Times* bestselling author

NORA ROBERTS

brings you more of the loyal and loving,
tempestuous and tantalizing Stanislaski family.

Coming in February 2001

The Stanislaski Sisters

Natasha and Rachel

Though raised in the Old World traditions of their
family, fiery Natasha Stanislaski and cool, classy
Rachel Stanislaski are ready for a *new* world of love....

*And also available in February 2001 from
Silhouette Special Edition, the newest book in the
heartwarming Stanislaski saga*

CONSIDERING KATE

Natasha and Spencer Kimball's daughter Kate turns her
back on old dreams and returns to her hometown, where
she finds the *man* of her dreams.

Available at your favorite retail outlet.

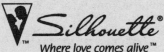

Where love comes alive™

The romantic suspense at

HARLEQUIN®

INTRIGUE

just got more intense!

**On the precipice between imminent danger and
smoldering desire, they are**

**When your back is against the wall
and nothing makes sense, only one man
is strong enough to pull you from the brink—
and into his loving arms!
Look for all the books in this riveting new
promotion:**

WOMAN MOST WANTED (#599)
by **Harper Allen**
On sale January 2001

PRIVATE VOWS (#603)
by **Sally Steward**
On sale February 2001

NIGHTTIME GUARDIAN (#607)
by **Amanda Stevens**
On sale March 2001

Available at your favorite retail outlet.